IN JAKE'S SHOES

A FATHER'S JOURNEY THROUGH LOSS AND REDEMPTION

ANDREW C. PHILLIPS

Black Rose Writing | Texas

ISBN: 978-1-68513-737-3
LIBRARY OF CONGRESS CONTROL NUMBER: 2025948402
PUBLISHED BY BLACK ROSE WRITING
www.blackrosewriting.com

Printed in the United States of America
Suggested Retail Price (SRP) $21.95

In Jake's Shoes is printed in Garamond Premier Pro

*As a planet-friendly publisher, Black Rose Writing does its best to eliminate unnecessary waste to reduce paper usage and energy costs, while never compromising the reading experience. As a result, the final word count vs. page count may not meet common expectations.

To My Family

Praise for
In Jake's Shoes

Quarter-finalist in a past Amazon Breakthrough Novel Award contest
2019 Semi-finalist for the Elixir Press Award
Selected to the Long List for the Page Turner 2024 Writing Award

"In Jake's Shoes weaves a story toward reconciling the past of a misunderstood son and reaching for healing and redemption. This is a poignant novel that acknowledges the need to face difficult truths for the chance to move forward, while at the same time forgiving others, including oneself."
–Linda Paul, author of *The Last Gypsy Queen*

"In Jake's Shoes is a moving story where heartfelt words uncovered in letters provide insight and a life-changing gift. *In Jake's Shoes* will pull at your heartstrings much like it did mine."
–Lucille Guarino, award-winning author of *Elizabeth's Mountain* **and the** *Lunch Tales* **series**

"Author Andrew Phillips brings the goods swiftly to the reader. Something special here, as your empathy will attach to Jake with only a small introduction, but here we are. Just Brilliant. In Jake's Shoes goes straight to the point with sharp, poignant prose and delivers a smooth, heartfelt story."
–Paul Jantzen, author of *Sour Apples*

"Andrew C Phillips has written a masterful tale of an agonizing venture of perception, understanding, and retribution. The device he deploys to advance the story is both unique and compelling as it slowly intensifies the reader's wonder. You'll be enthralled by his creativity and lyrical writing as you find yourself unable to put it back on the shelf unfinished."
–Bill Schweitzer, author of *Doves in a Tempest* **and** *The Valley of Horror*

Reader Comments

"I have wept through both of my readings of this novel."

"...begins us on a journey of what most likely will be a journey for every one of the family members."

"What a powerful beginning to a story of family, heartache, grief, war, loss, and the love that surrounds it all."

"It is a great coming of age tale in many ways. It's very tragic, but wonderful.

"What a touching, interesting book that touches on all the important parts of family-coming of age, understanding death, and healing - while unfolding a gripping story about a secret that lies deep at the heart of a broken family."

"This is a novel with a lot of heart."

"A heartfelt novel that conveys the pain of loss and regret in a skillful manner. The father-son dynamic reads as a realistic and relatable portrayal of how standards of masculinity can strain relationships."

"The emotions I felt lingered long after I finished reading."

IN JAKE'S SHOES

THE PRELUDE

Thursday, Early Midday
November 25, 2004
Forward Operating Base Salerno
Khost, Afghanistan

Working around dead people leaves a smell.

After a long day, I know the chow line's gonna be brutal. Better to stay behind in the tent to let it shorten. Nobody wants to stand or eat too close to anyone serving as a Mortuary Affairs Specialist. Idling away my time, I eye the table in the Mortuary Affairs Unit. A body bag lies stretched out flat on the table. Removing my boots and socks, I place them on the floor beside a chair at the end of the table. Hesitantly, I unzip the bag, climb inside, and pull the sides over me.

I'm like a bird dog on point—still as death. My eyes are open, but I can't see a thing. The heavy black plastic covering my body reminds me of the thick wool blanket Mama lay across me on cool nights when I pretended to be asleep. The body bag, smooth under my heels, settles loosely on the tops of my toes. Its weight and coolness are like ripples of shallow water on my naked forehead. Nose. Cheeks. Arms. Stomach. Legs. Feet. I take deep, slow breaths to try to keep my chest from heaving too much. It won't matter, though. Each breath moves me enough to crinkle-crackle the plastic. I imagine bone beetles scurrying across the outside surface searching for a way to get in.

Time stands still. No DD Forms wait for a signature or processionals of flag-draped transfer coffins to watch. No red dirt swirls up my nose, or dog tags lie crumpled on the ground to collect and catalog. No folded "Dear Son" letters to chase as they blow in the wind across the red dirt, or tattered pockets to search for hidden "I love you" notes from wives, or wrinkled, bloodied photographs of unseen babies to smooth and place in plastic baggies. No suicide notes soaked in blood to send home to grieving spouses or legless, foot-filled boots to unlace and remove ragged, bloody stumps. And…no dead eyes stare sightless up into mine. Nothing matters at the moment. Except for this brief escape from the random mortar rounds pounding somewhere in the distance. The incessant engine roars and the thick, pungent odor of diesel fuel are all in the world outside the one I now occupy inside this bag. Until my unit gets the call again. It can happen anytime. We'll ride out to the site. We'll search for and gather up and bag and evacuate and inventory everything. Everything that existed as a part of a living, breathing, feeling, thinking, missing and missed, loving and loved someone. Everything has to be bagged. *Everything.* There can be no more unknown soldiers. It's *our* job to make sure it never happens again.

A staleness consumes the air inside the bag, and my arm itches. Willing the itch away doesn't work. I give in and scratch. It's time to rejoin the other world…the real one. I unzip the body bag and sit up. Need to get outta this thing before somebody comes in.

Damn. Too late. It's Mack.

"Gatlin, that is some creepy shit, man."

I sigh, pull my legs up out of the black bag, and dangle them over the side of the table. Without looking at Mack, I jump, lightly, off the table and sit in the nearby chair. Reaching down, I grab my socks and slip on my right boot. "Don't worry about it," I say quietly.

Mack walks over. Slides his fingers across the black plastic as if it were a velvet seat cushion. He shakes his head, and his eyes narrow as he stares at me. "Don't let the NCO or anybody else in the unit catch you doing this. What's up with that, anyway? You got a death wish or something?"

I finish lacing up my right boot. My voice is barely above a whisper. "No. It's just…" I stop. Even if I try to put an explanation into words, I'm not sure

I want to. It's been a long time since I've been able to open up to anyone. Not since those letters to Gammy Gat back in the fifth grade. God, I loved that woman. Mama would've sent me to a shrink if she'd known I wrote letters to a dead woman. That was then. This is now. And I like Mack. We've talked before. Mostly junk and nothing worth anything. Still, we connected. Mack finally moves away from the table, pulls up a chair, turns it around, and sits backwards. I shift my gaze to keep from staring directly into his eyes as he leans forward onto his hands along the top rail. Before he can say anything, I preempt his response. "I needed to know what it was like," I say quietly, reaching down to tuck my pants leg down inside the top of my right boot. "We've zipped up so many 'angels' in these things." I pause. "And I can't help thinking Greeny put himself in there...on purpose."

"He still in your head? You gotta let go, man." Mack pauses. "You know, we can't let the personal stuff get to us. First thing they teach us."

I throw up my hands. "He's got a wife and a little kid."

Mack rubs his nose with the back of his hand. "We all got family."

My family's sorta like an old deck of cards with a tattered Jack, a faded Queen, and a rumpled-up King of hearts. My sisters are three solid aces. I chuckle quietly to myself, as I get this image of somebody dealing us out at a poker table. It sidetracks me until the thermostat on the portable heaters kicks in, and the purring fans push the image away. It takes a few seconds for the warm air to reach me, blowing against my cheeks as if I'd sneaked too close a peek beneath the lid of one of Gammy Gat's bubbling pots of spaghetti sauce. One of the units is close by. I stretch out my hands for a few seconds. Mack's gotta be thinking I've lost my mind or something. I look over at him and smile. "Did you read his..."

"Hell no!" Mack, restless, interrupts and moves to a stool. "Weapon under his chin? And in the port-a-john?"

I flick my eyes toward movement through the open window flap. Greeny's note? I'd read it more than once. "Want me to tell you what his note said?"

Mack smiles and does this thing where he puts his finger on his chin and looks up as if a light bulb or something suddenly appears over his head. "Let me think." He "thinks" for all of about three seconds, then throws up his hands, glares at me, and whispers this time, "Like I said, hell…no."

I tell him, anyway. "He told his wife and son he was sorry." Mack puts a finger in each ear and squinches his eyes shut. I know he can hear me. I keep talking. "He didn't know who he was anymore."

Mack removes his fingers and presses his palms against his cheeks, his mouth, and eyes as if his girlfriend has just let it slip she's pregnant. "That's a big, DUH."

"Don't be an asshole."

His hands fall from his cheeks. He shakes his head, stands up, walks over to the closest chair, and plops down. "Least I know I'm an asshole."

I shake my head and sigh. "You're not an asshole, you jerk. I'm sorry. I didn't mean it. It's just…" I don't know what to say next, but I want Mack to know about Greeny's note. Stalling, I walk over and straighten an evenly stacked set of DD forms. Glancing up, I notice the poster stuck on the tent wall behind the desk. In big letters, *Dignity, Reverence, and Respect.* I finally turn to Mack. "Last thing he wrote was they'd be better off without him." I pause. "The guy was a loner when he got here." Mack removes his service cover and rubs his balding head. I notice he takes a quick peek at the creed on the wall, then turns away and shakes his head. My nose gets another sleeve wipe before I reach out toward the heater again. "We should've made it harder for Greeny to feel alone."

Mack walks over and re-straightens the folders I'd just straightened. "Not our job, man."

"He killed himself, for God's sake," I mutter between clenched teeth. Mack runs his thumb up the side of the stack of folders, then shakes his head and gives them a shove, leaving them disheveled. He walks around the desk and sits in the chair again.

"You got a damn burr up your butt about these suicides," he says, his voice quiet. "What's that about, anyway?"

A Black Hawk flies overhead, and both Mack and I make eye contact. The glance lasts only for an instant, though. "I knew a guy who killed himself," I say, my voice quiet, too. "He was one of my classmates."

"No shit. How old were you?"

"Eleven."

Mack leans in toward me. "Jesus. How'd he, you know, how'd he do it?"

I shake my head and reach for a pen in the holder on the desk. Voices close by outside—guys walking by heading for the chow line—interrupt the momentary silence. "Found some of his mom's OxyContin. Took a bunch of 'em on purpose and overdosed."

Mack leans back and brushes his hand over his head once more. "That's brutal, man."

I finally lean down, finish lacing up my left boot, and adjust my pant leg. "Yeah, well, it was a long time ago."

"Why'd this kid do it? Did he leave a note or anything?"

"Yeah, sorta. The only note they found...was to me. All it said was, *'Tell Jake thanks for wanting to be my friend.'*" Mack just stares at me. "He was mixed up, and his family was messed up. Old man on drugs. Beat him and his mom. I think he figured things would never change or get better."

Mack puts his cover back on, stands up, walks over, and checks it out in the mirror. "You sound like maybe you were tight with this guy."

I make my way over to the table and smooth the wrinkles along the length of the body bag. For a brief moment, I imagine seeing Randy's skinny, eleven-year-old body stretched out in a bag pretty much like this one. "Yeah, I guess I was."

"How'd your folks feel about all that?"

I hesitate about how to answer. Turning, I look at Mack, shake my head, and say quietly, "It drove my Daddy nuts. He hated the kid 'cause he thought he was a bad influence."

"A bad influence?"

Just sayin' those words out loud brings back a memory I wish I didn't have. One night, Daddy and Mama were talking in their bedroom, and I overheard them. As if written with a permanent black Sharpie marker, my father's words remain imprinted in the back of my mind. I don't repeat them out loud to Mack, but they ring inside my head...loud and clear.

.   .   .   .   .

"Our boy's gonna drive me stupid, Millie. I don't know what's wrong with him. I don't know how to talk to him. Nothing I say seems to get him to change his behavior. He's damned exasperating, that's what he is."

.   .   .   .   .

I look at Mack and try to smile, then stare down at my boots. "Me and my old man didn't...don't...get along." I pause. "I, uh...I got into a bunch of trouble my fifth-grade year."

"Damn, man," Mack says, rubbing his chin. "What'd you guys do, rob a bank or something?" He chuckles. "Just shitting with ya," he says. "Ain't none of my business. But...you mean ever since you were in fifth grade, you and your pop...?"

"Yeah," I interrupt him, ignoring his robbery taunt. "It's not like we don't speak or nothing, it's just...we got this divide between us, you know, like some big ole' canyon." I pause and ponder Mack's tease. *If he only knew.* Randy and I did commit a crime. Mack's pretending he doesn't want to get into my "business," as he put it, but I know he's fishing for...needs...some kind of tidbit. Guess I owe him that. But I'm not willing to reveal the crime thing. At the time, we made a bad decision for all the right reasons. At least that's what I've continued to tell myself ever since it happened. So I tell him something I'd never told anybody. "My sophomore year, my daddy got so mad at me, he threatened to send me off to some military school if I didn't agree to join up after high school. I agreed, but was pissed at the time. During my senior year, I changed my mind. Decided it might be a good thing to "get with the program." I smile and sigh. "So, here I am."

"No shit," Mack said, his eyes wider than two sunny-side up fried eggs. "Again, ain't none of my business, but I'd love to know what happened to change your mind."

I smile. "Sort of a long story," I say quietly. "Kinda complicated. Don't think I'm ready to go into all that right now."

"Hey, don't mean to poke my nose where it don't belong," he says.

"No problem," I say, still smiling. "We're good."

Mack doesn't speak for a moment. The window flap flutters, and we both turn at the sound. I involuntarily wince as I think about the coming cold, winter breezes, they say will chill us to the bone. Mack stands up and walks toward me. He reaches up and lowers his palm gently on top of my shoulder. "Climbing inside that thing is still nuts." Pulling his hand away, he walks over to the table—where we all play cards in between recoveries—picks up a deck, and starts thumbing through it. "You scare the shit outta me sometimes."

The tent flap slaps open. It's Sergeant Danbury. "Get the unit together, girls. And grab your gear. We got a recovery site." Mack and I shoot glances at one another. Thanksgiving chow's gonna have to wait.

Sunday Night
December 5, 2004
Forward Operating Base Salerno
Khost, Afghanistan

It's late. Everybody's asleep in the barracks except me.

I'm still thinking about the Thanksgiving Day recovery. A member of the Afghan Border Police patrolling outside the base was hit by a sniper. Our unit assists when any of the allied military personnel are killed. Greeny's still on my mind too. Mack was right. Getting inside the body bag was one of my goofier decisions. I'd opened up to my friend a bit, though, and it felt strangely good. Mama would probably call it "therapeutic."

I leave my bunk, slip on my heavy jacket, and step outside. If I'd been a smoker, I guess I would've wanted to light one up. The image of my Gammy Gat dying from all the cancer gunk in her lungs pretty much kiboshed it as a habit for me. I pop a piece of gum instead and stick the wrapper in my pocket. Anyway, rule here at Salerno is blackout. With the blackout here on base, the clearest lights I see are from the stars overhead. Stars back home in Oakton, North Carolina, have never been as clear as they are in the skies over this place. The light from the stars provides just enough visibility to see the shadowy rows of sycamore trees along the nearby road. A grove of olive trees is a little further down.

My thoughts drift, again, to Gammy Gat, my daddy's mother. Her name was one of those wonderful southern double names—Mary Claire Gatlin.

After Grandpapa died, Mama and Daddy had added on a small, Grandmommy suite. I had just turned ten. Bunches of times I'd walk in and see her reading on her couch, puffing smoke like a steam engine, a menthol cigarette dangling from the side of her lips. I close my eyes and can even hear the sounds of her wheezing through the doorway connecting our part of the house to hers. I'll never forget the image of Mama and Daddy helping her into the car, around a year later. Gammy Gat turned toward my sisters and me. A pained smile eased onto her face. She waved a shaky hand. Mama stood at the curb with us while Daddy drove her to the hospital. My sisters and I made one visit. It was the only one Mama and Daddy allowed us to make before they insisted we stay home. For two weeks, I went to school with an aching stomach every day.

Gammy Gat never came home.

They held the funeral a few weeks before we moved to Oakton. The image of her casket blanketed by a flowing flower bedspread lingers in my memory.

    .   .   .   .   .

The gravediggers had disguised the open hole with pretend grass. The funeral home canopy shadowed the casket. Graying clouds had already begun to crowd the sun. A drizzle started. It was as if the clouds were a leaky ceiling, ready to burst open at any minute. When the watery burst came, the preacher kept talking anyway. Slender water tributaries slithered around my shoes like clear baby snakes. I remember lifting my shoes and resting them on the slanted legs of my chair. One shoe slipped off onto the wet carpet, and the chilly wetness crept into my sock. I muttered something I don't remember now. I do remember the elbow rebuke from my father.

    .   .   .   .   .

Gammy Gat's image fades like *she* did during the year she lived with us.

I spit out my gum—it sort of felt like it was beginning to chew me—and pop in a new piece. I think about those couple of months after the funeral, spent packing for the move. The next image to show up is one I knew would slip in—my best bud, Eddie.

.　　　.　　　.　　　.　　　.

He'd stood at the end of our driveway, unmoving. I could see him through the rear windshield, watching us leave. The moving van had gotten underway, and Daddy pulled our car out into the street to follow it. The moving van crept. We crept. It was like our car eased down the street with something hanging onto the bumper, trying to hold us back. Maybe the car just didn't want to go either. Eddie's figure had lingered behind us. Palm open, he'd raised his hand and held it up shoulder high. I'd pressed *my* hand against the rear windshield. Like a tiny octopus clinging to the side of an aquarium, I'd held it against the glass. I couldn't see if Eddie had any tears and hoped he couldn't see mine.

.　　　.　　　.　　　.　　　.

I pretend to shake the memory away and close my eyes again. When one of these memories, from my fifth-grade year, slips back into my mind, it always opens up a floodgate. They are always like dominoes falling in slow motion and just as unstoppable. I can't help thinking about Randy again. His image is faded. Like trying to make out the shape of your foot while standing in murky, shallow water. Randy had been a small, red-headed boy with freckles, crooked teeth, and funny-looking ears. He carried a major chip on his shoulder. I shake my head. Tired of this new piece of gum, I spit it out, too. Out of gum, I just sit and stare up at the stars.

Predictably, my mind takes me back to my conversation with Mack on Thanksgiving Day. The one where I'd told him about how me and Daddy didn't get along so well. And about his threat. What Daddy and I said, how we said it, and what he did feels like a tattoo I'll never be able to surgically remove.

·   ·   ·   ·   ·

"You're screwing up, son."

"If you say so."

"Always gotta have a smartass come back, don't you, Jake?"

"Whataya *want* me to say?"

"First off, I want a little bit of respect."

"Oh, okay. What would you like me to say, *Father*?"

Daddy shoved me. Not hard, but a shove, just the same. Standing firm and just staring at my old man, I didn't push back. His face turned pale. "Look, Jake…I'm sorry. I didn't mean to…"

I threw up my arms. "I'm outta here."

"You're what?"

"I'm outta here."

"What…now you're gonna run away? Where, in God's name, would you go?"

"I don't know. I'll go to Uncle Bobby's. He'll take me in. I'll get a job."

"Nobody…not even Bobby's gonna hire a high school dropout. And anyway, you're not sixteen yet. You can't drop out of school."

"Don't care. You can't make me stay."

"I can. And as soon as you turn sixteen, I'd just as soon send you to one of those military boarding schools for boys. They've got some here in North Carolina."

"No way."

"Yes, *way*. As far as I'm concerned, you can spend the rest of your high school in one of those schools."

"Daddy, you can't do that. Please."

"It's either there or you make a commitment to finish high school, here, then join up after you graduate."

"The military? Like Grandpapa? That's like asking me if I wanna cut off my arm or my leg."

"Your choice. Ever since fifth grade, you've done nothing but get by. In school and life. You're capable of making good grades. Every year, you passed by the skin of your teeth. You've developed a lazy-ass pattern of behavior. You sleep all the time. You don't talk to anybody. You..."

"Okay. Okay. So, I'm a loser. I'll finish school, then join the Army. That make you happy?" I paused. "Means you got to put up with my *pattern of behavior* for a couple more years. Then you'll have me outta your hair. It's what you want, isn't it?" I paused again. "If you won't tell Mama I threatened to take off, I won't tell her what you did."

.   .   .   .   .

Every time that memory shows up, this next domino image appears right after it. I see a piece of paper, inside a spiral notebook, with a date at the top. It's followed by words written in my scratchy, scribble handwriting. I can see myself writing them. It was the first one of nearly a year full of letters to Gammy Gat.

Sunday
December 24, 1995

Dear Gammy Gat,
I need to talk to somebody. It's got to be somebody who will listen to every word and won't tell me not to say what I want to say or not to feel what I'm feeling...

I shake my head. The rest of the words in the letter fade away. I think of my one final letter—the one I wrote my senior year in high school—the day before Thanksgiving. The words flow through my mind as if I wrote them yesterday.

Wednesday
November 27, 2002

Dear Gammy Gat,
Tomorrow's Thanksgiving. I'm sorry I haven't written to you in a long time. It's been hard because to write, I had to think, and I just can't think. It

hurts too much. I needed some time. Guess nothing's worse than an idiot who thinks he can figure out everything he needs to know about what to do with his life all by himself. Would you believe I'm a senior in high school now?

Mama's going to cook a turkey with all the trimmings. The weather is a bit "coolish" as you used to say, but it's not too bad. A sweatshirt and jeans work great for walks and playing football. You know, hanging around. Can't wait for the smells tomorrow. Especially the chocolate pie. Lisa learned how to make them like you did. Nothing better.

I have to admit something. Some of my memories of you are starting to get fuzzy. Like remembering when some things happened or exact details. It drives me stupid 'cause I don't want you to think I've forgotten the important stuff.

Sometimes, I try to remember what you looked like. Not when you were sick or when we visited you in the hospital, hooked up to all those machines. But when you were...you. Like the times you gave us birthday parties and made special cakes. Or when you worried if the birds were getting enough to eat in the wintertime. Or when you still treated Daddy like he was your little boy and teased him or fussed at him about something. Or when all we had to do was open a door at our house. A smile on your face is what I try to remember.

It's been about seven years since Randy died. Years, I know, of driving Mama and Daddy crazy. I do worry about not wanting to remember Randy. I get so confused about what's important to remember and the memories I want to go away. I think I haven't treated Mama and Daddy right about the whole Randy thing. I don't mean the dumb decision Randy and I made at the end of the school year. I know I embarrassed them and made their lives miserable. What I mean is, I still haven't been able to talk to them about everything. I don't know why. It's like I can't or won't. I don't know which. Mama told me they would be ready to listen whenever I was ready to talk. Maybe I'll be ready someday. Just not quite yet.

I think it's why I couldn't write to you for such a long time. I didn't know what to say or what to think anymore. I felt an emptiness that wouldn't go away. I think Mama thought I might go and do something stupid, and Daddy got on my case and stayed on it. I know they both meant well, and I guess I haven't done anything to help change their minds. Oh, I haven't gotten into trouble again. I have done what both of them think—coasted along with no direction. You know, through school and life. This was and is what mostly drives Mama so crazy. So many times, I can see it in her eyes. Even her hugs. I can tell she wants to hold on to me for a little bit longer than usual. I also know I haven't done anything to help her not feel, somehow, I'm slipping away from her or something. Daddy's eyes are different. Instead of wanting to hold on to me, he just wants to push me away. I confess I felt the same way for a long time.

Oh, I know, Mama's had big plans for me all along. Lisa's made for college, and it's made for her. I think the more successful she is, the more I'm sure I'm determined not to go. Remember my best friend, Eddie? He wants to go to college, too. I remember, at one time, we talked about trying to get in at the same place so we could room together. I think life has something else in mind for me. At first, when Daddy talked about me enlisting, I was angry. You don't know this, but when I was a sophomore, I got so fed up, I decided I was going to run off. I told Daddy I wanted to quit school and leave home. Anyway, he told me I couldn't leave and if I tried, he'd send me to some military boarding school. He wouldn't if I stayed and finished out high school, then promised to join up. I said sure, to get him off my back. At the time, I figured he had no right to "make" me do anything. Now, I feel kind of like Forrest Gump when he asked his mother to tell him what his destiny was. She told him he had to discover it for himself. You know, I never thought people were supposed to try to fit in somewhere. Destiny's got to be when you "fit in" without trying. How do you know where that is? Something has to let you know if you're on the right track, doesn't it?

Maybe it's why—would you believe it—I've decided I want to join the military. I know you know all about military life because of the first part of your life spent with Grandpapa. And I've been thinking real hard about it. Remember the last letter I wrote you after Randy died, and how I wished I'd been able to make it harder for him to believe he was all alone? Well, I've heard lots of soldiers come home from Iraq and Afghanistan and have problems "fitting" back into their lives. I learned this from my history teacher, Mr. Willis, this year. He's a Vietnam Vet. When he came back, he got his teaching degree. He's been here at my high school for several years. He does some coaching, too, and is a great guy. Remember, in one of my letters, I wrote that I didn't think I could ever be a teacher? Well, I've been rethinking it a bit after being in his class. I think I might join up and then maybe come back and do what he's doing. He talked about what being a soldier was like and how some of them struggle when they come home. It got me to thinking that being a soldier must make them feel alone. I know they have all their buddies around, and they talk about watching each other's backs. Maybe a special kind of feeling alone reaches deep into their souls—when they know every day could be their last. So many of them come home confused and depressed. It's gotta be the kind of alone Randy felt. I couldn't help Randy. Maybe my destiny is to join the military and then come back home and teach, because I know about this kind of alone and what it can do. I know Mama won't understand about the joining the military part. She'll freak out. Daddy will say the discipline will be good for me. Maybe so. I don't want to coast anymore or go after some career I don't have my heart in, or hang around and work at McDonald's until I "find myself." Anyway, just thought I'd throw that out as something to think about.

We went to the beach last weekend. November is a great time to go. Still warm enough to build a sandcastle and walk on the beach. We went back out Saturday evening to see if our sandcastle was still standing. Ship's lights dotted the dark horizon way offshore. The tide hadn't come in yet. We think the college kids we had seen walking on the beach, drinking beers, came by and knocked it down. It was like they didn't care someone had spent hours working and building something important. We sure wanted it to stay around a while longer. Those jerks tore it down too soon.

Your cancer was like that, wasn't it? It tore you down. And Randy's family was torn down by all their problems. I hope I haven't torn down my family. I have to be honest with you, I don't like going to the cemetery to visit your grave. Even though it's where your body is buried, I believe who you were, your essence, and your soul are not. Know what I mean? I often think about where you are, for real.

I remember when I first started writing to you, I thought maybe God would give you some kind of superpower so you could hear and see what I was writing to you. I know it was pretty much little kid thinking. Maybe, in some ways, you did read all my letters because I have this feeling in my heart I know what you'd be writing back.

You'd tell me to work hard and do my best. You'd say hard things are a part of life. And I shouldn't make them more difficult by worrying about them all the time. You'd tell me you were proud of me, and I can be anything I want to be if I work hard enough.

You'd tell me to listen to Mama and Daddy. Even though I may not agree with them or like what they tell me, they love me. You'd tell me to make sure I get along with my sisters. And it's okay to fuss with each other now and then. It's part of growing up. And you'd tell me you know I love them and they love me.

I think you'd tell me I shouldn't feel guilty about Randy and what he did. And, as terrible a thing as it was, all of us will learn from it. You'd tell me never to forget who I am. And to remember, people aren't perfect. You'd tell me I'll make mistakes, and I'll have to put up with other people's too. And I should never forget, feeling happy is better than feeling sad, although I'll always feel some of both. And it's a good thing. You'd tell me to say, "I love you," even when it's hard.

I think you'd tell me, too, not to worry about you or Randy. Your pain and his, your worries and his, are things of the past. I know it's taken a long time for my heart to listen to you, and I never told you thanks for being my "super" listener. I don't know all that's in store for me, Gammy Gat. Do you think I'm ready to face it now?

I'll try not to worry about stuff. If it's all right with you, now and then, when things aren't quite like I'd like them to be and a little bit of worry starts to creep in, I'd like to "talk" to you. Daddy used to after you died. He'd go outside and sit by himself in the dark.

Well, I'm getting sleepy. The night is clear, and I think I can see a zillion stars. It's nice. Real nice. I'm looking forward to tomorrow. Might even spring the military thing on Mama and Daddy then. If I do, I'll probably hold off bringing up the coming back to teach part. Still just keeping that idea on the back burner. Or the part about knowing what alone feels like. I still don't think Daddy's ready to hear me talk about Randy yet.

Wish so much you were here. Goodnight.

I think I'm finally ready to pick up some pieces,
Jake

P.S. I love you, Gammy Gat

P.P.S. One more thing I never told you about, but you probably already knew. I didn't get a baby brother, but...SHE'S pretty cool. Oh, yeah. They named her Mary, after you.

After writing the letter, I'd carefully folded it, slipped it into an envelope, and wrote, *Gammy Gat,* across the front. The next morning, while the rest of the family was outside enjoying the cool November morning, I'd sneaked up into the attic. Tucked it away inside a secret box. It's where I'd also hidden my notebook of letters to Gammy Gat.

I rub my fingers through my hair and sigh. The air in Khost, at this time of night, is cool enough to see my breath. Like those lingering ghostly shadows haunting old lithographs, more feelings from that year—and since—creep into my mind. Although I try to will away anything specific, one thing stands out. I suppose the anger I felt for my father, at the time, drives all of those memories. Our family had moved because he wanted a different job. A betrayal, as far as I was concerned. Do I hate him? Maybe hate and love him at the same time? Is it possible? He's my father. I'm his son. I'm just not sure if he likes me very much. Things happened during my fifth-grade year. Some bad. Some not fair. Some made no sense. Some just plain stupid. Some changed me...forever. An anger lingered with me for quite a while, but not so much anymore. I believe I've reached a point I can only describe as somewhere between mellow and anxious.

I quietly re-enter the barracks, undress down to my skivvies, and climb into my rack. Closing my eyes, the last thing I remember thinking about is challenging myself to put together a letter by the end of the week, so it'll get home before Christmas.

It's time to make things right.

Friday Night
December 10, 2004
Forward Operating Base Salerno
Khost, Afghanistan

Dear Mama, Daddy, Lisa, Beth, and Mary,

I can't believe it's almost Christmas. I know you'll be getting the tree pretty soon. Wish I could be home to decorate it with you.

Lisa, make sure to make one of Gammy Gat's chocolate pies. Since I won't get to eat one this year, it'll give you something to write to me about. Beth and Mary, you can describe how all the chocolatey goodness looked and tasted.

I do hate to tell you this next thing. I thought you should know, not too long ago, one of the guys in our company—Private Green—shot himself. Our MA unit had to process him. He had a wife and kid back in South Carolina. And now he's headed home, just not the way his family expected. I didn't know him very well. It didn't make what he did any easier to accept. You know, I even read somewhere, counting those who come home, more soldiers kill themselves than get killed in combat.

Mama and Daddy, I know I've never sat down and talked with you about my fifth-grade year. I guess when Greeny did what he did, it brought it all back, big time. It made me realize I owed you a long talk.

I kind of shut myself down then, I know. Like I wanted to keep everybody out. I haven't let anybody in on anything I've felt for a long time. And I know it wasn't and hasn't been fair. Being only eleven at the time, I guess I can convince myself I didn't know any better. I know I royally screwed the whole father-son thing, and I have awful regrets. Maybe if I'd known then what I know now…but things don't work that way, do they? Not sure what I'm getting at, except I think I'd like to try to talk about it, you know?

I didn't tell you all this because I want you to worry about me. It's, well, when I get back, I hope we can sit down and get to know each other again. Means even you girls (Ha ha).

Oh, yeah, one more thing. They say December is nasty over here. We thought the dust storms had been bad. All the red dust builds up and turns into a muddy mess because of all the rain and snow. It's cold, too, and going to be worse than Oakton in December.

We've been involved in a few recoveries these past few weeks. Don't fret, though. (I know you, Mama.) Khost has been pretty dull lately, and the road to Gardez has been pretty quiet for the most part. Before long, the weather will clog up the road, anyway.

Well, I've got to go. Sorry this one had to be so short. Didn't mean for it to be so mental either. This stuff's on my mind, and Christmas is tough enough without family around to spend it with. The holiday won't be the same without being at home. I miss you all so very much and wish I could be there with you. We have a job to do. Will try to write more later.

Love ya and hugs,

Jake

P.S. Merry Christmas

P.P.S. Don't worry about me. I'll be home before you know it.

Jake drops his letter off at the Military Post Office first thing Saturday morning. He knows about the eleven-day window of opportunity for letters to reach home.

Saturday
December 18, 2004
Forward Operating Base Salerno
Khost, Afghanistan
6:30 a.m.

The sun's rising.

I pull myself out of my bunk. Light blonde hairs growing across my upper lip feel smooth. I'd gone unshaven for several days and kind of hoped to find enough to keep my buddies from razzing me about my baby face.

A rooster crows somewhere.

The city's Afghan residents yawn awake too, getting ready for the day's market. All of us live and work under the constant threat of insurgents. These guys hide out along the road leading away from Khost and up into the mountains. Rugged terrain is hell along the road through the mountains leading to Gardez. Deep snow will pile up along the high embankments. It'll flow down onto the pass soon enough in this Southeast province. The snow, along with the rutted roadway, will make sections during the winter nearly impassable. Chilled air here, now, is nothing compared to the cold we all expect.

After morning chow, I head back to our unit's tent. Sarge is waiting for us. A Growler out on patrol hit an IED. There's a body. We gather gear and head for our Humvees waiting at the entrance of the installation. Just outside the base, a long coil of barbed wire loops its way along the rugged gravel road. Rocks scatter randomly, like freckles, on the dirt roadway. Concrete barriers stand like small, ancient stone monuments scattered among the scrub trees and bushes forward of the gate.

"Hey, Gatlin," the guard on duty shouts, "keep your head down out there. The road ain't no picnic, you know."

I commit a half-hearted smile. My warm breath visible, I aim a thumbs up at the guard and climb into the vehicle taking the point. Corporal Maxwell's driving. I slide in and slam the door. It makes a solid clunk even though these trucks have seen their best days. He grins. His pearly whites almost gleam beneath his dark black mustache. I roll my eyes and ask him a question I already know the answer to. "What's the skinny on getting them new MRAPS?"

He reaches through his open window and slaps the side of our truck. "Aw, you know the drill, Gatlin. We'll see 'em when we see 'em. Typical SNAFU at HQ. Till then, we'll have to ride in *this* piece of shit."

Friday
December 17, 2004
Gatlin Home
Oakton, North Carolina
A Little Before 10:00 p.m.

Marshall Gatlin smiled at the view looking down from the top of the tree. He could hardly tell his wife, Millie, from their three daughters. The oldest, twenty-three-year-old Lisa, home from her first year as a Kindergarten teacher, stood below, staring up at him. Her heritage from her mother was her beauty, her auburn hair, and her gift for *reading the room*—a trait which was going to make her an excellent teacher. The strands of her hair hung long and as thick as a Wiccan besom. She pulled them into a lengthy ponytail down the middle of her back. The steaming mug of cider in her hand and the wafer-thin Moravian ginger cookie she munched on looked tempting. Beth, their third-born, recently turned seventeen and was a junior in high school. She swiped, unsuccessfully, at her sister's cookie. Big-boned like her grandfather, Cole Gatlin—and the recipient of a bit of his wonderful *snark* DNA—Beth was destined to be tall like her older brother. She flicked her bobbed—more red than auburn—hair, and it flipped across her freckled face. The "pixie" and late addition to the family was eight-year-old Mary. As well as her Gammy Gat's first name, she inherited her curly, dark-brown hair and unyielding sense of fair play. Marshall smiled, but the view from the top of the tree was incomplete. One child was missing. Twenty-year-old Jake.

"Daddy! Pay attention! You're gonna break the ornaments." Beth turned and pleaded with her mother. "He's gonna break 'em, Mama."

An indignant glare from Marshall flashed across his face before segueing into a smile. "I'm not gonna break 'em, sweetheart. I'm not one of Lisa's kindergarteners, you know." He paused. "Can't get this damn stepladder close enough to reach the top."

"I'm with Beth, on this one. And watch your French, Marshall."

He ignored Millie's admonition and evil eye. "The tree's too wide at the base, my dear, and this wonderful stepladder is inadequate for the job."

"Not the only thing too wide at the base."

"I heard that, Beth."

"WHAT? What did I say?"

"A little respect would be…you know…nice."

Marshall climbed down and moved the ladder in closer through the branches. It meant having to suffer the prickly needles. He tugged at his pull-string jeans and stretched his sweatshirt sleeves down over his wrists, all the while silently cursing his beer paunch. If his belly plopped onto the top of the ladder, like a flood-stopping sandbag, he'd never live it down.

Too late.

He rolled his eyes at the sounds of the familiar, and if he were honest, expected snickers behind his back. "Oh, you think this is funny, huh? I thought, at least, my youngest would have more respect for her old daddy."

Mary's older sister, Lisa, saved her. "We haven't seen any letters from Jake, lately."

Millie jumped in. "I'm sure we'll hear from him soon enough. He's busy, you know."

"That is no excuse," Lisa chimed in.

"Give him a break," Marshall said. "He's a guy."

"*Because* he's a guy?" Beth snarled. "Here we go." She threw up her hands and nodded at Lisa.

"It's on." Lisa dropped down on the sofa and crossed her arms across her chest.

"Hold it, you two." Millie held up her hands. "We are not going there tonight."

"Aw, Mama. You're no fun," Beth said, frowning.

Millie cast a fake grin at Lisa and Beth and handed Marshall the Moravian Star. After his father died, when Marshall's mother lived with them, he'd taken over the ritual of placing the star on top of the tree.

"Mary Claire Gatlin will not be happy if you drop this, Marshall Gatlin."

"Better listen to Mama, Daddy." Beth poked her father on the leg. "Gammy Gat's watching."

"Everybody got to know Gammy Gat but me," Mary said, her lips turning down in a sad frown. "It's not fair."

Millie grabbed her youngest and hugged her. "She would've loved knowing you, little girl."

Mary smiled and looked at her father. "Be careful, Daddy."

"I will, little girl," he said.

The high expectations for successful accomplishment of the ritual drove his effort. He'd watched his father grimace dozens of times. Not once had he fallen short of the deed. For Marshall, the nature and intensity of the grimacing and tooth gritting had to be the key. He clenched his teeth, contorted his lips, and stretched to place the star over the topmost branch. The star swayed slightly to the left, then back to the right—albeit slightly ajar—atop the tree. After another heart-stopping lean, the star righted itself for good and perched at the top of the tree as the beacon for which it was intended. Marshall turned and grinned.

"Ta-da."

Millie tugged on his pant leg. "Okay, hot stuff, come down from up there. I don't trust this stepladder." Millie's lack of trust proved well-placed. The thing wobbled more than one of those dashboard hula dancers.

Once back on the floor, Marshall moved the ladder out of the way. He grinned as he felt an imaginary congratulatory slap on the back from the weighty hand of his old man. "Anybody see the remote for these lights?"

"Uh, it's right beside you, Daddy," Beth said, rolling her eyes. "If it'd been a snake, it would've bitten you." Marshall rolled his eyes and snarked a grin at his oldest. The multi-colored lights exploded around the tree. The nine-foot Fraser fir and the entire family room glittered like a miniature theme park's holiday celebration parade. Fire snapped, crackled, and popped in the fireplace as hickory smoke perfume permeated the room.

Millie leaned against Marshall and took his hand. "Nice." She knew he wasn't going to put his arm around her. Not a hugger, he had inherited this trait from his old man. Something unexplainable held Marshall back from what should have been an easy, intrinsic physical expression of emotions—hugging, pulling someone in close, and well-timed kisses on the cheek. He struggled between worrying whether heartlessness or ineptness defined him as a human being. Marshall's desperate tendency to lean toward the ineptness moniker kept him sane. Heartlessness would be unforgivable. From time to time, it helped to chuckle about his apparent phobia, wondering which category seemed most likely to describe his father. The girls chastised him mercilessly about this character flaw every chance they got. It didn't rear its head tonight. A few streaks of unwanted gray from Millie's auburn hair fell across her face. She blew it away and up and sighed audibly. "Wish we'd found the little cherub ornament your mother gave me."

"I promise I'll go back up in the attic to see if I can find it." He sneaked a peek around Millie's back and cast a pleading glance at his daughters.

Ignoring him, Beth plopped down on the sofa. "I'm beat. What time is it, anyway? And for Christ's sake, where'd all these ornaments come from anyway?"

"Watch your language, Beth." Millie reached over and tugged at her hair. "Ouch!"

"Almost 10:00," Millie said, dodging the swipe back from Beth. "And I'll have y'all know, young lady, someday all these wonderful ornaments and decorations will be divided up among all four of y'all."

Lisa stuck out her tongue at her sister. "They're great, Mama. Don't listen to her." She plopped. "What time is it in Afghanistan, Daddy?"

"Well, let's see, I think they're about eight and a half hours ahead of us. So, I guess...let's see, must be about 6:30 tomorrow morning, December 18th."

Mary moved over to put her arm around her mother's waist. She didn't disguise her whisper. "I wish Jakey was here."

Marshall placed his hands on his hips and stared back at the Christmas tree. "I do too, little girl," he said. "I keep telling myself, he's where he oughta be. And if he's making the most of it, he'll come back here a better man."

Millie socked him on the arm.

"Ow, that hurts."

"Well, you deserve it." She paused. "And he is a better man, already."

Marshall winced. "Ouch to that too."

She patted his stomach and smiled. "I didn't mean better than *you*."

Marshall frowned and scrinched his nose. "Something insincere about your grin."

Millie stuck out her tongue at Marshall and gave Mary a squeeze. "We're thankful you three are here."

Saturday
December 18, 2004
Gatlin Home
Oakton, North Carolina
12:01 a.m.

The quarter moon hung in the sky like a honeydew melon sliced through the middle. Old Man Winter had finally chased the red leaves on the maples and the golden reds on the post oaks to the ground. A slight breeze squeezed through a tiny crack in the original bedroom window in their 1917 bungalow home in Oakton, North Carolina. The cool nights appeared regularly now.

Marshall relished them. As if in defiance of his asthma, the crisp, winter air filling his mildly diseased lungs invigorated him. He took the three or four steps between the bed and the old window and leaned in until he stopped an inch or so from the small glass crack. Seeing the life-affirming mini-clouds appear on the glass from his warm breath stirred his soul. With eyes closed, he breathed in the trickle of coolness as it slivered through from the outside. Millie, periodically, requested a replacement window. Marshall kept finding excuses to hold off. History mattered too. Someone, long gone, had also stared through the now murky glass. Maybe a frightened bird had slammed into the window. Perhaps in an argument, someone had thrown something. He would love to know the story.

Marshall missed his son. He didn't understand him and, for a long while, just hadn't liked him very much. He missed him just the same. Millie would've told him it was Jake's behavior he didn't like, not him personally. He bought the explanation, but the depth of his sentiment he tried to camouflage, especially from the prying mind of his wife and his daughters. Marshall's inability to spontaneously express physical emotion didn't help his capacity to reveal his deepest thoughts. For several years, now, his son lived immersed in a story Marshall just didn't understand. It seemed the first chapter began during Jake's fifth-grade year. Experiencing this story had opened a floodgate into Marshall's perception of his parental effectiveness. According to Millie...ineffectiveness. His relationship with his son portrayed a narrative whose chapters had left Marshall unfulfilled as a father. If not unfulfilled, it left him perplexed. Perplexed at how little control he had over circumstances he believed he had an obligation and a right to control.

Marshall opened his eyes and leaned in closer to the window. His breath fogged another small circle on the glass. He frowned at the thought of how the first chapter—the fifth-grade year from hell—could be such a driving force sending his son careening toward such a potentially convoluted, unknown ending. Marshall had made decisions then, and subsequently since, based on solid principles. Black and white, right and wrong principles he vowed would hold up in any court of public opinion. These principles existed to be applied to circumstances requiring circumspection, prudence, and foresight. His father, Cole, had lived by just such a creed, and creeds provided frameworks. Frameworks could be malleable, certainly not breakable. Marshall sighed and rolled his eyes. Periodically, Millie called him out for this bullshit explanation he maintained was, in her words, an excuse to rationalize his total lack of empathy for his son and his inability to recognize the gray areas within any framework of principles.

He and his principles had been the driving force behind Jake's decision to join up. On the outside, he embraced the choice. He tried to downplay the confrontation the two had experienced when Jake was in high school. It had certainly been the catalyst. The incident, however, churned in his gut, messed with his mind, and saddened his heart. He would never forgive himself for the shove—his spur-of-the-moment physical outburst. Sighing, he turned away from the window and stared at Millie. Hunkering down beneath their comforter, she stared back, smiled, and motioned for him to join her. "For goodness' sake, Marshall, get under the covers and get me warm."

He rolled his eyes and made his way to his side of the bed. *If anything happens to our boy....* He refused to finish the thought, reached the bed, and slipped beneath the sheet and comforter. Millie locked legs with him and snuggled close. The girls had crashed soon after they finished decorating. Both Millie and Marshall had piddled around for a while in the kitchen, spent time admiring the tree and its decorations again, and then, cups of spiked eggnog in hand, sat by the dying fire until it finally burned itself out. Now, finally ready for bed, neither of them could drift off. Millie, uncharacteristically, remained too quiet for him. Before he could speak, true to form, she muttered, "If Jake hadn't enlisted, he'd be here, with us, right now. And I can't believe he volunteered for that dreadful Mortuary Affairs duty." Millie paused. "I wanted him to go to college."

A finger from Marshall gently poked its way into her side. "It's what he wanted."

Millie smiled, grabbed the finger, and pushed it away. "We shoulda changed his mind." She sat up on her elbows, pushed both her pillows behind her back, and sat up.

Marshall shoved his pillow behind his back and scooted against it. "You *keep* bringing this up." Not wanting to make eye contact, he stared out the window and said the words he'd convinced himself were true. "Military service will help him to grow up, be a man, and think about his future." He paused and took a breath. Told himself not to say what he thought next. He did it, anyway. "His decision would've made my old man happy."

Millie shook her head and chuckled softly. "Your father served in the military during a whole different time in this country. And, as I seem to recall from your stories about growing up, you weren't particularly inspired by his experience." She paused. "You forget. You told me that your father called you 'soldier' throughout your childhood and up until you were in your early teens. Until you begged him to stop."

Marshall snorted. "When I got older, I started to worry maybe he'd forgotten my name." He puckered his lips in his best little kid imitation. "When I was wittle, I wiked it."

Millie smacked him lightly across the chest. "Cute. He *was* a piece of work." Marshall chuckled. Millie reached up and brushed back the few strands of hair Marshall still had. Her fingers tickled, and he didn't want her to stop. He closed his eyes. Frowned when she pulled her hand back. Millie took a deep breath, reached around, and patted her pillow again. "I still think about his fifth-grade year, what with your mother dying, the move, the new school, everything he experienced with Randy, and our family expecting a new baby, and ..." She paused. "It would've been a lot for any kid to handle."

Marshall mumbled, "I thought we'd taught him to handle it."

Millie shook her head and glared at him. "You don't *stop* teaching your children. He was growing up, but he wasn't grown. You've forgotten what it was like to be his age."

A deep sigh escaped from Marshall's mouth. "It's not a matter of my not remembering. It's a matter of knowing what's right and what's wrong."

"Growing up is something more. Your mother taught us that."

"Yeah, well, Momma was a piece of work, too."

The softer of Millie's two pillows had squished itself nearly flat beneath the firmer one. Millie tugged it out from behind her and hugged it like a favorite stuffed animal. "It's why Jake loved her so much." Millie burrowed her chin into the softness. "And when she died and we moved, he grew distant. Like someone beamed away his soul."

"We all had to accept her death and the move," Marshall said, turning over on his side and facing Millie. "It's a part of growing up, too, isn't it?"

"Kids aren't supposed to have to deal with it all by themselves." Millie rearranged the pillow beneath her chin. "We can't treat them as if they already know what it is we're supposed to help them learn. It's why they have us. When he was struggling, we should've..."

Marshall reached out his hand and gently covered her mouth. "Don't say it, 'cause I *know* what you're gonna say. We should've talked to him more. Listened to him. Damn it. I did bring it up now and then."

Millie moved his hand away. Her voice louder than she had intended. "You mean, you *threw* it up at him."

"You're not being fair, Millie, and you know it." Marshall's frown preceded an immediate switch so his back faced Millie. "C'mon, he wouldn't talk much to you either." A pause. "And anyway, kids his age don't talk to their parents."

Marshall felt Millie's hand on his shoulder as she whispered. "He had a tough year."

He reached out his hand and found hers. "Who hasn't had at least one tough year growing up?"

Millie caressed his fingers, then slipped her hand away. "I'm sure you weren't the model of behavior when you were his age."

Marshall turned his head and muttered between slightly clenched teeth. "My old man was tough as hell, and I toed the line."

Millie started to laugh, then caught herself. "Really? You wanna rethink what you just said?"

Marshall turned, lay flat on his back, and stared at the ceiling. "I wasn't perfect, I'll admit it." Another pause. "After the fifth grade, Jake just wasn't the same. He lost his great smile and just seemed angry all the time. Sometimes the look he'd get in his eyes scared the hell out of me."

"He struggled with what he wanted to do with his life," Millie whispered. "Like any kid."

Marshall kept his gaze on the ceiling. "Yeah, well, his struggling led him to a bunch of dead ends."

Millie perched up on her elbows. "And the military was his answer?"

Marshall turned to face her. "It was his choice."

Millie caught his gaze, then glanced away. "I think he hid how he was feeling all through the rest of elementary school, middle school, and high school." She paused. "Going into the military was his way of running away."

Marshall threw the covers back, and sat up on the edge of the bed. He stood up. "How many times are we gonna have this argument? I'm telling you, most kids don't talk about touchy-feely kinds of stuff with their parents. And he can go to college *after* he gets out." He took a couple of steps toward the window. "Anyway, what the Mortuary Affairs Unit does is important work."

Millie patted an invitation back to the sheet he'd vacated. "Discussion, sweetheart. We are *discussing* our son. And I don't care how important you say it is, preparing bodies to be sent home is awful duty. Now, please get back in this bed."

Someone coughed. Lisa had been nursing a bit of a cold. Chasing five-year-olds around day in and day out surely took its toll. A siren whined somewhere off in the distance, then faded.

Movement caught Marshall's attention outside their window. Rustling boxwood leaves and branches stretched up below the sill, like shadow fingers attempting to reach the glass. He chastised himself for not cutting them back like the pest control guy suggested. In the spring, sugar ants would use the branches as bridges to break into the house. Marshall sighed and accepted Millie's invitation. "I know what your kind of *discussion* means," he muttered. "It means we're tallying up all the things *I* did wrong."

Millie touched his shoulder. "Let's not go *there* tonight."

Marshall turned and looked at her. Even in the dim light, the two caught each other's eyes and held their stare. Marshall finally said quietly, "He was a tough kid to raise back then." He received an unexpected crab pinch on the arm. "Ow."

Millie turned away and stared out the window. "I don't care what you say...what happened then changed our son's life forever." She paused and whispered. "And he kept it all inside."

Marshall reached over, touched her chin, and gently eased her back around. Even in the dark, he noticed the tear leaking down her nose. It moved slowly, like it couldn't decide whether to make the journey down her cheek or not. "We couldn't *make* him open up, sweetheart."

Millie snuffled. "Well, how we responded was a big part of it."

He tamped the tear with the tip of his finger. "I worry about him, too." A pause. "I do. You raise your kids the best you know how. And you hope to God they turn out all right. Know what I mean?"

She kissed him on the cheek. "Yes, honey, I think I do. Now, close your eyes. Let's try to get some sleep."

Both of them adjusted pillows and turned on their sides, backs toward the middle of the bed. A long pause followed. Marshall closed his eyes and waited for the last word. He didn't have to wait long. Millie whispered, "For somebody to want to talk, there has to be a listener." Marshall remained silent. He lay still. After a few moments, he heard the soft breathing affirming Millie had drifted off to sleep. His thoughts immediately accessed a memory. The day for Jake to head back to Fort Lee for his deployment to Forward Operating Base Salerno near the city of Khost, Afghanistan, flashed in his mind. The family had gathered around Jake's car.

▪   ▪   ▪   ▪   ▪

He had stood silent, almost as if at attention, while Millie fussed with his uniform, pretending to polish his buttons and smooth out his collar.

"You sure you didn't forget anything?"

Jake rolled his eyes at his sisters.

"Yes, Mama, I'm sure."

Millie started to run back inside the house. "Stationery. We forgot stationery."

"No, we didn't, Mama. Remember...you packed three boxes under my socks."

Lisa, leaning on the car, spoke up. "Do you have your contact solution and extra contacts?" She smiled a facetious grin.

Another eye-roll from Jake. "Got 'em."

His mother grabbed his cheeks. "*Promise* me you'll write."

Jake gently removed her hands. "I will. I will."

Millie put her hands on her hips. "Say it. Say, 'I promise.'"

Jake saluted his mother. "I promise."

Beth whispered, "And you'll change your underwear every day."

"Beth!"

"Say it." All three girls at the same time.

"I promise," he shouted. Then, under his breath, "Unless I'm going commando."

"Eww!" All three girls again.

Millie put her hands on her hips and glared at him. "Jake Gatlin...I'm gonna forget you said such a thing."

Jake pointed his finger at his sister. "She started it."

Millie stepped close to him, gently pushed his finger away, and gazed up into his eyes. "Promise you'll come back to me safe and sound."

Jake looked down at the ground.

Millie socked him on the arm. "Say it."

"Ow!" He rubbed his arm. "I promise."

She threw her arms around him and held on. "I love you, honey."

"I love you too, Mama."

Marshall reached out and touched Millie's shoulder. "He's gotta go, Millie."

She wiped her tears on his shirt. "I know. I know."

Marshall stuck out his hand. "All right, son, you take care now."

Jake's firm grip matched his father's. "I will."

An awkward silence followed. "Uh, son."

Jake stared at his father. "Yeah, Daddy."

Marshall reached and massaged the back of his neck. "I, uh..." He stared down at the ground and then sneaked a peek at Millie. He wished he hadn't, because she gave him the "say the words" glare.

"Sir?"

"Uh...don't you break *any* of those promises you made to your mama. Like my daddy used to say, 'That's an order.'"

"Yessir," Jake said, casting a glance at his mother. Holding the glance for a brief moment, he then turned, waved, and got in his car. Marshall let him drive off without saying those three words.

Millie had waved goodbye to Jake, then stood watching until his car disappeared around the corner. She turned around and looked Marshall square in the eyes. "I hope to God you don't come to regret not telling him."

·   ·   ·   ·   ·

A single, high-pitched whistle from a Millie tongue snore brought Marshall back from his memory. He listened for a second to see if she would follow it up. Luckily, it appeared to be a one-off. He closed his eyes, hoping the voice in his head would remain silent.

No such luck.

Saturday
December 18, 2004
Gatlin Home
Oakton, North Carolina

Marshall woke up, summoned by a 4:00 a.m. bathroom call. After coming back to bed, he tossed and turned. Allowing himself to get caught up in the fretting and worrying about everything and nothing always made it so difficult to fall back asleep. Eventually, he did, and before he knew it, a buzzer buzzed. Millie tapped his shoulder. He mumbled, "What's the alarm doing coming on so early in the morning? And when did the damn thing start sounding like the doorbell?"

Millie jumped up out of bed. "It *is* the doorbell." The clock read 8:00 a.m.

Marshall threw his bathrobe on over his pajamas. "Who, in God's name, would be ringing our bell this early in the morning?"

Millie dashed to the bathroom. "I don't know. Go and find out. I'm not dressed."

"Who is it, Daddy?" Lisa's sleepy voice sounded from her bedroom down the hall.

Marshall's knees ached like hell in the morning, a condition he took advantage of, periodically, to pronounce how getting old hurt everything, even his feelings. He hobbled his way out of the bedroom door. "Don't know, honey. Go back to bed."

He made his way downstairs and peered through the living room window out onto the front porch. Those gimpy knees buckled. Millie had followed him partway and sat on a step midway down the stairwell. "Who is it?"

Marshall glanced back at her, his face pale, his breaths in quick succession. "You...you'd better come here."

Saturday
December 18, 2004
Gatlin Home
Oakton, North Carolina
8:02 a.m.

"Mr. and Mrs. Gatlin, we regret to inform you..."

The army officer's teleprompter words spun in Marshall's mind like a broken record stuck on a spinning turntable. Millie whispered, "Are y'all sure, Pastor Gordon?"

"Yes, Millie, they're sure."

A gasp broke the tension. It wasn't Millie's voice. Somebody said something about the body...arrival back in the US, within two days...Marshall thought the girls might have been standing in the doorway. He didn't see them. Millie clutched his arm. She said something he didn't understand. Another voice spoke. It sounded like the officer. He couldn't be sure. Millie's voice and the other voice were both talking. He couldn't understand what they were saying. Millie whispered something again, but she wouldn't release his arm.

Why is she holding me so tight? He thought. *I need to comfort her. She might faint or do something drastic.* Marshall tried to tell them, then the air stopped. He couldn't breathe. Millie said something about his rescue inhaler.

Tuesday
December 21, 2004
Dover Air Force Base

Jake's flag-draped transfer case containing his body arrived. The carry team passed the remains to the medical experts of the Armed Forces Medical Examiner System. After their work was complete, the remains were released back to the Port Mortuary in Dover. Their specialists preserved and restored Jake's body and sent it to the Smithson's Funeral Home in Oakton, arriving late in the day, December 22nd. Not wanting to go through Christmas in anticipation of the funeral, Millie and Marshall asked Smithson's if they could schedule it on Christmas Eve afternoon. Smithson's assured the Gatlins they would be able to comply.

Friday
December 24, 2004
Oakton Methodist Church
2:00 p.m.
Meadowview Memorial Park
3:00 p.m.

The church service passed like a blur. Several school friends and family members spoke. The congregation stood for a couple of hymns, and the preacher shared several appropriate Bible verses. All Marshall remembered was sitting in the front pew beside Millie and his daughters, staring at the flag-draped coffin.

At the interment, Pastor Gordon's words flowed over Marshall like a wispy fog and drifted away as if he never heard them. An honor guard detail performed its ritual as if programmed by a computer. Marshall's eyes followed their slow and deliberate salutes. Rifle volleys pierced the silence, followed by the long, lonesome notes of a bugle. The wail reached through the frosty air and grabbed at Marshall like dead fingers threatening to steal his breath away. Two honor guardsmen lifted the flag from the casket. Their white-gloved hands performed those agonizing thirteen, slow-motion folds. Marshall counted them, not realizing he breathed in and out with each fold. The senior officer handed Millie the folded flag and Purple Heart. His quiet words played and replayed in Marshall's ears.

"On behalf...please accept this flag and medal...as symbols of our appreciation...your loved one's honorable...faithful service."

Everyone left from beneath the canopy, except Marshall and Millie. She had motioned for the girls to make their way to the waiting limousine. They had hesitated. She shooed them on. "We'll be there in a minute," she whispered. A cold, trickle rain began. Millie hurried to the funeral home's black Cadillac, stopped short, and glanced back. Marshall hadn't moved. She shouted at him. "Marshall! Please come and get in the car. You're going to catch pneumonia."

The weather channel predicted thirty-six degrees, cold even for the middle of December in Oakton, North Carolina. Marshall's overcoat remained draped across his arm. A silent sentinel, he stood guard a few paces outside the twenty-by-twenty canopy tent. The near-freezing droplets splattered against his balding head. Icy trails of tiny rivers flowed down his forehead, seeped through his bushy eyebrows, and plopped onto his cheeks. His lips quivered. He *wanted* to feel the cold rain. He wanted it to punish him for sending his son to his death. It wouldn't be enough until the muddy slop soaked through his shoes and socks and oozed between his frozen toes. The stark, glossy brown casket, waiting to be lowered, perched on top of the metal frame. An image from around ten years ago of yellow and white blossoms crept into his mind. Flowers draped across and trailed off the sides of another casket. Two symbols of death merged into one. He had to close his eyes as he pictured his mother's funeral and now Jake's. His son's letter from Afghanistan arrived two days *after* the devastating news. It remained stuffed in his pants pocket. He pulled it out and unfolded the crumpled paper. Raindrops smacked onto the surface. Marshall, trying to protect it from the rain, read the words.

For the umpteenth time.

When he finished, he closed his eyes. It only enhanced an image he could not make himself unimagine—his twenty-year-old son sprawled on the cold, hard Afghan ground, body twisted and broken by an IED. The irony of his son's own words created the image. *Don't worry about me. I'll be home before you know it.* Little muddy rivers sloshed against his shoes, escaped around the makeshift shoe dam, and raced helter-skelter away. The sludge pit kept growing larger. Sighing, he folded the soaked paper and stuffed it back in his pocket. He felt Millie's touch on his shoulder again. It should have been his cue to turn, reach out, and pull her to him. He couldn't move. Even then, he couldn't bring himself to return a consoling embrace. With gentle pressure, her fingers closed around his arm. "Marshall. Marshall, honey, please come with me. You've got to get in the car."

Marshall whispered, "He's gone." He paused. "And *who* he was is gone too, Millie. I pushed him to go out into the world, be a man...and find himself. Now he's gone, and we'll never get to know who he really was...or could've been."

"Shhh." Millie kissed his cold, wet cheek. "If I don't get you in out of this weather, I'm gonna lose you too, and I'm not about to let that happen." She placed her arm around his waist. Marshall's throat tightened. He tried to speak. His voice shook, and no words formed, only quickened breaths. He placed his hand over his eyes, trying to stop what followed. He choked slightly, then began to cry uncontrollable, quiet sobs. Millie pulled him away from the canopy. They waded through the puddles to the sanctuary of the black limousine.

Christmas Eve
December 24, 2004
Gatlin Home
4:00 p.m.

Marshall had convinced his sister's families, both of whom lived out of state and had flown in for the funeral, to catch return flights immediately after the funeral. Older sister, Helen, and younger sister, Alice, had initially insisted on staying over. In the end, they had relented and returned home. In the south, church members and friends dropping by with food items after a funeral was, typically, an honored tradition. Marshall had initially balked at the idea, expressing to Millie that folks would want to spend their Christmas Eve with their own families. The outpouring and support, however, had been impressive. He'd let himself be talked into honoring the tradition. Now, the doorbell rang and a steady stream of mourners entered with armfuls of such southern delicacies as squash and green bean casseroles, Tupperware containers of potato and chicken salad, spiral hams, plates of fried chicken, homemade biscuits, fruit plates, barbecue, boiled potatoes, pigs in a blanket, baked beans, slaw, sweet potato pies, deviled eggs, and ham biscuits.

His kitchen was filling with more food than his family could ever eat, and the house was filling with more folks than he wanted to see. Ignoring the doorbell, he slipped into his home office and quietly closed the door. Crossing over behind his desk, he reached down and pulled open the large file drawer on the right side. He scrunched the rack of files forward and reached into the back of the drawer. His fingers found the unopened bottle he'd hidden. Wrapping his fingers around the black label on the fifth of Jim Beam, he pulled it up and out of the drawer. Checking one more time to ensure the door was closed, he started to twist off the cap. Hesitating, he shook his head and set the unopened bottle on top of his desk, making a mental note to himself to return it to the bar later. Sneaking a few swallows of courage behind the closed doors of his office wasn't exactly a social drinking experience. And he decided he wasn't about to let himself get started on such a foolish journey. He left his office and made his way to the kitchen.

When he arrived, he found himself weaving in and around the crowd, like a football halfback juking his way through a defense, until he finally made it to Millie. She looked up from stirring her wassail—a favorite of Jake's—and greeted him with a half-smile. An apple, orange, burgundy wine, nutmeg, and allspice perfume filled the room. The fragrant aroma wasted itself on Marshall. Tension raised hell on any breathing disorder. His asthma raised its ugly head. The rasp in his throat rattled like sand in a paper bag. Marshall endured three hacks trying to cough up the phlegm. Millie's stare offered no opportunity to hide the spit, so he swallowed.

"Agggh!"

"You all right?"

"Sure," he whispered in her ear. "It's Christmas Eve. We buried our son. Our house is full of people. This is a wonderful celebration. Why shouldn't I be all right?"

Millie hissed a whisper reply. "Everyone is only trying to help."

Marshall leaned back on the counter and threw up both hands, in one of those "Whatever" gestures.

Millie gritted her teeth. "You can be such a jerk sometimes." She pulled the spoon from the wassail and jabbed it at him. "And anyway, please don't talk so loud." Her tone softened, the angry look on her face eased, and her words pleaded instead of seethed. "They'll hear you."

Marshall flicked a loose bread crumb into the disposal. "Well, maybe they should," he whispered, "and they'll all go on home." Millie's face turned ashen, and a tear trickled down her cheek. He'd crossed the line and knew it. He wiped the tears off her cheeks. She turned away and churned the wooden spoon in the wassail again. "Millie, I'm sorry." She spun to face him and accidentally dropped the spoon into the pot. She gave him a quick, unexpected kiss on the cheek. When she leaned slightly forward, she allowed her hair to brush beneath his chin. The fragrance of her cucumber shampoo filled his nostrils. "You dropped your spoon in the wassail," he muttered. She retrieved it.

"I hate a cold rain." Marshall's voice rose barely above a whisper. Frigid plinks struck the kitchen window in rapid succession. "Snow would sure be better." Even in the slowly diminishing light of the late afternoon, the bare trees in the backyard glistened from the drenching. Branches grasped at the air like an old man's gnarly-knuckled fingers. Unraked red maple and post oak leaves covered the once green zoysia, having turned brown already from the changing weather. The long boxwood hedge fronted the fence like a prickly green belt holding up the stand of old Loblolly pines planted long before Marshall's family had moved to Oakton.

A half-smile crossed Millie's lips. "Well, this is good old Oakton, North Carolina, for ya." She resumed stirring in large, slow circles. "The temperature'll have to drop a little bit more for the white stuff." Marshall sighed and shook his head. Millie stopped stirring. She left the spoon immersed in the wassail, reached up, and placed her hand against her husband's cheek. "Everybody here loved Jake, too, you know." Her voice broke.

Marshall searched for his bald spot, found it, and rubbed. "I know," he said. "I know." Millie's hand still rested against his cheek. He gently removed it and looked away. Several more folks found a spot on the counter, dropped off a dish, smiled at both Marshall and Millie, and then left to join others in one of the other rooms, all rapidly filling with visitors. For a moment, the kitchen was empty, except for Millie and Marshall.

"Have you, uh, been in Jake's room, yet?" Millie turned to stir the wassail once more. "I put the flag and his Purple Heart on his pillow," she said, her voice still struggling. She spied a clove sprig hiding beside the spoon-rest on the stove and dropped it into the wassail.

"No."

"You got to, sometime, you know."

Marshall hesitated. He wanted to go in. Guilt kept him out. "I'm, you know, not ready, sweetheart," he whispered. Unresolved issues remained. His son had referred to them in his last letter. Issues, now, which could never be resolved. Marshall had dried the letter after returning from the cemetery and placed it under a heavy book to smooth the wrinkles and flatten it out. Afterward, he'd carefully folded it and slipped it into his shirt pocket. He'd kept it with him ever since receiving it, removing it only at night, when he placed it on his bedside table beneath his phone. Just then, a man whom Marshall and Millie did not recognize entered the kitchen. He carried an apple pie in his hands.

"Mr. and Mrs. Gatlin," he began, "My name is Tom Willis."

"You were one of Jake's teachers," Millie said, turning and smiling at Marshall.

"I was Jake's American History teacher," Mr. Willis said. "I was so sorry to hear about what happened." He paused and handed the pie to Millie. "I baked this. It's my, uh, grandmother's apple pie recipe."

"Thank you so much, Mr. Willis," Millie said.

Marshall reached out and shook the teacher's hand. "Nice to, uh, meet you," he said. "And thanks for coming."

"I want you to know your son was one of my more perceptive and thoughtful students," he said.

Millie placed her hand on her heart and glanced at Marshall, a look of anguish on her face. Turning back to Jake's teacher, she said, "You are so kind to share that, Mr. Willis. You don't know how much it means to us."

Tom Willis nodded and sighed, a look in his eyes suggesting great sadness. "Well, I just wanted to stop by and give my respects. And again, I am so, so sorry." With that, he turned and left.

As he disappeared around the door, Marshall, a questioning look on his face, looked at Millie. "You knew he was one of Jake's teachers?"

"Jake mentioned him once," she said. "Was nice of him to come by."

"Yeah," Marshall said, rubbing his chin and shaking his head. "Seemed like a, uh, nice guy," he said quietly.

Stepping away from Millie, he moved to the sink and fiddled with the spigot. The hot water from the water heater, located a long way from the kitchen, required an unrelenting wait until it finally reached the sink. A small, steady stream of lukewarm water finally spilled from the faucet. Soapless, Marshall scrubbed his hands red as if rubbing away imaginary dirt. Millie stood in silence and watched him. The soft murmur of voices from other rooms drifted into the kitchen, as if someone had turned up a volume dial a couple of notches. The wassail simmered in the pot on the stove until small bubbles appeared at the bottom, followed by a rapid boil. Millie immediately turned the heat down. The constant plinks of cold rain against the windowpane completed the symphony of soft voices, boiling wassail, and pinging drops. She stared into Marshall's eyes. He knew her well enough to know what to expect next. "Oh, God, Marshall! Oh, God! Oh, God! I wasn't ready for him to go!" Tears streamed down her face. She reached for him. Awkwardly, he pulled her to him, and they stood together, twisted, like Virginia Creeper clinging to a trellis. One of them needed the touch, the other one uncomfortably complied. An exaggerated southern twang broke the spell.

"Where y'all want me to put this?"

Millie turned and wiped away her tears. She pulled away from Marshall. "Oh, hi Emma Kate."

Their neighbor tried to smile, managing only half of one. "I am so sorry," she said, her eyes a bit teary. "Are y'all okay?" She offered up a Pyrex dish of sweet potato casserole. All of Marshall's and Millie's friends knew about his "touchy-feely" phobia. Seeing them wrapped around each other would have been quite a shock. Marshall's cheeks warmed up to a full blush.

"We're okay, sweetie. It's just been a long day for all of us," she said. "Here, I'll show ya where you can put it."

Marshall backed away. He lingered for a moment and watched as the casserole finally found its way in-between a basket of homemade rolls and a pickle tray. The kitchen resembled Cracker Barrel and the Golden Corral buffet all rolled into one. A plate of country ham biscuits rested temptingly beside a small platter of asparagus and ham roll-ups. He frowned at the asparagus and selected the country ham. Picking it up, he squished it slightly between his fingers and started to take a bite. Changing his mind, he dropped it back onto the plate. He didn't deserve comfort food yet.

Not tonight.

On the other side of a recently renovated kitchen pass-through loomed their large den. Marshall glanced at the three Gatlin girls hovering together on the floor in front of the Christmas tree. Lisa comforted Mary. Beth clung to them both. All three sported tear-stained cheeks. Each girl's best friend remained close by. No one talked. They hugged, snuffled into each other's shoulders, and wept quietly. The crackling fire and the muffled small-talk of well-meaning neighbors pretending to enjoy what they were eating constituted the ambiance in the background. A voice from Marshall's heart told him he should walk in immediately and gather his girls up in his arms. *Hold 'em tight,* the voice whispered. The *hold your emotions in check* voice from his head vied for time, as well. Marshall listened to the latter and convinced himself his girls would forgive him if he left them in the hands of their friends. He turned his attention back to the kitchen.

Another neighbor, Gillian, had brought a bowl of bread pudding. She dipped a spoonful, intending to feed a bite to Millie. It missed her mouth, and Millie dripped a bit on the floor. When she reached down to clean the spill, she noticed Marshall's stare. She rolled her eyes and attempted a grin. *Love you,* she mouthed. Marshall smiled and mouthed it back.

He glanced once more at his daughters and made his way past the girls down the hallway to his home office again. Hesitating, he reached into his pocket and pulled out his cell phone. He switched it off and stuck it beneath a stack of folders piled onto the corner of his desk. Picking up the bottle of bourbon, he decided to return it to the file drawer. After taking a deep breath, he stepped into the hallway and headed toward the foyer and the front door. His ultimate destination? The attic and escape from hearing "So sorry for your loss" over and over, from greeting woe-stricken faces, and feeling the weight of the pervasive pall-drowning grief that permeated the entire house. He couldn't bring himself to go into Jake's bedroom, but the attic held boxes of his children's childhood memories. Perhaps spending a bit of time revisiting his son's would be easier to face than the grief represented by the live faces and comments of his family and friends. His parka hung on a peg as well as his UNC ball cap. Glancing around, he made sure no one saw him, then took his parka and hat and sneaked upstairs. After using the bathroom, he left the light on and closed the door behind him. He did this to make it look like he'd settled in for one of those "long haul" contemplations his family knew him for. It would keep folks from bothering him. Crossing to his dresser, he pulled out a heavy sweatshirt and slipped it on, followed by his parka. He didn't plan on staying too long, but knew the cold would settle in throughout the attic. Before he left, he searched in his dresser's catch-all drawer for the unused hand warmers they had bought for Oakton's Christmas Parade. Picking them up, he started to put them in his pocket, then changed his mind. *Won't need them,* he thought. *Not for the short time I'll be up there.* As he started for the door, he hesitated. Re-opening his drawer, he reached in and grabbed the hand warmers anyway. He left his bedroom and walked the few steps to the middle of the upstairs hallway and slowly pulled down the attic access door. He cursed the creaking springs, pausing once the steps were down to ensure no one had heard them. Convinced he was clear to climb, he made his way up the ladder. Upon reaching the top step, he scrambled onto the plywood flooring and managed to pull up the ladder without too much noise. His knees cursed him for the climb and scramble. He begged them to stop their grumbling. The pain eased, so they must've bought his argument. As the attic was a stand-up space, he pulled himself to a standing position.

All the empty Christmas decoration boxes lay strewn on shelves and a long table he had built for Millie. He meandered his way through a maze of shelving, the table, and the scattered mess to reach where he headed. On his journey, he bumped the table. Something fell. When he glanced back, he muttered a quiet "Damn," and shook his head. Two glittery red-gowned ceramic cherub bodies lay side by side on the floor. Millie's small ornament had broken in two. It would take Super Glue, he hoped he could find later, to put them back together. Picking them up, he set them carefully on the table, telling himself to be sure to retrieve them when he left.

He eased himself beside a stack of old mattresses, which were probably a nice cozy home for some miscreant mice. Beyond those were shelves he had built for all four of their kids. Millie stored all the growing-up stuff the kids, more than likely, didn't want, but would be expected to take off their parents' hands someday. He had placed an old, wooden barrel directly in front of these shelves for Millie to sit on when she wanted to go through some of the kids' boxes. It's where he intended to sit for his anticipated, brief escape from the gathering below.

After he sat down, a shiver ran down his back, either from the cold or from being so close to Jake's stuff. He wasn't sure and second-guessed his decision to come up to the attic at all. Sighing, he figured he'd made it this far and would at least stay for a while. He gazed around at all the labeled boxes. This evidence of Millie's anal-retentive organization gene made him shake his head and chuckle. His eyes immediately scanned the boxes Millie had designated for their son. *Jake's Trophies, Jake's Stuffed Animals, Jake's Old Shoes, Jake's Favorite Books, Jake's Hot Wheels Collection, Jake's Baseball Stuff, Jake's Art Masterpieces, Jake's Misc. Stuff.* Instinctively, he reached for Jake's trophy box. It wasn't too heavy. He hesitated. One of those inner voices of his—he wasn't sure which—kicked in and asked him if looking inside would bring back happy memories or nightmares. The voice suggested, with his luck, probably both. He sighed and rubbed his finger across the tape. Dry and crackly, the tape proved to be a real bear to remove. Halfway through making a mess of the removal, he noticed an unmarked box tucked behind the trophy one. The tape job crisscrossed every which way. Not one of Millie's. Marshall set the trophy box back and concentrated on the unmarked one. With his small, red Victorinox knife, he slit the cracked and split tape. Removing it, he folded and pressed the flaps down so they wouldn't flip back. A few empty manila folders lay stacked on top. Something rested underneath them. With already cold fingers, he lifted the manila folders, set them aside, and reached back into the box.

"What's this?" His voice startled him. His son's familiar elementary years' chicken-scratch handwriting jumped out at him. He picked up the thick, spiral notebook with the words *Letters to Gammy Gat* scrawled on the cover. He started to read the one on top.

"Unbelievable."

Marshall, his eyes still on the first letter, slowly removed his watch, almost as if unaware of his action. Continuing to read, he gently stuffed the watch into his pocket.

Den

"Have you girls seen your father?"

"He stuck his head in here a while ago," said Beth. "Didn't say anything. Just left down the hall."

"When I saw him walking around earlier, he seemed like he was walking around in a daze," Lisa said. "I know he's so sad. I just hope he's okay."

Mary reached out, grabbed her oldest sister's hand, and squeezed.

A quiet voice from the kitchen caught Millie's attention. She smiled. "Oh, hi, Maysie. Thanks so much for being here."

"I made a chicken pie," she said quietly. "I'll just go and stick it in the oven for a bit."

Millie turned back to the girls. "Gotta go," she whispered. "How 'bout looking for him, will ya? Tell him to come find me."

THE LETTERS

Attic

Sunday
December 24, 1995

Dear Gammy Gat,

I need to talk to somebody. It's got to be somebody who will listen to every word and won't tell me not to say what I want to say or not to feel what I'm feeling. So, I decided to write you a letter. Because you're in heaven, I'm hoping God gives grandparents special superpowers, so you can hear the words your grandkids might write to you. By the way, it's me, Jake, your grandson, and it's Christmas Eve.

I have a bunch to tell you. A lot of stuff has happened since you died. I miss you a lot. Guess it's the first thing I want to say.

Marshall stared at the date. His son wrote this to his dead grandmother, around nine years ago, at the beginning of the year from hell. They had moved to Oakton soon after his mother's funeral. Reluctantly, he shifted his eyes away from the page. A lump filled his throat, and a shiver ran down his back.

Again.

Marshall thumbed the edges of the pages filling the notebook. He closed his eyes and imagined a Twilight Zone episode where an eleven-year-old kid wrote letters to dead people. Chuckling to himself, he decided the script for such a show would even be far-fetched for Rod Serling. The rational message in Marshall's head told him nothing was to be gained from reading these letters. What they contained would only confirm everything he believed about Jake's fifth-grade year. They were bound to be nothing more than shallow, poor me reveries. A rebellious son had misbehaved badly and blamed his belly-aching on everyone but himself and his own decisions? Life wasn't fair, and mine was a mess because of my terrible parents? My parents loved my sisters more than they loved me? And why couldn't I do what I wanted to do?

Close the notebook and put it back into the box, Marshall. Eleven-year-old boys are incapable of writing anything of substance.

This inner voice, coming from his head, kept repeating that only more heartache and despair would result if he read them. The voice in his heart whispered relentless pleas to indulge his curiosity. This message began to gain traction. Perhaps satisfying more than his curiosity was at stake. The notebook appeared to hold countless letters containing the thoughts and words of a child he believed he had lost even before his untimely death. The conundrum was clear. He couldn't bear to look back down at the first letter, nor could he close the notebook and set it aside.

While Marshall's head and heart continued their quiet bickering, an October memory blew in like a breeze through an open window. His nostrils embraced the memory, for it was filled with the sweet fragrance of burning cherry wood from their neighbor's wood-burning fireplace.

■　　■　　■　　■　　■

A smoky aroma greeted him after he opened the car door upon his and Millie's return from the hospital. A brief, chilly rain had fallen earlier in the day, and his pants had brushed against the door. Under his breath, he'd cursed the cold wetness. Millie had shot him one of her "watch your language" looks. Side by side in silence, they had made their way up the sidewalk. Jake had opened the front door before Marshall finished turning the key. His eyes stared straight into his father's, his jaw set, and his shoulders squared. "Gammy Gat's in heaven, isn't she?" His older sister,

Lisa, and little sister Beth had stood together in the hallway. One of Beth's hands entwined with her sister's.

Marshall had taken a step forward to hold the door for Millie. Jake didn't move. "Son, she...uh..."

Millie placed her hand on Jake's shoulder. "Yes, Jake, she's gone to live with God."

Sobs from the hallway interrupted, and both Lisa and Beth ran to their mother. Jake had sidestepped his sisters and walked out the door.

"Where're you going, son?"

"I'd like to go for a walk, Daddy."

Marshall turned. "Hang on, I'll..."

Jake interrupted his father. "By myself." He paused, turning, his face set, his eyes clear. "I won't go far. Promise."

"Marshall?" Millie grabbed his arm.

"Let him go, honey. He'll be all right."

Jake made his way down the front walk, turned left onto the sidewalk. His hands in his pockets, he took measured steps along the concrete walkway. His chin drooped to his chest.

. . . . .

The chill in the attic eased Marshall back to the present. The image faded. His eyes still closed, he thought about how they had moved to Oakton two months later. When he opened them again, he reached up and lightly placed his hand over his heart. A slight grin crossed his lips, as if acknowledging the outcome of his internal, head vs heart battle. The two had compromised. He sighed and shook his head. He couldn't keep his eyes away from the letter.

I'm not so good at writing letters. I guess the first thing to tell you is we moved. Not too long after you...well, you know. We got out of school for the holidays, and then we moved. I had to leave Eddie. You remember Eddie, don't you? He's my best friend, ever. We stared at each other like jerks or something. And then we shook hands. I said, "See ya." He said, "Yeah, see ya." Then we all got into the car and drove off and left Eddie standing on the curb. I looked out the back window. He waved. I didn't wave back. I wanted to. My hand wouldn't move. I'd just pressed it up against the window. Lisa asked me if I was crying, and I told her to shut up.

Daddy got a new job. Mama said she wished she didn't have to quit her job in the lawyer's office. She did it to support Daddy. They both said going to new schools was like our new jobs. Even though they asked us what we thought, we knew they had already decided to move no matter what we said. Everything's different here. And I don't know anybody.

Accepting the job as the new district manager for a North Carolina food service supplier meant the family had to move. Although Millie had to leave a law office job she loved, she secured a position in Oakton as a Family Law Paralegal for a local attorney. Marshall's message to all of them had been one of learning to adapt to what life threw at you. The kids' job entailed understanding that everyone had to face stuff like this from time to time. He reminded himself he had told them it either made a person stronger...or...a self-pitier. He believed his son had chosen the latter. Seeing what Jake had written, juxtaposed against his message about adapting, made this stance seem a bit harsh at the moment.

We're renting this big old white house. Some rich guy in town's mother's grandmother used to live in it. It has a big front porch and high ceilings. Daddy had to use a ladder to put up our Christmas tree. Every room has a fireplace. Mama thinks it's neat because it's right in the middle of town. We even watched the Christmas parade from our front porch. Lisa thought it was cool to be able to drink hot chocolate, eat cookies, and watch the parade pass by. Mama said, "Now this is the way to watch a parade."

Marshall almost retrieved the handwarmers but stopped himself. *Not yet.* He rubbed his hands together to keep them warm and thought of the house they had rented when they first came to live in Oakton. Visualizing the home, he could almost see it as if it stood before him on the front walkway.

·　　　·　　　·　　　·　　　·

Round fluted columns supported the wide front porch. Four steps up led to the wide, gray-planked flooring surrounded by a white balustrade picketed by white custom-milled balusters. Flaky chips of weathered and decades-old white paint curled up like chisel shavings. Deep enough to accommodate rockers, the porch stretched across the front of the house with room enough to hold a dozen such chairs. The porch became a natural family gathering place. Its owners said the house had been the family home for three generations of old Oakton gentility. They weren't interested in selling it. Marshall's family stayed in this house for over a year until they found a place to buy across town.

•   •   •   •   •

Marshall smiled as he remembered this wonderful old house. The creaky floors, old plumbing, sagging door frames, and endless repairs were offset by its history of elegance and location in the middle of a quaint, tree-lined downtown in a small city in the south. His eyes eased back down to the scribbled words on the page.

Lisa and Beth have their own rooms on the second floor. Mine's on the third floor. I guess it's the one neat thing about this house. The way you get to my room is you have to go up this winding staircase. Nobody can walk on the creaky steps without me hearing them. The reason I'm telling you about my room is that I'm up here right now. And it's late. I can't sleep. Guess it's because it's Christmas Eve. Mama and Daddy said I had to turn off the lights. I've got my flashlight. They know I have it, but always say, "Just don't let us hear you." I can be quiet as a mouse when I want to be. Sometimes, I like to hide and spy on everybody when they think I'm not around. I like to spy on Lisa and Beth the most. Daddy catches me a lot. He says he can smell me.

Daddy likes to stay up late at night, too. He told me sometimes he talks to you, then. It's the clear nights he likes the best, when he can see lots of stars. I believe maybe he thinks you might have superpowers too, because he has a smile on his face when he comes back inside.

Marshall chuckled. During many a cool, backyard night ever since his mother's funeral, Marshall had reclined in one of their old Adirondack chairs. He'd convinced himself the way to hold on to her memory meant to avoid acknowledging her death. For a while, following her funeral, he'd talked to her during those late-night opportunities. Whenever he could sneak away with a glass of the port she used to drink, he'd slip into a silent stream of consciousness dialogue. Somewhere along the way, those talks stopped. These letters indicated Jake had taken up the mantle for him. He wondered if his confiding in Jake had permitted his son to take up the conversations he had let slip away.

For several months after her death, thoughts and memories of her often popped into his mind. The way she smiled or tossed an errant curl out of her eyes. The sound of her voice, seldom raised in anger and always controlled. Mary Claire Gatlin had been an open vessel ready to take on any and everyone's problems. Marshall's inability to visualize his mother crept into his psyche over time. The memories surfaced less often. Although his sisters kept him apprised of the need to recognize her approaching birthdays, his visits to the cemetery dwindled. Neither his mother nor his father had wanted to be cremated. At one point, he couldn't remember the last time he'd been by the graveside. The idea of picturing a casket in the ground containing bodies he had once hugged haunted him. He wondered, again, why he stopped talking to her during those alone times, especially about Jake and what happened during the year. An inner voice whispered, *Did you decide you didn't need her, Marshall?*

He figured her words would have cut to the chase if she were sitting beside him, now, a glass of port in *her* hand. She would have questioned him, back then, mercilessly, and accused him of being sanctimonious, expecting too much, and misreading his son's behavior. Sentiments Millie had felt free to express incessantly. All sentiments he hadn't particularly cared to hear. He groaned out loud again. It seemed his whole world was threatening to flip upside-down. He didn't know whether he was coming or going or in some sort of state of suspended animation. When he talked to his mother, whether in life or death, Marshall believed she listened to him. To realize his son felt the same way comforted him. He glanced down at the letter. Was this his opportunity to reconnect with both of them at the same time? Or a chance he was going to drive himself crazy from guilt?

A "Momma" memory window opened.

.   .   .   .   .

Mary Claire Gatlin sat on a step halfway up the stairwell, a glass of rotgut port in one hand, a menthol cigarette in the other. A sturdy, yet slim woman, her head was full of brunette curls spilling across her head like breaking waves in the ocean. Her face, with its permanent smile, never met a stranger. And she loved late hours with anybody who could keep up with her. The conversations usually meandered around nothing in particular, because it wasn't about the words spoken, but the bond created during those tipsy times. Millie, his fiancée at the time, had sat mesmerized. She had loved those chats. After their initial toast, kicking off the chat session, the two women shooed Marshall away.

Those late-night sessions were as much a reflection of his mother's need for companionship as they were for the sheer joy of the booze and banter. His father, Cole, spent time away about as often as he spent time at home. After his stint in the army, he'd gotten a job as a traveling salesman with a local seed company outside of Kernersville, a small town not far from their home in Winston-Salem, North Carolina. His mother and father had been happy, even though they were apart so much, and his father wasn't much of a late-nighter. Cole Gatlin's image appeared before Marshall's inner eyes. It seemed like one memory triggered another. Clear as day, a big man with thinning hair and hands like snow shovels entered his mind.

.   .   .   .   .

His old man always sprawled in his easy chair right after supper. A full stomach revved up a snore machine inside his head. Before he settled into his La-Z-Boy naptime ritual, he pulled out his shirttail. When his chest breathed out, his shirt spread open. Some of his bare belly squeezed out between the buttons like a glob of peanut butter oozing through a split in soft bread. Sprigs of black hairs, plenty ripe for the picking, curlicued up. His mother had dared him, and Marshall took the bait. He'd reached out, at first, to tickle those hairs. He couldn't resist and plucked one. Cole Gatlin rose out of his chair like a bass hitting a jitterbug.

"Soldier, you're cruisin' for a bruisin'."

Marshall's dash for his bedroom proved unsuccessful. Those massive knuckles inflicted a brutal noogie. He remembered believing he'd received a permanent indentation in his skull.

·　　·　　·　　·　　·

Icy rain plinking on the attic vent eased Cole Gatlin's image away. For a fleeting moment, Marshall imagined his mother sitting right beside him. The plink sounded like the clink of his mother's port glass as she and Millie had toasted one another while sitting on the stairway. A shiver skittered down his back. It wasn't from the cold. His mother used to tell him the shiver meant a rabbit was running lightly across his skin. He glanced up toward the vent opening. *Momma's not here*, his head told him. His heart, however, challenged this contention. Marshall smiled as he turned his attention back to Jake's letter.

She *was* with him.

Well, guess I'm getting sleepy. I'll write to you again. Lots of stars are out tonight. Oh, yeah, is it okay to hate your parents sometimes? Especially when they decide to do something and you have to do it, too, whether you want to or not?

Thought I'd ask.

Your favorite grandson,

Jake

P.S. I love you, Gammy Gat

The words, "hate your parents," jolted Marshall's memory. This time, the incident revolving around the memory was not as clear as what he remembered doing after it happened. He couldn't remember how old he was. His father had done something or told Marshall to do something he didn't want to do. Or maybe it had been to stop doing something he didn't want to stop. What he did remember was what he had done about it. He'd stomped off to his room, slammed the door, and attacked his pillow. Every time he'd hit it, he'd said the words, *I hate you*. His father's "head" took some pretty tough beatings back then.

Marshall sighed and traced his finger over Jake's handwritten name. Thinking about his son's teenage years, Marshall figured Jake's signature hadn't changed much since he'd signed this first letter. For a moment of respite, Marshall stared away from the notebook and glanced around the attic. Reading only one letter Jake had written had already stirred several memories about things during his own life, not unrelated to what his son had revealed as a youngster. An inner voice muttered, *Maybe Millie's right. Think you've conveniently forgotten what it was like to be Jake's age, Marshall?*

Recalling memories from life at ten or eleven or whenever, out of the blue, wasn't easy. Reading a few lines revealing his own son's thoughts sure seemed to stir something inside him, though. Jake's letter from Afghanistan crackled in his front left coat pocket. He reached in, carefully, and unfolded it. His care had kept the words from fading. Even though he'd memorized them after about the umpteenth read, he read every word again and agonized over the irony.

Jake *had* come home.

He had come home...just not the way he'd planned it or the way Marshall and Millie and the girls had planned it. What Marshall had on his lap embodied the essence of the *talk* Jake had promised. Reading these letters, however, might take him somewhere he was unprepared to go. One of those inner voices slipped in another word or two. *Don't you think you should stop right here and include Millie in on this?*

Marshall shuffled through the notebook one more time. Not yet.

This first letter was the tip of the iceberg.

Den

Millie stuck her head back in the den. Beth noticed her and asked, "You still looking for Daddy?"

"Just wondering where he might have sneaked off to."

"We still haven't seen him," Lisa said. "Do you think he might've slipped into an empty room for a few minutes? The stress of today might've aggravated his asthma, and maybe he just needed to get away, calm himself down, and breathe."

"That's a thought," Millie said, a slight smile across her lips. "Or maybe he's hiding out, reading a magazine, in the bathroom."

"Gross," Mary said.

"Want me to go get him?" Beth said.

"Don't bother him. He'll come out sooner or later." In the back of her mind, Millie thought, *Better be sooner.*

Coping with the personal emotions surrounding a child's death, well-intended neighbors and friends whose every look reminded you of the depth of your agony, and providing the love and support for three children who had lost a sibling was difficult enough. Having the child's father appear to lose his capacity to assist you during this time, when all hands on deck was a no-brainer, set a whole different bar of difficulty.

Attic

Monday
January 1, 1996

Dear Gammy Gat,

It's me, again. Mama and Daddy let us stay up late to watch the ball of light go down the pole to celebrate New Year's Eve. I'm supposed to be asleep, but I'm too awake. I needed to write you.

I like it when everyone else has gone to sleep. But you know Daddy. He's sitting up by the fireplace and reading, even after midnight. He won't last long, though. Mama usually goes to bed early, so staying up tonight was weird for her. Beth fell asleep before the ball of light started to go down the pole. She used to fall asleep in your lap. Remember? Lisa's in bed. I'm sure she's not asleep. She likes to listen to music and paint her nails.

I've got to tell you about Christmas. Of course, don't listen to Mama and Daddy. They think Santa rips his bag and everything falls out at our house every Christmas. We probably got all the stuff we got because they were feeling bad about making us move.

Daddy set up his old electric train. It was the one he had when he was a little boy. You remember, don't you? I got to work the controls all by myself. It didn't work so great, though. It kept falling off the tracks. Daddy thinks maybe the tracks were too rusty.

Marshall immediately glanced toward a stack of boxes. The large, heavy-duty cardboard box, with *Train Set* written in black marker, sat between a trunk full of old picture frames and a trash bag full of dried flowers. He still loved that train. A memory rolled into his head like a diesel pulling a mile of cars along an endless time track.

·   ·   ·   ·   ·

A long line of anxious kids wrapped around the Belk's Department Store cosmetics department. His mother held his hand. "It's a long line, Marshall. It'll be a pretty good wait. You sure you don't hafta go to the bathroom?"

"I'm okay, Mommy. I can wait."

She had planted the thought. He started squirming, but if he got out of line, he'd lose his spot. He'd had to hold it. Finally, when it was Marshall's turn, the elf lifted him up the two green carpeted steps and deposited him onto Santa's knee. The knee started bouncing as soon as Marshall touched down.

"And what do you want for Christmas, little man?" The nasty odor of burnt tobacco had rushed into Marshall's nose. Creepy, yellow-stained teeth hid behind the old man's fake beard.

Marshall had closed his eyes and whispered, "A train."

"Speak up, sonny. Old Santa's ears aren't what they used to be." The old faker leaned forward until his mouth almost touched Marshall's nose. Some spittle landed on his cheek. He'd been afraid to wipe it off.

·   ·   ·   ·   ·

The memory brought a chuckle. Instinctively, Marshall reached up and wiped his cheek, as if the bit of spit still clung to it after all these years. It had been no laughing matter back then. He'd nearly peed his pants. Marshall took in a deep breath and exhaled. As he watched his hot breath shoot out into the cold air of the attic, he knew this one train memory would trigger another one. It chugged in, chasing the Santa image away. This one occurred on Christmas Eve, a couple of days after the visit with Santa.

.   .   .   .   .

His father sat on the edge of his bed. "You know, sometimes, you don't git everthin' what you want for Christmas, little soldier. Lots of kids won't get nothing."

"Why not, sir? Don't Santa know where they live?"

"Well, Santa can't give toys to every boy and girl. If everybody got toys, there'd be nothing special about getting 'em. So, some get 'em and some don't."

To Marshall's delight, the train had appeared the next morning in front of the Christmas tree. His father had flipped the transformer handle until the train eased into a chug around the track. Cole had pressed a red button, and the whistle sounded. An orange-yellow, American Flyer cargo train engine pulled a flatcar, a boxcar, a tank car, and a caboose. A miniature conductor leaned in and out while the train rushed down the track. A station box announced destinations.

.   .   .   .   .

A whistle from a boiling tea kettle from downstairs in the kitchen brought Marshall back to the present. He thought about his father's ass-backward logic back then. Messed with his mind, even today. Shaking his head, he chastised himself for not taking care of the train. His children would've loved to watch it tote its cargo around the track, whistling and chugging all the while. He glanced at the box one last time and made himself a promise to take all the train pieces, cars, and tracks out and clean them up. He sighed and went back to the letter.

Our tree was the tallest one we've ever had. They don't last very long, though, do they? I hate it when the needles start falling off. It's sort of sad, too, know what I mean?

I got clothes, books, a remote-control car, and some skates. What I wanted was a pony. Every letter I ever wrote to Santa, I asked for a pony. I even made promises I might have kept. I knew right where I'd keep the pony. One good thing about this house is, it has a big backyard. Daddy could build a barn. We could grow some hay. I'd ride him when I got home from school. It would be a piece of cake. Mama didn't buy any of it. Neither did Santa. I keep thinking this was our first Christmas without you. I have to admit, even a pony wouldn't have helped. No matter what, nothing will ever be the same without you.

Marshall shook his head. Jake's emotional hammer made a direct hit on the nail. Nothing was the same without his mother. After his father died, Marshall feared she might waste away. He didn't give her strength enough credit. He and Millie had talked her into staying with them. With the help of the sale of his folks' house, they had enough to add on and build a Grandmommy Suite. The grandkids loved having her living just a room away. She made their birthday cakes, helped with school pickups, and was home when the kids got back from school. She even tried yoga for a while, until the tobacco did its job on her lungs. When it did, the cancer showed no mercy. This woman of strength, determination, great heart, compassion, and love slipped away from them. An image crept in he preferred to keep away. He closed his eyes, hoping the image would disappear. Thinking that closing one's eyes could block an image from one's mind's eye rose to the heights of stupidity.

■　　　■　　　■　　　■　　　■

The image? A layer of green carpet spread below his mother's casket. It was a typical fall day in North Carolina. Nature dressed the oaks, hickories, gums, maples, cedars, and pines in golds and reds and greens and brilliant oranges throughout the old Chapel Hill Cemetery. A low, rambling stone and rock wall meandered a circle around the entire historic resting space. Several generations of both of his parents' families had lived in Chapel Hill, and many were buried there. The sun's rays searched through the trembling leaves, found openings, and shined down onto the feathery mosses, black dirt, solemn monuments, and gray fieldstones scattered throughout. Marshall, however, knew his mother's sun-flooded Carolina day image would linger only briefly. The babbling, stuttering mess of rain drenching the mud-stained green carpet beneath Jake's casket washed it away.

.   .   .   .   .

Marshall brought himself back to the attic. One memory had been a glorious send-off into the light of eternity. The other one blanketed Marshall's mood with clouded doubts, lost opportunities, and unfulfilled dreams. He gazed around the attic for a full five minutes. He tried desperately to stifle those conflicting images. Reading these letters wreaked havoc with his psyche like some sort of morbid test. He couldn't even get past the first two.

"Take a deep breath, Marshall," he whispered out loud to himself. Even doing this proved difficult. Asthma pretty much dictated the depth of such efforts. He took whatever his affliction allowed, then turned to the letters. Like a magnet, they drew his eyes back to his son's written words.

I'll tell you two neat things about Christmas morning. The first one was something special from you. All the girls got necklaces made with some of your pearls. Daddy and I got tie pins. I'm saving mine for later when I have to wear a tie. It made us all happy. It made us all sad, too. The next neat thing was Santa left us something special. It was something we read about in a Christmas story. He left us bells as gifts from his sleigh, and we had to find them. He wrote a note telling us they might have dropped into the ashes in the fireplace. And they did. If you believe in Santa Claus, you're supposed to be able to hear the bells ringing. Daddy and Mama had told us the gift of the bells represented how important the spirit of Christmas and giving to others was. They said the day we stop believing will be the day Santa won't stop at our house anymore.

I believe in you,

Jake

P.S. I love you, Gammy Gat

The Polar Express had provided the perfect Christmas ploy for Marshall and Millie to spring on their kids. In fact, to this day, no Gatlin kid had ever acknowledged a belief that Santa Claus might not be real. He smiled at the memory of this particular Christmas morning, and how the Christmas bell caper and the gifts created from Gammy Gat's pearls had made it extra special. Marshall's mother had kept one set of her mother's lovely, upscale, cultured pearls. It was these pearls Marshall and Millie had used to make the girls' necklaces and Jake's tie pin. Marshall promised himself he would look for Jake's tie pin when he finally got up enough gumption to go into his bedroom. His son had probably tossed it somewhere with the stuff on his dresser. He quickly pushed the task out of his mind. He wasn't ready to enter for any reason.

Not yet.

Main Floor Hallway

After Jake's untimely death, Millie desperately needed some semblance of family harmony to return. To face this incredible tragedy, she needed everyone to work together, to be at least somewhere on the same page, provide shoulders to lean on, be free to vent or share, or be available as listeners. Be anything but gone. An exasperated Millie, dish towel across her shoulder, walked by Marshall's office and peeked in.

Empty.

For better or worse, Marshall and Millie Gatlin had functioned for nearly twenty-five years as partners in life and love, duty and decisions. Their only true departure from harmony had been the strategy for facing the trials and tribulations of their second child and only son, Jake. During and after what he called Jake's year from hell, Marshall had allowed his perception of how to deal with his son's behavior to devolve into the mental rigidity of black and white thinking. Millie's eyes, mind, and heart had discerned the grays and nuances of the life of a young child. The two might not have always been on the same page. At least neither of them had thrown up their hands and walked away.

And at the moment, their house was full of people.

Where the hell are you, Marshall?

Attic

Saturday
January 6, 1996

Dear Gammy Gat,

Even though it's been the new year for almost a week, it doesn't feel so great. I want to have another year where we used to live.

I can't stop thinking about how much I miss you. An old man down the street died on Tuesday this week. People visited his house all day long. Mama took some food. It made me remember what I didn't want to remember. I had never been to a funeral before until I went to yours. I don't want to go to another one.

I know you're in a better place. Daddy said you can visit your daddy, who died when you were twelve years old. And he said your mother is with you too. And Grandpapa. Daddy said we should be happy for you. I am happy for you. I'm just not happy for me. How can I miss you and be happy at the same time? And I can't help thinking, before you died, HERE was a better place.

I remember when you came to Grandparents' Day at my other school. I hope they don't have a Grandparents' Day at this new school.

Marshall winced and hung his head. How to measure the "how can I miss you and be happy at the same time" factor didn't seem to have an answer. A few answers revealed themselves in these letters. More uncomfortable questions remained unanswered.

I want to tell you something else I thought you might be interested in. Tuesday was my first day at the new school. I met the principal and everything. Mama filled out some papers and stuff. We walked around the school. I learned where the cafeteria was, the gym was, the library was, the music room was, and where my classroom was. They didn't show me a bathroom, so I pretended to have to go so I could see one. This school's bigger than my other school. It has more hallways, more kids, and more teachers. I really liked my old school. My teacher was great.

I still can't believe Mama and Daddy are making us go to new schools, live in a new town, and a new house, and have to be around new kids.

I hate cancer,

Jake

P.S. I love you, Gammy Gat.

The memory of an icy conversation with Millie swirled into Marshall's head.

▪   ▪   ▪   ▪   ▪

The Monday evening before Jake's first day at his new school, Millie had stood in the bathroom doorway, brushing her hair. In between downward strokes, with her grandmother's antique silver hairbrush, she surprised Marshall with a request he had not anticipated.

"Both of us ought to go with Jake on his first day."

"You go," Marshall had responded, a bit too quickly. "You're the one who's good at all this kind of stuff." He remembered smiling one of those smartass, "Please don't ask me to go," smiles. "Anyway, I've got enough paperwork here to choke a goat."

"The issue is not who's good at it." Millie had chewed the words like they were old gum. "And it's not like I don't have a mound of paperwork to complete, either." She paused and glared into his eyes. "It's the opportunity to support our son in a pretty scary situation."

"Aw, he'll be all right, sweetheart. He's a big boy, now. He doesn't need me."

"Be careful," she had said. "You may get what you wish for."

•   •   •   •   •

Marshall smelled fresh-baked pumpkin bread escaping from the kitchen up through the intake grate and into the attic. He recognized he hadn't eaten squat since they'd received the news, and the aroma wafted sweet and spicy. He sighed, thankful for the memory interruption of Millie's prognostication about wishes. Speaking of wishes, he regretted not bringing the ham biscuit with him. Just then, the wind whistled under the eaves, and Marshall zipped up his coat another notch or two. When he moved, some of the pages broke free from the notebook. He re-adjusted the metal spiral coil and slipped them back in place. During that fifth-grade year, Marshall believed his son had put him through hell. After reading the first of these letters, he wished he wasn't starting to believe the opposite contention.

On to the next one.

Main Floor Hallway

"I'm going upstairs to check to see if he's in the bathroom," Beth said.

Mary reached out and held her sister's arm. "Mama said not to bother him."

Beth scowled. "Well, he's being rude staying up away so long."

Lisa shook her head and sighed. "Maybe he just needs some space."

Beth frowned and gently removed Mary's hand. "Reading a magazine on the toilet for this long? I don't think so." She took the first step up. "Anyway, something might have happened to him."

Attic

Wednesday
January 10, 1996

Dear Gammy Gat,

I guess you knew I'd have to talk about Eddie. You remember him, don't you? He has brown hair and a cowlick right in front. He's my best friend ever. But he's back at my real home. It was neat to be able to walk down the street to each other's houses. When I got my bike, it didn't take any time at all. We used to meet behind our houses, too. We would dam up the creek in the woods. And we nailed some ladder steps to a tree. A bunch of times, he'd be waiting for me. Sometimes I'd be waiting for him.

Marshall smiled. Eddie was one of those kids who pulled his pants up so far, you couldn't tell where his waist stopped and his chest began. He notched his belt so tight, the end must've hung ten inches past the last hole in front. His ball cap was constantly scrunched down against his ears and set crooked over his cowlick crew cut. The boy was a piece of work.

I remember when we found a beer can on the side of the road. I hope you don't mind me telling you about this. I do know kids aren't supposed to drink beer. We dared each other to open it and messed with the pull-tab so much it broke off. Eddie got a rock and punched in the top. It made a little, raggedy hole. Not much would come out, so he held up the can so he could get it to drip on his tongue. He said it couldn't be called drinking the beer. I knew better, and so did he. When it was my turn, I held it up too. The drops landed on my tongue, and boy, was I sorry. I think maybe you're not supposed to drink it after it's been sitting in the hot sun. Eddie said it tasted great. He didn't taste another drip, though. We looked at each other, then dropped the can and ran like crazy, laughing and pretending we were drunk all the way home. I went straight to the bathroom and brushed my teeth. I was afraid Mama would be able to smell beer on my breath.

Marshall second-guessed his decision to put the Jim Beam bottle back in the drawer. He figured a little sip might've actually made a positive contribution to all those inner voice conversations he seemed to be having. He chuckled to himself. Jake's "alcohol consumption confession" opened a memory window about a football Sunday in November.

.   .   .   .   .

Ten-year-old Marshall sat on the floor. He and his father were gearing up for a big game. Cole Gatlin had put out a great spread—Salted peanuts in the shell, hot dogs, chips, a bottle of Coke, and a Miller High Life beer. His carrot-thick fingers wrapped completely around the damp, glass beer bottle. With a church key bottle opener in his other hand, he popped off the cap and smiled at Marshall.

"Slicker'n snot," he'd said, as he relished watching the wisp of beer breath seep out. He'd raised the bottle rim to his lips, sucked on it, then eased away like he'd been in some movie kiss scene.

"Nectar of the Gods, soldier. Nothing better."

Marshall took a sip of his drink, set it down on a coaster, and turned to his father. "Can I taste some, sir?"

His father stared at him for an instant, then nodded. "Why, sure thing, soldier. Let me fix one right up for you."

Cole Gatlin rose from his seat and walked back to the kitchen. Marshall heard him open the refrigerator and then move around. A cupboard opened, and a glass clinked. Waiting for him to return, Marshall's excited heart beat like a little rabbit. He wondered if his father was teasing or if he'd actually do it. Shortly, he returned with a small glass, half-full of what looked to Marshall like some beer.

"Here, soldier. Drink up."

Marshall had taken a big swallow, then promptly threw his guts up. He found out later his father had salted it, big time.

.   .   .   .   .

Marshall chuckled as he readjusted his seat on the barrel. To this day, he couldn't bring himself to gargle with salt water. But even though the salted beer tasted pretty nasty, the experience had not dampened his propensity, since then, to down a few during many a weekend of sports watching. Jake had never asked him for a taste. Marshall had never offered him one. At the moment, he didn't know what he would've done. He licked his dry lips, immediately regretted the chapped condition sure to follow, and returned to the letter.

I keep thinking about what it was like to eat dinner at Eddie's house. I think I ate there more than he ate with me. He had a big and a little sister too. His mama was a great cook. First place I ever ate pizza was at Eddie's house. His mama made peanut butter and marshmallows on a cracker melted in the oven. I even tried broccoli. I didn't know people ate fried bologna. It curled up. Seems like I had lots of firsts with Eddie. It won't ever be the same. He's gone. Like you.

I miss you both,

Jake

P.S. I love you, Gammy Gat

Reading Jake's words at the end, silently, didn't seem to do them credit.

"It won't ever be the same," he read again, aloud. "He's gone. Like you. I miss you both." One of those inner voices sneaked in a thought. *Sounds like you're reading about a kid who didn't like you very much, Marshall.* He shook his head, in an effort to rationalize the normalcy of a kid angered by any number of their parents' decisions. He'd convinced himself he'd tried to have productive conversations with Jake about things going on in his life. But they had always seemed to devolve into lecture fests from him. It appeared Jake's solution...his outlet? A dead woman was easier to talk to than his father.

His nose started to run. Cold air brought out the worst in Marshall's nasal cavities. His sleeve did what he figured sleeves were designed to do. Gritting his teeth, he shook his head and kept reading.

Den

"Is something wrong with your daddy?" It was Sally Anne, one of Beth's friends, who'd stayed a little longer. Several had already left to go spend the rest of Christmas Eve with their families. She had just come out of the kitchen, a doughnut in her hand, and met Beth walking down the hallway.

Beth reached out, snatched the doughnut, took a bite, and returned it. "No, why?" Beth mouthed, between chews.

"Ya'll keep looking for him, and I wondered if something was wrong."

Beth swallowed. "Naw, he's probably hiding out in his *thinking* place, if you know what I mean. Mama just needs to talk to him for a minute."

Attic

Saturday
January 13, 1996

Dear Gammy Gat,

I got a letter from Eddie on Thursday. He said he missed me and things weren't the same. I showed Mama and Daddy the letter. Daddy didn't care. I could tell. And if you won't tell anybody, I cried a little bit. His letter made me happy and sad at the same time. It's kind of like now. It makes me feel good to write you letters. It makes me sad too.

Marshall remembered this. The entire incident whiffed into his mind like a brisk face-wind from a downhill bicycle ride.

■   ■   ■   ■   ■

Jake had ridden his bicycle after school. A coolish day, but not too cool for a kid who wanted to ride his bike. Millie had opened the front door for a bit to let some fresh air flow through the screened door. Marshall, in his La-Z-Boy, had about eased into a before-supper snooze when he heard the screen door slam.

"Mama, Daddy, look, it's a letter from Eddie." Millie clapped her hands together and smiled. "I'm so glad Eddie wrote to you, Jake." Her voice sounded upbeat…sincere.

Marshall's eyes, in pre-snooze mode, focused on nothing in particular through eyelid slits. "That's great, son. How's he doing? He was a good, best friend, wasn't he?"

Jake had gone silent. His face turned red. Marshall, reluctantly, shifted out of recliner mode and transitioned from pre-snooze to something akin to almost alert. The letter had already started to float from Jake's hands to the floor. On the way down, it wavered in the air and finally slid under the coffee table.

"He's not a *was* best friend, Daddy." A tear trickled down Jake's cheek. "He's an *is* best friend." Jake wiped the tears away on his sleeve. He searched for and found the letter, picked it up, and ran from the room.

"What'd I say?"

Millie scowled and jumped to her feet to go after her son. As she darted down the hall, she turned and shouted at Marshall. "You can be so insensitive, sometimes."

Marshall sat back again. "Aw, let him go. It's a man thing, my dear. He doesn't want us to see him cry."

Millie stopped short. Jake slipped into his room and slammed the door. "I don't want him to not want us to see him cry."

Marshall shook his head, reclined again, and closed his eyes. "Sometimes, you got to let kids work stuff out for themselves."

.   .   .   .   .

The lack of a cushion on his attic barrel seat reminded Marshall of the comfort level of his recliner. It revealed the painful reality of the cold and harshness of the attic. Jake's January 13th letter exposed how easy it was to cross the fine line separating Jake's *working stuff out for himself* from *Daddy didn't care.* Perhaps another painful reality reflecting coldness and harshness. An inner voice kicked in again. *Think it might be possible to let 'em suffer a little bit without making 'em think you don't care, Marshall?* From what he was reading, it appeared he had allowed himself to be less than aware of the extent of his support for the former and woefully lacking in his efforts to project the latter.

He just shook his head and recalled how the two boys had written to each other from time to time and even swapped pictures. During those early years, Eddie never seemed to change. He wore the same old hat hanging the same old way. He wore the same old-man pants riding high on his waist. Later, in middle school, the letters and visits were fewer and farther between. It wasn't until high school when the two boys hooked up again.

When Marshall and Millie had informed Eddie's family about Jake's death, they learned Eddie was out of the country. He was participating in an education abroad program with a family in France and would not be able to come home for the funeral.

Marshall shook his head and sighed. He let his eyes fall back on the letter.

I haven't made any new friends yet. I don't know why I should. I've decided friends don't make. They just are. Anyway, I don't want to make any, or find any, or work at it, or be one, or whatever. If it can't be Eddie, then I don't want one.

I'll never forgive Mama and Daddy for making us move. They must not have cared about any of their friends.

Your friend,

Jake

P.S. I love you, Gammy Gat

Marshall stared at the words. *They must not have cared about any of their friends.* Marshall had read, somewhere—when facing challenging situations such as tough crowds, difficult scenes, and important presentations—presenters, performers, and actors should be sure not to "show their seams." Appeared the definition of "seams" included such things as your shortcomings, your frailties, your imperfections, feelings of inadequacy, and fears. Misconstruing this advice, he figured it applied to raising kids. Marshall had convinced a leery Millie the best strategy for dealing with their children about the move was to act strong and not allow their own sadness to show. Perhaps this particular calculation had, ironically, been their biggest seam of all. Sharing their feelings of sadness and heartbreak and emotional traumas associated with the move were not seams to hide. *How did* not *sharing your kids' anxieties—especially Jake's—work for you, Marshall?* Jake had hopped an angry train he couldn't get off, and Marshall chastised himself for not being willing to share that he was riding on a pretty anxious train himself. He rubbed his brow and moved on to the next letter.

Living Room

One of Marshall's co-workers walked up to Millie. "You looking for Marshall?"

Millie, who had been standing in front of the large bay window, just staring, turned at the sound of her name. "Uh, just needed to tell him something, Allen. Has he been with you?"

"Nope, not with me. Is anything wrong?"

She smiled and patted his arm. "No, it's, uh, nothing. Just needed to tell him something."

Allen rolled his eyes. "Probably in the bathroom. Anything I can do?"

Millie forced a smile. "Thanks, but no." "I'll see him when he gets out."

Attic

Wednesday
January 17, 1996

Dear Gammy Gat,

A new kid came into my class at school. His name's Randy. He's new, like me. He's only been here for three days. He's kind of a short guy. And he's got big ears. They stick out even worse than mine. Something about him makes me want to get to know him. Of course, he's nothing like Eddie, so don't get the wrong idea. I haven't even talked to him or anything. I did notice something. He seems angry all the time. I think he might be a little bit like me.

Marshall had expected the Randy kid's presence to slap him in the face in the letters. Predictably, it proved as painful as he had imagined it would. Jake had loved school up until the move. Both Millie and Marshall had been at wits' end about how to explain the apparent change in their son's attitude. Marshall had to blame somebody—certainly not himself—for Jake's anger at the world and what he considered the belligerent nonsense going on in Jake's mind. This kid, Randy, a head full of Irish red hair and a face full of freckles, provided the perfect scapegoat. He scooted around on spindly bowlegs, wobbly as unstaked tomato plants. He wore raggedy hand-me-downs. Sporting a mouth full of unbrushed teeth, the guy didn't wear a chip on his shoulder. He carried around two oak logs. A floodgate of memory windows started to open. Marshall attempted to shutter them and hold them at bay for as long as he could. He needed to go back to the letters. Maybe the act of reading would temporarily keep the memories from materializing.

I think I saw the principal's office in one of those magazines. You know, one of those house decorating kind. When we were looking for pictures to cut out in art class, I saw it. Not the principal's real office. It just looked like hers. It had all these matching colors and everything in the right places. Pictures and stuff hung all over the walls. Not kid pictures and stuff, though. And vases and pottery things were on the tables and shelves. Her office sure looked like the picture in the magazine. You know, look at but don't touch kind of stuff. Guess if I went in the room in the magazine, it'd be hard to breathe in there too. Speaking of the principal, I bumped into Ms. Ledbetter in the grocery store. I remembered HER name.

I hope you've met some of your old friends, and they remembered you. Guess I better go. I've still got some homework to do.

I remember,

Jake

P.S. I love you, Gammy Gat

Marshall found himself shaking his head after almost every sentence. Sentences full of revelations, they triggered a constant flow of flashbacks, attempting to smash through those previously shored-up memory windows.

During his first few school years, Jake's behavior reflected Millie's DNA. School had been a good experience for her. She'd been one of those kids with an instinct for how to be successful when it came to "playing the school game." Marshall, although a good student, had played at being the rebel from time to time because he thought it made him look like a cool guy. He'd known how to play the game. He just chose not to, sometimes. Like Millie, Jake had everything it took upstairs. During his fifth-grade year, he'd changed. Bent, bound, and determined, it seemed going to this school just angered Jake. Marshall had believed Jake had never given it a chance right from the git-go. As a result of their move, it seemed some of Marshall's pretend rebel DNA had kicked in on Jake, with a vengeance. Only, Marshall wasn't reading anything that sounded like Jake had inherited any notions of wanting to be perceived as a *cool guy*.

The notebook discovery was shaking him to his core. Like a redbone hound on a scent, the letters were forcing him to search his mind for the trail to understanding those truths. Marshall couldn't resist staring at this notebook. *Let the memories in, Marshall. Quit fighting and let them in.*

His heart and his head agreed. This notebook told *Jake's* story. Jake's *version*, of course. Separating the version in his son's head from the one he remembered was going to be the problem. A problem he was determined to solve, because a definite dichotomy prevailed between those two versions. And, at the moment, the reliability of Marshall's version was being severely challenged. He figured some memories would slip in he didn't even know he didn't know he had. One proved to be a conversation with Jake.

. . . . .

Marshall could see Jake's eleven-year-old figure stretched out on the floor. He had been sitting in a lounge chair right beside his son. A crumpled-up math homework assignment lay tossed on the carpet like an errant deli sheet at a picnic.

"Why's school so dumb, Daddy?"

Marshall had lowered his newspaper. "You got to learn to play the game, son. School's not supposed to be all fun and games. You got to work hard and take care of business."

Jake scowled and chewed on his lip. "School's stupid." He flicked at the rolled-up math assignment with his finger. It rolled out of sight under the couch. "They make us do dumb things."

"That's to make you tough and learn what life's all about."

"Well, it's still stupid..."

. . . . .

Marshall took a deep breath and stared at the notebook sitting in his lap. Just this short time reading Jake's thoughts and rehashing some of his own memories reverberated like a truck's backup beeper alarm in his head. Over and over, the letters were warning him that his son's perceptions of the version of his life, as a member of the Gatlin family, were wildly in conflict with those of his father. *Who are you to argue, Marshall? Think it might have been important to recognize perceptions matter? You figured all your son's issues required specifically "black and white" responses, didn't you? Think you might have discovered some gray answers worth considering?*

Those annoying inner voices weren't going to shut up.

Dining Room

Millie made her way back toward the dining room. Several friends sat around the table, talking quietly. "Thanks for being here, you guys," she said, smiling. She looked at her watch. It read 5:00. "It's Christmas Eve, and you know you oughta head on home to be with your families."

"We're just so sorry," Ashley, her neighbor from down the street, said. "And...and we all wanted to be here for you today." Millie reached down and hugged her friend. "Have you eaten anything?" Ashley asked.

"Not really hungry."

"You should eat something."

"I will." Millie smiled and turned to walk away.

"I looked for Marshall," Ashley said. "Haven't had a chance to talk with him. Is he close by?"

Millie rolled her eyes. "I think he's in the bathroom."

"Don't leave," Ashley said softly. "Sit down for a minute." She reached out, took Millie's hand, and gently pulled her over to the chair beside her.

Attic

Saturday
January 20, 1996

Dear Gammy Gat,

Guess what? Remember the new kid, Randy, I told you about? His mama and daddy don't live together. I heard some teachers talking in the hall on Thursday. I shouldn't have been listening. They didn't know I was timing out on the floor around the corner. The teachers said something about his daddy might have been hitting him and his mama. She took Randy and left in the middle of the night to come to Oakton. The teachers were talking about how terrible it was to come from such a home. Randy didn't say anything to me about it. He hardly talks to anybody.

Oh, yeah, remember when I told you about living in this old house? Well, this bathroom upstairs has a big, walk-in closet. It doesn't even have a light. When you close the door, it's so dark you can't see a finger in front of your nose. Beth and I did a dumb thing. We went into the bathroom while we were playing, decided to hide in the closet, closed the door, and got locked in. We screamed, and Beth cried. Well, I did too. Daddy had to take a hammer and a crowbar and knock the door down. I think I wiped away the tears in time. He was too busy telling me what a dumb thing I had done, anyway.

Marshall closed his eyes and recalled the old, booby-trapped bathroom. He remembered that day—a memory he wished would stay hidden away.

. . . . .

He and Millie had stood, just staring at the closet door. She'd tried to tell him what to do and calm Beth, all at the same time. He'd left, in the middle of a suggestion, to retrieve some tools. When the door finally dropped off its hinges, the sight of Beth screaming, huddled on the floor, left them speechless. It took them both over an hour to get her to stop sobbing. She had nightmares for two weeks and spent every one of those nights snuggled in-between the two of them.

. . . . .

Sitting on the barrel, Marshall rubbed his forehead in an attempt to push out the memory of Beth's terror-induced screams. The tears in Jake's eyes had not gone unnoticed, either.

You had yelled at him, Marshall.

During a traumatic moment in his son's life, Marshall had made it worse. Like a goofy, bobblehead character tapping his own head, Marshall tried to shake away the sound of the recurring, inner voice. Unsuccessful, he sighed and went back to the letter.

It makes me think about Randy's parents. When you grow up, I guess doing dumb things doesn't change all that much.

I don't understand why my teacher thinks she has to be so mean. She makes you think going to school is supposed to be hard. And I'll bet she can't be having fun. Maybe she is. I guess not smiling, making somebody put their nose in a circle on the wall, telling everybody to stop talking and get back to work, telling everybody all the fun we had in the primary grades was over because now we're in real school, must be fun for her. I did hear her talk happy on Friday to some of the other teachers, though. She even smiled at us on Friday. It seems like she thinks if she didn't have to put up with all us kids, school would be a pretty cool place for her. Don't ask me if I want to be a teacher when I grow up. I couldn't stand all the FUN.

I hope you are having fun.

You deserve it,
Jake
P.S. I love you, Gammy Gat

Marshall reached back and rubbed his neck and shoulders. If anyone deserved fun and happiness in the afterlife, his mother met the criteria. Her weakness for nicotine in no way qualified as a disqualification. He had no reservations about where he thought the guys who manufactured those chemical-filled death sticks ought to be serving their time. Both his parents grew up in a generation duped into addiction, one on nicotine and the other one with a fried food obsession. Cole Gatlin had died from a heart attack, they told him he would experience if he chose not to find the will to push away the fried chicken and fried okra and fried chicken livers. The threat of a heart attack or heart disease wasn't incentive enough. One morning, his father woke up alive and kicking. A few hours later, the alive and kicking stopped in one fell swoop.

With his mother, it had been different. For days, she had tried to endure the pain after the cancer diagnosis. The initial progression flowed downhill, like a pinball rolling into bumpers—hopeful obstacles—stalling the journey to the final drain hole. Once she went to the hospital, everything tumbled downhill in a hurry.

Marshall shook his head. He attempted to prepare himself for the next memory to rear its ugly head. The image he knew he'd never be able to *not* see.

He took a breath and let it in.

． ． ． ． ．

The lights had been dimmed in her single room. Her frail form, visible beneath the hospital sheet, had seemed to waste away by the minute. Watching her struggle, going from breath to breath, proved to be pure agony.

. . . . .

As he sat in the attic, Marshall agonized over what he imagined her breath-to-breath struggle would have been. It was an agony he had experienced, coping with his asthma. Of course, the cancer attacking her body would have exponentially raised the level of that trauma. *At the time, you blamed her for being weak, Marshall.* Having to listen to those inner voices was going to be a real pain. Not in the ass but in his heart. He sighed, though, and glanced back at Jake's letter. His son had been right. If anyone deserved to have fun, his mother fit the bill.

Marshall stood up to stretch his legs, under the notion he needed to stand to make sure he still could. A soft crack whispered from inside his left knee. It was one of those "good hurt" stretches. He set the notebook on the barrel and took a step or two away. A few steps would loosen up his piss-poor knees, so he meandered by the kids' treasure shelves. Jake's school comments had certainly rejuvenated some of his perspectives on the school experience.

When their kids were young, Marshall thought more than one story existed when they got into trouble at school. The proverbial kid's perspective versus the teacher's. At the time, he'd figured the lean ought to be toward the educators, the folks who were supposed to know better. Their job was to know what transpired throughout the day. Jake's versions, at least about his teacher, seemed to be punching holes and putting the kibosh on this perceived default approach. *Parents are supposed to know better, too. Right, Marshall?*

Now, his predictable answer of *"We do"* sounded lame, terse, and a bit sanctimonious. He made his way back to the barrel and reached into his pocket for the hand warmers. The chill had pretty much made its way to all ten digits, so he figured it was time for them. But his fingers felt the outline of his watch, instead. The hand warmers were in his other pocket. He rolled his eyes and quickly released the watch. He didn't want to know the time, for he figured he had pretty much blown passed his original plan to stay in the attic for only a short while. Coming across Jake's letters had changed everything. An entire notebook of revelations about his son rested on his lap. And from what he had read, so far, the pressure of anticipating what was within the large number of remaining pages posed too great a conundrum to ignore. He couldn't leave now. Wriggling his fingers, he retrieved the hand warmers from his other pocket. Kneading them for a minute or two, he pressed them between his hands, their warmth quickly soothing his palms. He held them for a few moments, then returned them to his pocket for later use. Picking up the notebook, he returned to the letters.

Dining Room

Both Lisa and Beth looked up from where they sat on the floor and spied their mother standing in the doorway. Standing, they stepped away from their friends and walked over to her. Beth whispered in her mother's ear, "He wasn't in the bathroom, Mama."

Millie, smiling at her daughter's friends, ushered both girls out of the room. "I need them for a minute to check on something in the kitchen."

Once in the kitchen, Lisa, her eyes starting to tear up, reached out for her mother's hand. "Where is he, Mama?" She said it louder than she had intended. "He's hiding somewhere, isn't he? Or he's sneaked out. All these people are here...and...and it's not like him to..." She stopped herself and rubbed her hands across her face to keep from crying.

Taking a deep breath, Beth placed her hands on her hips and glared at her mother. "You better sock him hard when he shows up."

"I'm sure he just needed a little breathing space, honey," Millie said. "He'll suddenly turn up like he's never been away, you'll see."

"Still...you better sock him."

Millie rolled her eyes and turned to go back to the dining room.

Attic

Wednesday
January 24, 1996

Dear Gammy Gat,

I need to tell you about something that happened at school this week. Randy got into a fight on Tuesday. This other kid said something stupid about his dad. Randy socked the kid. The kid hit Randy back, and then they had a real fight. Ms. Murray (she's my teacher) stopped the fight. The other kid said Randy started it, and Ms. Murray believed him. I think it was because Randy wouldn't say anything. He stared real mean and hateful-like. Ms. Murray took both kids to the office. Randy got paddled. The other kid had to talk to his mama on the phone and tell her what he'd done.

I talked to Randy later. I told him I thought he was right to clobber the other kid for being nosy. Randy didn't answer me. He did smile. For some reason, I think maybe we could be friends now.

I was the other kid.

Marshall's eyes opened wide, and he raised his more than abundant eyebrows. Millie had not shared all the details about this incident, an oversight he thought he might have to bring up later.

Or not.

Jake had never punched out a classmate before. It was a totally out-of-character move. His confession proved even more fascinating. Marshall re-

read, *Maybe we can be friends now.* It was clear Jake had started a fight with this kid because he thought it might be the only way to get his attention. Being seen and heard echoed the essence of basic human needs. Recognizing it didn't only apply to oneself required a high level of empathy.

How loud did Jake have to shout to get your *attention, Marshall? Is he getting it now?*

Marshall winced and read on.

Randy waved at me today. Well, it was sort of a wave, and he had a half-smile on his face. I sort of waved back. Ever since we had the fight, he hasn't been such a jerk to me. I caught him staring at me a couple of times. He'd look away real quick, though, when I looked at him.

None of the other kids like him. They think he's weird. They pick on him all the time. If he'd stop getting so mad when they do, they'd stop. He does what they want him to do. They win every time.

I remember when you told me about the winning and losing game. How the only way to win was not to give somebody who picks on you what they want. You said the best thing to do was to do the opposite. Like if they're trying to make you hit back, don't. If they're trying to make you cry, don't.

He must not have had a Gammy Gat who told him this kind of stuff. I guess it'll have to be me. Maybe a guy can make a friend after all.

Trying to be a friend,

Jake

P.S. I love you, Gammy Gat

Marshall shifted uneasily on the unbearably hard barrel seat. He'd started to worry about the prospects of receiving an apparent permanent wedgie. Maybe even a hemorrhoid problem. The shift and reach-around skivvy readjustment seemed to do the trick, at least temporarily.

No stranger to his mother's "win-lose" game, he had sat on the toilet seat top, more times than he could count, and been privy to the eloquence of her famous lesson. One conversation, during the administration of her painful, iodine, cure-all therapy, he remembered clearly. He'd been running to catch a friend, who had called him a name. Being called a "Dooky-Head" pretty well forged itself into a person's memory bank forever.

.　　　　.　　　　.　　　　.　　　　.

"He wanted to make you chase him, didn't he, Marshall?" His mother said quietly. She dabbed iodine on his knee after he'd received a nasty scrape.

"Yes, Mommy, but..." She'd apply it, then blow the sting away. He hated to admit he whimpered like a weenie every time. He'd pull his shin into his body, trying to squeeze away the pain of the cure.

"You did what he wanted you to do, didn't you?"

"Yes, Mommy, but..."

"Who fell and cried all the way home, and who ran and laughed all the way?"

.　　　　.　　　　.　　　　.　　　　.

The sound of a box falling to the floor—evidently teetering on a shelf edge after he'd fiddled around the boxes—snapped Marshall away from the memory. Sidetracked, now, he sighed and turned his attention to the fallen box. *Jake's Old Shoes,* written on the side in Millie's handwriting, denoted the contents. The crackly tape split open, and several pairs spilled out. Deteriorating rubber bands snubbed most of the pairs together. Some bands had already snapped, clinging to the dusty surfaces from having partially melted during the stifling heat generated in the attic during the summers. Millie had labeled each pair accordingly, by year. Some small, hospital white, high-top Stride Rites perched right on top. He and Millie had stuffed Jake's little feet into those during year one. Wearing them, he'd been as cute as they wanted him to be. The discomfort level had to have been hell. And they weren't cheap, especially when the small window of wearability required frequent purchases. Millie had tied a pair of miniature Brogan boots together, using their tubular-looking shoestrings. Tiny scuff marks decorated the toes. She had also packed up his old pair of black dress shoes. They matched the suit she made him wear to his school's honor assembly in the third grade. Marshall had begged Millie not to embarrass the guy. She had insisted. He spied several versions of discount store sneakers. The pièce de résistance pair was a pair of black, high-top Nike knockoffs, his fifth-grade shoe of choice. A memory, like a snapshot, whisked into his mind. Three-year-old Jake, wearing only a pull-up, shuffled around in Marshall's bedroom slippers.

.   .   .   .   .

"I wearing your shoes, Daddy."

.   .   .   .   .

Now, years later, Jake's toddler Stride Rites stared up at him. Marshall cradled them in his hands and rubbed the leather, still stiff after all these years. Although a bit scuffed, they felt almost new. His eyes caught a glimpse of something stuffed inside one of them. He pulled it out and discovered a pair of tiny white socks, the kind you could never keep on a toddler's foot. He shook his head, sighed, and started to return the shoes to the box, thought better of the idea, and set them down beside the wooden barrel. Folding the flaps closed on the box, he placed it back on the shelf. An inner voice suddenly butted in, reminding him he'd let himself be sidetracked by the shoe box. *Reading these letters is a bit like being caught up in the "win-lose" game, isn't it, Marshall? What do you think wanting to read them is going to make you do? After reading them, what would winning look like? Or losing?*

He rubbed his head.

Your son learned about this game from your mother, Marshall, not from you. How does that make you feel?

At this point, reading the letters was like running a marathon with no end in sight.

Laundry Room

Millie pulled Beth into the laundry room and pushed the door shut. "Are you sure he wasn't in there, sweetheart?"

"The bathroom door was closed, Mama. When I knocked, nobody answered. I, uh, listened at the door. Didn't hear anything. So, I opened it. Empty."

Attic

Wednesday
January 31, 1996

Dear Gammy Gat,

Daddy doesn't play as much as he used to. You know, tickle fights and stuff like that. We used to play monster too. I'd hide under the covers, and he'd come in growling. I'd scream. Sometimes Daddy would hide under the covers, and I'd be the monster. "Who's there!?" Daddy shouted when he heard me growling. Then I'd get him. We don't throw Frisbees as much anymore, either. Or build as many sandcastles. Is it because he's getting too old, or am I? Seems like either way, getting old isn't much fun.

I know you were kind of old. When you get old, I wonder how far back you can remember. When I get older, will I remember what it was like to be the age I am now? Will I always remember you?

Randy and I had our first real talk on Monday. I said, "How's it going?" He said, "Who's asking?"

I wrote to Eddie and told him about Randy. Of course, I told Eddie he was still my best buddy of all time. I hope Eddie understands about Randy. I know you can have all kinds of friends. Like the friends we made at the beach, we knew we'd never see again. Mama called them our "little while friends." And then you got friends like Eddie. He's like my best ever, number one, all-time friend. Even when we get grown-up, I know it'll be this way. And then you have just the guys. The ones you hang around and do stuff with every now and then.

You won't believe what happened. The school has this fountain I forgot had water in it. I didn't see the ice. I was walking around the edge on Tuesday, minding my own business, when the fountain leaped out and grabbed me. It pulled me in. I'm kidding. I slipped. Nobody knew until I showed up at my classroom door. Mr. McQueen, the custodian, had to mop up the puddle where I was standing. Golly, it was cold.

Ms. Murray took me to the principal's office. She said I jumped in on purpose. She held my arm tight while we were walking. And she didn't say a word. Neither did I. I didn't know it was such a long way. Ms. Ledbetter talked to me in her office. I remember the whole conversation.

Ms. Ledbetter: "Well, young man, what did you do your teacher didn't like?"

Me: "I don't remember."

Ms. Ledbetter: "Well, why was she angry?"

Me: "I don't remember."

Ms. Ledbetter: "Did you do something you weren't supposed to do?"

Me: "I don't remember."

I knew she wanted me to say it. Adults always try to make you. You know, tell on yourself. I did tell her Ms. Murray grabbed me. This thing called "pleading the fifth" was on a TV show, and Mama explained it to me. I guess it's only for grown-ups.

When I think about you, now, sometimes it feels like you're far away. When I write you letters, it feels like you're here with me. When I remember the fun things we used to do or when I tell you stuff, it makes me feel like you're close. When I remember the funeral and seeing you in the hospital, it feels like you're far away. Sometimes I get a kind of goose-bumpy feeling when I'm writing to you. I wonder if this is how you use your heaven superpowers to let me know you know?

Trying hard to remember the good stuff,
Jake
P.S. I love you, Gammy Gat

Marshall went back and re-read, *When you get old, I wonder how far back you can remember. When I get older, will I remember what it was like to be the age I am now?* Reading it again made him think about his conversation with Millie, the night before finding out about Jake's death. "He was growing up, but he wasn't grown," she had said. "You've forgotten what it was like to be his age." He remembered his reply. "It's not a matter of my not remembering. It's a matter of knowing what's right and what's wrong."

Are you oversimplifying, Marshall? You know, rationalizing your inability to think beyond your shallow response to your kid's issues?

The "kid" stuff in those early elementary years proved easiest to remember for Marshall. The anticipation of tickle fights, Chutes and Ladders game board nights, homemade pizza suppers, trips to the playground, and all hands-on deck Taco Tuesdays were staples in the list of family together events. When the enthusiasm started to taper off, Marshall couldn't recall. He knew, at some point, it was all but gone. Of course, he accepted that parent-child relationships adapted and modified and changed over time. During Jake's fifth-grade year, it seemed like Johnson's fable purported, "the cheese got moved" for the Gatlin family. Changes happened. Changes so shocking, a normal "take them in stride" attitude didn't cut it. A parent and a grandparent died. A move to a new town left old friends and comforts behind.

You were the adult, Marshall. How did you deal with the changes? You certainly didn't like how your son dealt with them, did you? How'd you help him? Criticizing him for being angry and upset and struggling to deal with those changes worked, didn't it?

At the moment, he didn't think it was in his own best interests to provide an honest answer to any of those questions. And then he admitted to himself, honesty wasn't the issue. Just coming up with *any* answer was boggling his mind.

Main Floor Hallway

Millie checked out the clock over the kitchen sink. 5:25.
"Where is that man?" She whispered to herself.

Attic

Sunday
February 4, 1996

Dear Gammy Gat,

Guess who I sat with at lunch on Friday? Randy. We talked and everything. We even swapped desserts. When we finished lunch, I asked him if he wanted to mess around after school, sometime. You know, play some ball, and maybe hang out at our house. His trailer park is not far away. He said, "You want to play with me?" I said, "Sure."

We haven't done it yet, though. Making friends can be a slow business.

Ms. Murray embarrassed me on Friday in front of everybody. She asked me if I was paying attention. I was sitting, doing nothing wrong. I wasn't bothering anybody. I was thinking about stuff. Mama left on Saturday to go on a business trip for a couple of days. When she gets back, we're all going to the circus. We haven't been in at least a hundred years. I was thinking about Daddy telling us we have to clean our rooms when we get home after school. I was thinking about seeing if Randy could spend the night sometime. I was thinking Daddy says my hair is too long. I was thinking we've got clothes to wash, because I'm not going to wear those pants Mama bought for me without my permission. Anyway, I already knew how to do those math problems on the board.

I've got a feeling they're starting to think I'm a troublemaker at school. I know they think Randy is. And they know we've been hanging around together.

Even when I'm doing nothing and somebody else starts something, I'm getting the look. I'm getting the stare from Daddy all the time, too. I guess I should cool it. It won't make any difference.

I'm doomed.

Marshall stopped reading and looked up. Jake was right about the troublemaker label. And his relationship with this Randy kid bothered him. Marshall had aimed his anger at both of them, but Randy wasn't his. He'd wanted his kid to be better. An inner voice kicked in.

You wanted him to be better? What did "better" mean? Your definition? His? From what you've been reading, are you getting some idea of how he defined himself as a young boy, growing up? Do you remember how you defined yourself at his age? By the way, did you want your kid to already know what it was you were supposed to help him learn, Marshall?

The questioning from his inner voices shouldn't have stunned him. He'd heard Millie express some of these same thoughts or something akin, at least a thousand times. His eyes returned to the letter.

I need to tell you about something that happened with this other friend. His name's Willie, and he's shy. Here's what happened.

We were playing kickball with this older kid and some other guys. Tucker, the big kid, (who's a jerk by the way) didn't like something Willie did. I forget what. He started pushing Willie around. Willie had a real scared look in his eyes, like he wished he could disappear. He just stared at Tucker. Tucker didn't like it one bit, either. He said, "What you looking at, tiny?" Willie stood like he was frozen. Then Tucker socked him in the eye. I heard his fist hit. It knocked Willie down. I wanted to do something. I didn't because Tucker was bigger than me, too. I stood and watched. Then I helped Willie get up after Tucker ran off laughing.

I felt bad. I think I have what Mama calls mixed feelings. You know, sometimes it's hard to tell the difference between being afraid, or believing it's wrong to fight, or wondering if you have to fight to stand up for yourself sometimes. I know you must be thinking about the day I hit Randy. For some reason, it seemed different. I don't know why. Maybe it's a heart and head kind of thing. Mama's right. Mixed feelings sure make things awful confusing.

I found our family picture album on Saturday. I saw lots of pictures of Lisa and Beth and some of me. Mama and Daddy, when they were little, were in it. You were in the album too.

Sometimes I want to grow up, and sometimes I don't. The things I like, I don't want to change, like hugs from Mama (a real hug from Daddy's not gonna happen)and surprises from the grocery store. And sneaking money out of Daddy's pocket when he pretends not to feel me doing it. And jumping on the trampoline and helping to cook dinner and playing restaurant for Mama. And riding dirt bikes and skateboards and climbing trees and grossing out your dumb sisters. And horse books and watching old Tarzan movies with Mama. And writing to you.

Daddy says things change. People change. And when you grow up, you do grown-up things and feel different about everything in your life. I think I want to do lots of new things. I don't want to forget or give up the good, old ones, though.

I hope when I get older, I won't think writing to you was stupid. If I do, you have my permission to jerk a knot in me. I heard Ms. Murray say she was going to "jerk a knot" in Walter for messing around in the lunch line.

Not a jerk,

Jake

P.S. I love you, Gammy Gat

Marshall glanced at his son's closing salutation. Instinctively, to verify one more time, he glanced to make sure Jake actually wrote these letters. Because they read like words written by a stranger. Jake's ruminations reflecting his own truths and mixed feelings were like a wall suddenly appearing on a path Marshall thought he could easily navigate. The bundle of emotions generated from acknowledging that his son had written these letters continued to befuddle him. Challenged everything he believed he believed.

Being reminded about their family album brought a smile to his face. He set Jake's notebook of letters down and stood up again. The crackle from his left knee prompted another scowl on his face. He didn't let it stop his search. He knew where to look. After moving four or five boxes around, he found it. Millie had put together several family albums. The one he looked for, Millie had made right after Beth's third birthday. Like salt and pepper squares on the pages, the pictures were a sprinkled smattering of old black and whites amidst a plethora of color photos. The one Millie took of his mother on her 70th birthday appeared particularly representative of his mother's personality. Her grandkids loved the goofy faces she used to make. Just before the camera clicked, she'd strike a pose. Photos of her sporting a typical, expected, generic grinning face were few and far between. The one on her 70th birthday had embarrassed him. For a reason he probably couldn't explain to this day, he blurted out his concern at the time. His only explanation to himself, now? Acknowledgement of a brain fart.

"Pooh on you, Marshall," she had told him. "We're having a *specialicious* good time, aren't we, kids?"

One of Marshall's mantras to his children was, "Life's not all fun and games." He'd figured you had to tell them this little tidbit to get them ready for life. One of those voices in his head butted in again. *Did this black and white view of the world suck a bunch of wind out of the fun your kids had when they were little, Marshall? You thought the act of adapting and accepting change had to be void of fun, didn't you? And was everything they did a part of the process of getting ready for life? Weren't they also living a life at the moment?* Marshal shook his head, as if attempting to shake out the noise from the voices. But they weren't done. *Jake's been talking a lot about dealing with changes, hasn't he? How is it an eleven-year-old knew more than you about the importance of keeping the new things in perspective and not forgetting some of the good, old ones?*

The list of questions he didn't want or know how to answer was piling up.

Dining Room

"Hadn't talked to anybody who's seen him in a while," Beth said, as Millie approached her three daughters.

"Everyone has asked about him, though," Lisa said. "I'm worried about him, Mama."

"Where did Daddy go?" Mary asked, a frown on her lips. "Why isn't he here?" She rubbed her eyes, and her lips started to quiver.

"Walk around again," Millie said, reaching out and pulling her youngest daughter to her. "And sneak a peek in the closets."

"Really?" Beth said, rolling her eyes.

Millie just shook her head and whisked away the two oldest. "Whatever," she whispered. "Just do it. Quietly." She paused, and her face softened. "Please." Shrugging, both Lisa and Beth turned slowly and shuffled away. Millie, still holding Mary, reached down and smoothed her daughter's hair. "I'm sure he's okay, sweetie. He just needs to be alone somewhere for a bit. That's all."

She wasn't ready to reveal the nagging, uncomfortable feeling in her gut.

Attic

Wednesday
February 7, 1996

Dear Gammy Gat,

Ms. Murray does something I wish she wouldn't do. She walks around with a ruler in her hand all the time. I think she thinks it keeps the mean kids from being bad. It doesn't. They still do mean stuff and only hide it better. By the way, Mama's back.

We had a pop test in Social Studies this week, too. It's like being punished for not being interested enough to read the stupid chapter.

Ms. Murray asked Randy why he hit somebody. She asked me why I didn't do all my homework. Mama asked me why I didn't clean my plate. Daddy wanted to know why I didn't study more. Ms. Murray asked why I had to go to the bathroom so much. She wanted to know why Randy couldn't sit still. She even asked him why he came to school if he wasn't going to try any harder than she thought he was trying.

They ask why all the time. And they want some big, fancy answer. When I ask "Why?" Daddy mostly answers, "Because I said so."

Just wondering why.

Marshall shook his head. One of those inner voices whispered, *Where's the real controversy here, Marshall? Answering honestly or skirting the issue because it's an easier answer?* "Because I said so" made for an easy answer. Admitting to having no substantive reason, even close to sounding rational to an eleven-year-old, not so much. Having to listen to these inner tidbits was like listening to Millie, albeit even more relentless. Sighing, he finished the letter.

Something's been bugging me. Randy gets himself in trouble all the time. I've had my share, but nothing like him. I did tell him what you told me about the win-lose game. He doesn't get it. It is kind of hard to do sometimes. The other kids make him angry all the time. And Ms. Murray always catches him hitting or pushing back. Mama calls it staying in control and making good decisions. It's not easy. Randy doesn't even try. It's like he wants to get in trouble. They have to call his mom a lot, and then she comes to school. Sometimes she takes him home or talks with Ms. Ledbetter, and he gets to stay. Sometimes I see his mom crying.

I wonder if Mama has ever cried because of me? She and Daddy made us all cry when we had to move.

Maybe fair's fair,
Jake
P.S. I love you, Gammy Gat

The tears Millie had cried over all their kids would sink a boat.

Not wanting to dwell on this thought, Marshall raised Jake's notebook to his chest and, absent-mindedly, flipped through the family album pages again. He stopped at a photograph of Jake. The toddler was blowing out candles on one of Mary Claire's cakes at his three-year-old birthday party. Marshall shook his head. He remembered Beth's comment after learning her grandmother had died. "Gammy Gat can't make my birthday cakes, no more, can she?" The top right corner of the next page held another photo of Jake at his three-year-old party. The little guy had stared right at the camera, a baby tooth grin on his face and a blond tuft of wild grass cowlick sticking up on his head. The spin from an inner voice spun relentlessly. *Wonderful innocence...and you let it...watched it...helped it...slip away. Why, Marshall?*

He reached down and allowed his fingertips to brush lightly across Jake's picture. As if, once again, he could brush his son's wonderful cowlick flat and then watch it pop back like he used to do when Jake was little.

Kitchen

Millie pretended to wash some dishes. One by one, their friends stopped in to offer to help clean up. Millie refused them all. "It's almost 5:45," she said. "Y'all really don't need to stay any longer. The girls and I are gonna take care of it," she said. "Gives us something to do tonight. Thanks anyway. Love you guys. Sorry, Marshall isn't here to send you off. He's...uh...upstairs, back in the bathroom. Stomach a little queasy. He'll be all right."

She hated telling this white lie. Confessing she had no clue where he might be—and signs were pointing more and more that he wasn't anywhere in the house—proved to be a truth she wasn't yet prepared to acknowledge. Whether Marshall was somewhere with a queasy stomach, she couldn't guess. *Her* stomach? Mere queasiness didn't come close to defining the condition *it* was in.

Attic

Sunday
February 11, 1996

Dear Gammy Gat,
I had to wait late at school on Friday. All the other kids had gone home or to the babysitters or the after-school program. Daddy said he was going to pick me up right after school. "Be looking for me," he said. "I'll be early."
I waited. The buses were long gone. Ms. Murray said I could wait inside the front doors and watch for him. The office called home. Nobody answered. "Must be on his way," they said. When he finally drove up, Ms. Ledbetter was not happy. He said he was sorry, and he had forgot.
Daddies aren't supposed to forget. Are they?
Jake
P.S. I love you, Gammy Gat

Marshall wished he'd tucked this next memory somewhere hidden deep where it couldn't find its way up through the mishmash he called his brain.

No such luck.

.   .   .   .   .

Frantic to finish doing something at work, he lost all track of time on this particular day. By chance, he glanced at the clock. He actually said, "Oh shit," out loud. He made a quick call to say he was on his way. It only took six minutes of the eight-minute drive to reach school. Jake, a scowl on his face, leaned into and held onto one of those metal posts propping up the covered walkway. Ms. Ledbetter stood, arms crossed, and no smile. Jake didn't say a word as he climbed in the back seat. Marshall thought he heard a grunt. It was more than likely a deliberate, exasperated "huff." When Ms. Ledbetter started to say something, Marshall butted into her lecture with an "I'm sorry. It won't happen again." He'd rolled up his window and pulled away before she could reply. Millie's wrath had been something to behold.

"You *forgot* him?"

"Now, Millie."

"I'll bet you didn't *forget* to buy beer for this weekend."

"Look, you have my permission to take my name off the list for the Father of the Year awards."

Millie's consequence for his severe encroachment, lack of judgment, and selfishness was nearly apocalyptic. "This is no joke, Marshall Gatlin," she had said. "And since you're into lists, I believe I'll remove this weekend's date night from mine."

■　　　■　　　■　　　■　　　■

A mini-burst of chilled wind slipped in beneath the eaves. Marshall shuddered and almost dropped the album and the notebook on the floor. Re-adjusting his backside on the hard barrel seat, he scrunched his nose and frowned at what this stupid indiscretion had cost him.

Den

"All our friends have left, Mama," Beth said. "Whataya want us to do?"

"You girls keep looking," Millie whispered. "And keep an eye on Mary. I don't want her getting too upset about her Daddy."

"Will do," Beth said.

Millie glanced at her watch again. 5:55. "We still have a few folks here. I'm gonna shoo 'em away. They need to go home to their families."

The nagging feeling in Millie's stomach had begun to inch itself upward toward migraine territory. Marshall's near collapse at the funeral messed with her mind. Damnable guilt at not reading it as a potential crisis point crept into her psyche. His behavior, from the very beginning at this gathering, telegraphed evidence his head was not in a good place. And now, he'd taken off to God knew where and was doing God knew what.

Attic

Wednesday
February 14, 1996

Dear Gammy Gat,

An embarrassing thing happened to another kid on Tuesday. He peed his pants. I remember it happening to me in kindergarten. When it happened to me, I was doing stuff and playing and everything. I knew I had to go, but I was having too much fun and all of a sudden it was too late. I was a little kid, though. And little kids don't make it all the time. This guy in my class tried to hide it. I could see the wet spot on the front of his pants and the look on his face like he wished he was dead. He even pretended like nothing was wrong. I'm glad it wasn't me again. I felt embarrassed, almost like it was.

Ms. Murray sent me to the principal's office again. She didn't go with me this time. She made me give Cynthia her pencil back. And then she shouted, "Out! Out of this room and straight to the office, young man! And when you arrive, you tell Ms. Ledbetter what happened." There's lots of ways to get to the office. I decided to take the longest one, so I'd have time to figure out what happened.

Still trying to figure it out,
Jake
P.S. I love you, Gammy Gat

Marshall shook his head and looked up from the letter. He'd consistently fought hard to convince Millie she was better equipped to deal with Jake's indiscretions at school. Confrontation was just not his thing. However, this particular bullshit rationale fell on totally deaf ears. This had been one of those times he felt Millie had snookered him into making the trip to school to meet with Ms. Murray and Ms. Ledbetter.

.　　　.　　　.　　　.　　　.

When he arrived, Marshall spied Jake sitting on a bench outside the office. His strategy had been not to speak to his son as he walked by. Jake hung his head and never looked up, anyway. Marshall rolled his eyes, took a deep breath, and dug deep to look for the gumption he figured he would need to make it through this ordeal. Jake's teacher and principal, backs straight, hands in their laps, sat and waited. Jake was in trouble. Marshall was the one with sweaty hands. Like someone trying to lift her chin above water, Ms. Murray began.

"I will not tolerate this kind of behavior in my classroom," she had said before Marshall even got comfortable in the chair.

"Whoa, Ms. Murray," Marshall said. "I, uh, understand you're upset. Let me at least sit down." He sat back, crossed his legs, and folded his arms across his chest. "What exactly did he do, anyway?"

"He stole a pencil."

Marshall remembered thinking she pronounced it like an accusation of murder. "I beg your pardon?" The stunned look on his face probably appeared a bit more shocked than he had intended. He looked first at Ms. Murray and then at Ms. Ledbetter. "From the school store?"

"No. From one of his classmates."

"We give him plenty of pencils at home."

"He didn't take it because he *needed* a pencil."

"What you're telling me is, he took a pencil from someone for no reason." Marshall kept his hands tucked under his armpits. He knew the sweatiness factor had risen to a level he did not want to reveal.

"It appears he took it to aggravate his classmate, Mr. Gatlin." Ms. Ledbetter paused. "It's not so much this particular incident which concerns us. A pattern of behavior is developing, we believe, is not in Jake's or the school's best interests."

Marshall uncrossed his legs and leaned forward. He kept his arms folded across his chest. "What did he say when you talked with him after he came to the office?"

"When I asked him what happened, he shrugged. Refused to say much of anything." She flicked her eyes toward Ms. Murray. "I'd like to ask Ms. Murray to have him come in here and join us, so we can talk about this together."

Marshall kept thinking he needed a towel. Jake shuffled in, slouching and hanging his head. Ms. Ledbetter directed him to a chair beside his father. "Have a seat, please, young man," she said, her voice calm but intentionally firm. "We're all here to talk about your behavior, Jake." She turned and nodded at Marshall.

He took the cue, breathed a deep breath, turned toward Jake, and leaned in close to his face. "All right, son, tell me what happened. What's goin' on? Why'd you do it?"

Jake merely shrugged and stared at his father.

■   ■   ■   ■   ■

Marshall stared down at the letter once again and shook his head. Those damn blank stares. Unreadable. He'd stared those stares, too, years ago. One particularly mind-numbing incident rushed through a memory window.

■   ■   ■   ■   ■

His goofy, ten-year-old self stood in a field behind his house in shoulder-high, wavy grasses. A young girl, Melanie, who lived across the street, stood beside him. Marshall held a box of matches, earlier hidden inside his father's top right desk drawer. The two children stood before a small, clear-cut area, about five feet in diameter. Dried grasses, short twigs, and hollow reeds from the creek across the other side of the meadow were bunched in a heap in the middle of the circle.

"Lite the match, Marshall," Melanie encouraged in her slow, southern drawl. Marshall slid the kitchen match across a flat rock he'd found in the driveway. The wind blew it out.

"Try agin," Melanie pleaded.

"I'm trying. I'm trying."

This time, Melanie cupped her hand to block out the wind. It worked. A thin column of smoke rose, followed by a burst of hungry flames. As if starved, the flames made a pig of themselves and started chowing down on the entire meadow. Melanie shouted over her shoulder as she dashed away.

"Run, Marshall!"

Still clutching the box of matches, he had taken off in the opposite direction. Breathless, he reached a house at the end of the block and hid. Scrunched up behind the prickly limbs of some boxwoods, he realized he still held on to the matches and dropped them like they'd burned his fingers. A covering of fresh mulch surrounded the base of the boxwoods, so Marshall shoved them down beneath the wood chips. Neighbors, on both sides of the street, who had spied the smoke, rushed out of their homes and dashed toward the meadow. Within minutes, fire trucks screamed into the neighborhood. Marshall curled up like a grub worm under those shrubs and closed his eyes. He rationalized if he couldn't see, maybe nobody could see him.

"Marshall. Marshall Gatlin, is that you?" An old man reached down, grasped his arm, and helped him to his feet. "What in the world are you doing here?"

"I don't know, Mr. Barlow."

Walter Barlow, a retired mail carrier, lived alone. Tall and lanky, the skin on his arms and neck was as wrinkly as baby pig snouts. The old man pressed his hand against Marshall's head. "You sick, boy?"

"Nossir."

Mr. Barlow ran his hand through his straggly white hair. "You know anything about the fire down the street?"

"Nossir."

"What's this?" The old man pointed to the poorly hidden box of matches, which Marshall could still see peeking out of the mulch. "Are these yours, son?" Marshall couldn't stop staring at the matchbox. Even though his lips moved, he didn't say a word. Mr. Barlow pocketed the matchbox and took hold of his arm. "I think we'd better go find your daddy, young man." When they reached the Gatlin house, five houses up from Mr. Barlow's, Marshall spotted his father pacing in the front yard, all the while staring out toward the burning field. Mr. Barlow handed him the matchbox. "I believe this young man has something to tell you, Cole."

Those carrot fingers squeezed tight around Marshall's shoulder, and Cole leaned in close to his son's face. "All right, soldier. Tell me what happened," he said, a daunting grimace on his face. "What's going on? Why'd you do it?"

Marshall had merely shrugged and stared at his father.

.　　　.　　　.　　　.　　　.

Marshall shivered himself back to the present and thought a roaring fire might be rather nice, at the moment. Then he chastised himself for making light of the rather traumatic incident from years ago, which could have proven to be an even worse disaster. An inner voice whispered, *Maybe 'I don't know' is the only answer to why, Marshall.*

He pondered the message from the voice. Does *'I wanted to'* count? He shook his head and sighed. To this day, he couldn't honestly justify or give a definitive answer that even remotely made a lick of sense.

Main Floor Hallway

By 6:00, their minister was the last to leave. "I'm heading out, Millie," he said.

"Thanks for staying, Pastor Gordon," Millie said, smiling. "I know you need to get to the 7:00 service."

"Would you join me in prayer before I go?" He asked.

"Uh, sure." Millie glanced at the girls and nodded for them to gather around her.

"Is Marshall close by?"

"He, uh...is struggling, as you can imagine," she said quietly. "I think he just wants to be alone for a bit."

"I understand." He gazed around at each one of the Gatlin girls and smiled. "Please join hands." After the prayer, he walked over and hugged each of the sisters. Then he turned to Millie. "Let me know if there's anything I can do."

"Thanks for being here." Millie hugged Pastor Gordon.

"Please give Marshall my best," he said.

What I'm going to give him is a piece of my mind, she thought. She immediately berated herself for jumping to anger at Marshall. Still, the irritation stuck in her craw was going to negate an automatic forgiveness pass after he finally showed up.

Attic

Sunday
February 18, 1996

Dear Gammy Gat,

They told us tonight. Mama's going to have a baby. My order's in, and you can sure guess what HE better be.

It's going to be another little sister, I know it. Well, if it is, yuck. I say having a little sister is unfair. Little sisters don't have to clean up their rooms by themselves. They don't have to take out the trash. They get their own way. And big sisters are a big yuck, too. They get more allowance. They get to stay up later and have more sleepovers and a telephone in their room. Daddy never gets mad at my sisters like he gets mad at me. I made a list of some of my "never get to's."

I never get to sit in the front seat.

I never get to stay up late.

I never get to eat what I want to eat.

I never get to be first.

I never get called on when I know the answer.

I never get to do what I want to do.

I never win.

Mama says I better be careful. Never say never, she says.

My order's in. No offense. It's got to be a brother. If you have any pull in heaven, I'd appreciate some help. Anyway, please do what you can.

I've got to tell you about this drug program at school. It's where this policeman tries to be your friend and dares us to say no to drugs. I hear stuff, though. Some of the older kids talk about smoking. Well, Mama drops us off at the movie theatre downtown sometimes. The bathrooms are gross. Lots of times, these big kids'll ask me if I want a cigarette. They smoke in the stalls. When they ask me, I mumble something dumb. I do turn and walk away fast. It's one of the things they tell you to do. I never tell Mama or Daddy about this kind of stuff. Daddy would probably yell at me for putting myself in such a position in the first place, instead of being happy I walked away. I'm sure he would've told me I can't go to any more movies. I still wish I could've stared this guy right in the eyes, though, and said something like, "Don't be a dope, Dope." If Clint Eastwood was my daddy, I think I would've said that. (I watched a Dirty Harry movie on TV.)

You make my day,

Jake

P.S. I love you, Gammy Gat

Not realizing Jake had been involved in a drug program at school struck Marshall like a slap in the face. *How could you not have known this, Marshall?*

He shook his head. Jake's assessment of his potential reaction would have been more than likely dead-on. Acknowledging the truth of this admission heightened his guilt about saying or doing something he never did or said. *Words work in mysterious ways, Marshall.*

The girls had been excited about getting a new little sister or brother. Jake's reaction had been difficult to read. Of course, Marshall assumed his son wanted a little brother. His druthers leaned toward the avoidance of raising another boy. At the time, it sounded too risky because of his perception of his lack of success with the first one. He closed his eyes. Reading these letters continued to punch holes in that perception.

Another memory, framed in pink and baby blue, whispered in.

.   .   .   .   .

His father sat wedged into an overstuffed chair, his legs propped up on a round, camel-skin ottoman, a newspaper spread open across his lap. Eight-year-old Marshall lay stretched out on the floor, a set of plastic cowboys and Indians in a battle to the death inches away. The screen, on a black and white television, shifted from the Ed Sullivan Show to a commercial. A young mother appeared and spooned baby food into a toddler too cute to be real. Cole Gatlin peered over his newspaper.

"How'd you like to have one of those, soldier?"

"Sir?"

"One of those babies...like in that commercial." Cole pointed at the television.

Marshall reached for one of his plastic rearing horses and looked at the images on the screen. "What do you mean?" he said.

"Your mother's going to have a baby."

"Will it be a little brother like Grover's got?"

"I don't know. We'll have to wait and see."

When he'd heard his new baby brother had popped out as a baby sister, Marshall had packed some clothes in a small backpack and told his mother he was running away to stay with Grover.

.   .   .   .   .

This bittersweet memory lingered like a bite of tart, vinegary pork barbecue, as he glanced down at the album in his lap. He discovered pictures he hadn't laid his eyes on in a long time. Scratching his chin, he looked for one in particular he thought he remembered. As he turned the somewhat crimped pages of the album, he displayed the care of a museum curator viewing an artifact. Some crinkled from the gentlest of touches. Others, secured on the page by inserting the corners into tiny stick-on triangle slots, remained precariously in place and in danger of slipping out. After a few delicately executed turns, Marshall found what he searched for—an old black and white picture of himself in a fedora. He held a new baby sister, awkwardly, in his arms. His goofy, proud kid smile smeared across his face as oversized as the suit hanging on his skinny frame.

Kitchen

"Everybody's gone, Mama," Beth said, then whispered, "Finally."

Millie frowned. "They were just showing they cared, Beth."

"I know, Mama," she said. "I didn't mean…"

"I know what she meant," Lisa said, interrupting and smiling at her sister. "It was just so hard, Mama. Having everyone here. Looking and feeling so sad. It…it just doesn't seem real." She paused and started to say something else, but Beth interrupted her.

"Not to mention that our father is nowhere to be found."

"Where's my daddy?" Mary whispered, burying her head into her mother's waist.

"He's probably hiding out in the garage," Millie said, putting her arms around her youngest and rolling her eyes at Beth. "And he's gonna burst back in here like he's never been gone. You wait and see."

"Shouldn't we check to see?" Beth said, throwing up her hands.

Millie put her hands on her hips. "Not gonna give him the satisfaction of thinking we ran around like chickens all night looking for him."

Lisa caught her mother's eyes, reached out, and pulled Mary to her. "I think we should keep cleaning up, baby girl, don't you?" Millie mouthed a silent, "Thank you."

"Let's all pitch in and get it done fast," Lisa said.

Attic

Wednesday
February 21, 1996

Dear Gammy Gat,
I told you some "I never get to's" last time. Here's some "I hates."
I hate having to keep my shirttail tucked in.
I hate lectures about being good.
I hate calling home to tell on myself.
I hate trying to keep my eyes open during Social Studies.
I hate feeling like a troublemaker.
I hate why adults get to tell me what to do all the time.
I hate that we moved to a new town.
I hate school.
I hate that you're gone,
Jake
P.S. I love you, Gammy Gat

Reading the word "hate" squeezed another memory trigger.

. . . . .

Marshall's mind's eye conjured an empty street, tree-lined by hundred-year-old oaks, whose gnarly roots cracked through the surface of the concrete sidewalk, like thick, brown zombie snakes escaping from beneath the ground. Around six years old, he sat none too happily on a brand-new bicycle.

"Daddy, please don't let go."

"I'm holding on right here beside you, little soldier." Cole Gatlin puffed beside his son, each breath a labor from hell. "You...keep...pedaling."

"Please don't let him fall, honey." Mary Claire stood on the curb.

"I won't let him fall. He's got to learn to ride this thing on his own, sometime."

"Don't let go!" Marshall screamed.

"You're doing fine." His father continued to hold on to the back of the seat. "Don't stop pedaling, and stop looking at your feet."

"Oh, Cole, he's wobbling."

"It's what they do...sweetheart," he wheezed.

"It's too hard."

"Soldiers don't give up. Keep going."

"Mommy, where are you!?"

"I'm right here, honey. Daddy's got you."

"All right, little soldier. I'm gonna let you go."

"No!"

"You can do it. Keep pedaling and hold those handlebars straight."

"I'm gonna fall!"

"No, you won't. Concentrate. Be a big soldier." Cole still held on. "I'm letting go...*now*."

"I'm riding it, Daddy! Look, Mommy! I'm riding it!"

She clapped her hands.

"Yippee! You did it!"

"Little soldier! Don't look at me! Turn! Turn! You're gonna hit the curb!"

Too late.

"Ow!"

"You alright?"

Mary Claire Gatlin covered the short distance down the road in a few brief seconds.

"Cole...is he alright?"

"He's good. Come here, little soldier."

"Stupid bike."

"Whoa, now. Don't kick it. It's not the bicycle's fault."

He grabbed Marshall's arm and jerked him away from the bike.

Marshall stomped his foot. "I *hate* it!"

.   .   .   .   .

What must've been a small, dead tree limb landed on the roof, startling Marshall. He glanced up, then returned his gaze to the letter. To hate seemed such a powerful and defining act for Jake. As a sentiment, its strength and depth of feeling seemed to drive so many of his decisions. Marshall had hated a bicycle—an inanimate object, incapable of any sentient act—and blamed it for his own shortcomings. He looked back at the end of the letter and re-read, *I hate feeling like a troublemaker. I hate why adults get to tell me what to do all the time. I hate that we moved to a new town.* Realizing Jake had blamed school—and him—for a lot of his troubles, troubled Marshall. Big time. What the next inner voice blurted at him was not unexpected. *What didn't* you *blame him for, Marshall? Were you so callous and unfeeling as to not see and understand what he was feeling?* Words like clueless and heartless came to mind.

Kitchen

A noise, like something falling or banging, came from the garage.

"See," Millie said. "I'll bet that's him, now. Probably got in the back seat of the car, to hide, and fell asleep." She walked quickly over to the door. When she opened it, she noticed the broom, supposed to be hanging on one of those pressure pegs, had slipped off and fallen to the floor. She picked up the broom and rehung it.

"Check inside the car, Mama," Beth suggested. "I'm betting he probably did sneak in there. Remember, he could fall asleep standing up."

Millie flipped on the light switch. On first glance, she saw no one in the car. Thought perhaps Marshall had stretched out in the back seat. She stepped down the two steps leading into the garage and made her way to the minivan. The three girls crammed into the doorway and watched, anxious eyes wide, as their mother peered through the car window.

Attic

Sunday
February 25, 1996

Dear Gammy Gat,

Ms. Mitchell is the art teacher. She looked at what I was painting and said she loved the colors I was using. She also said she liked my use of space. She said she thought my dog needed a little more detail. I thought I'd done everything I could to make it look like a horse.

I wonder sometimes what things look like where you are. I've heard those stories about how some people died for a few minutes. Then, some doctor saved their life. And the people remembered seeing a bright, white light. Sometimes their relatives who had died might be walking around. And they remembered not hurting anymore. You died but didn't come back. You know for real, don't you? If you can let me know, I'd sure appreciate it.

Mama wants Callie to have kittens. She's a pretty cat. It's why Mama is being picky about who the daddy cat's going to be. The neighbors across the street have a cat too. Mama says he's not the right one.

I heard from Eddie. He broke his wrist riding his bike.

Remember when I broke my collarbone when I was little? It was a mean, older kid, Brian, who jumped on top of me and threw me down on the driveway. I remember getting up and running and crying all the way home. It hurt bad. I haven't broken anything since, except when a bench fell on my big toe. The doctor heated up the end of a paper clip and burned a hole right through my toenail, before I could even ask him what he was doing. Blood went everywhere, but my toe felt better.

Remember when Daddy was mowing the yard, and he slipped on the steep bank by the street? He fell on his ankle and broke it. He said the doctor told him he was lucky the break wasn't any worse than it was. Come to think of it, neither Mama or Lisa or Beth has broken any bones. Daddy says Lisa is going to break some hearts, whatever that means. It's Beth breaking stuff right now. Like boards in her karate class. I tell her, whenever she starts acting goofy, she breaks me up. Mama says to give her a break whenever I'm picking on Lisa and Beth.

I may have to wear glasses. When I read stuff, things get a little blurry. I think it's because I don't like to read. Mama says if I could see better, then maybe I would like to read. She promised me everybody would think my glasses were great. You told me about piecrust promises, one time. Was this one?

That's the breaks,

Jake

P.S. I love you, Gammy Gat

According to Millie, piecrust promises were Marshall's specialty. He remembered one he'd hoped would stay hidden deep in his memory file. Come to think of it, he had a file drawer full of those. This one came floating up out of its folder and loomed particularly painful.

.   .   .   .   .

On Sunday evening, Millie had helped Jake pack for his deployment. The whole family had stayed up late. By midnight, the kids had gone to bed. Millie and Marshall lay wide awake. She grimaced and rubbed the bridge of her nose.

"I can't get control of this one. Will you get me one of my migraine pills...please? They're in the side zipper pocket of my purse."

Marshall located the miracle, migraine drugs and returned to the bed. A few strands of hair lingered across Millie's forehead, which he gently brushed away. "Here. Think it'll be gone by morning?"

She swallowed it dry and collapsed on her pillow, her arm stretched across her eyes. "This'll take care of it." The pressure from the weight of her arm helped to ease the pain too. She whispered. "Our little boy is going to war. It's not quite the dream I had for any of our kids."

"It's the best thing for him...and us," he answered. "He's still drifting. Something's gotta get him anchored." Marshall remained silent for a moment. He wanted to measure his next words carefully, knowing they'd touch a nerve with Millie. "He needs to get away from here."

She whispered, her words more sorrowful than angry. "You mean *you* need him to get away, don't you?"

Marshall didn't want to take the bait. "He, uh, made a choice."

"Bad choice."

They both lay silent for a few awkward moments. Millie lowered her arm and turned her head toward him. "Have you said it to him yet?"

Marshall didn't answer and looked away.

"He's leaving in the morning," Millie whispered.

"I know," he replied, staring up at the ceiling.

She paused and reached over to place her hand on his arm. "I know you. Don't you dare let him go away without saying...you know...*it*. He needs to know you still do."

"Millie..."

"Promise me."

"I said I'd take care of it."

■　　　■　　　■　　　■　　　■

Marshall turned quickly to the next letter. *You were...are such a wimp, Marshall.*

Dwelling on how his piecrust promise turned out would drive him stupid. Jake's little white shoes sidetracked his journey to stupidity. He couldn't stop looking at them...touching them. Damned if he did and damned if he didn't, he kept opening those memory windows. He knew something about the little Stride Rites contributed to making that happen. He sighed, rubbed his eyes, and scratched the hair he had left on his head. *These issues Jake had been living through and dealing with? His letters are revealing your son to you. Bringing up those memories is a good thing, Marshall. Don't you realize they're revealing you...to you?*

Kitchen

"Damn it, Marshall. Where are you?"

"Have you tried calling his phone?" Lisa suggested, ignoring her mother's unexpected outburst of profanity.

"He probably turned the volume down and forgot to turn it back up," Beth said. "It's not like he hasn't done that a thousand times."

"Already tried," Millie said. "He's not answering. It goes straight into his answering machine." She paused. "Beth, go check your daddy's office again."

"What for?"

"I don't know," her mother quipped. "Look for something. Anything. Just go."

His phone better not be in there.

Attic

Wednesday
February 28, 1996

Dear Gammy Gat,

Randy hasn't been at school so far this week. I guess he's sick. Ms. Murray has been in a better mood.

If Ms. Murray could've picked, I think she'd have chosen which kids she wanted to teach. She'd make two big groups. All the kids she thought were the good kids would be on one side. All the kids she decided were the bad kids would be on the other side. And she'd pick the good kids to be in her classroom. I wonder who'd get all the losers?

I have a good idea which group I'm in,
Jake
P.S. I love you, Gammy Gat

A memory tumbled into Marshall's head. This one revealed words, no image. Marshall had said them to his eleven-year-old son. "People are gonna *think* you're a *loser* because of the way you're acting."

Distinguishing between the damned if he did and damned if he didn't act of dredging up these memories swung Marshall back and forth from regret to yearning like a pendulum. It didn't matter, though. Reading the letters had opened the memory slough wider than Shaquille O'Neal's shoe size, and they were going to keep flowing in. Sounds and smells accompanied this next one.

•　　　•　　　•　　　•　　　•

Mr. Martin's tractor growled and spit white smoke as the old codger cut the outfield grass on the Miller Park baseball field. Fresh cut grass full of wild, spring onions and dusty red clay was what springtime and baseball smelled like. The guys gathered in front of a tall backstop, whose wire mesh peeled away from the top left corner post and drooped toward the ground like a load of needles weighing down a limb on an old pine tree. Choosing captains was the first item on the agenda.

"I wanna be captain," Marshall said.

Grover chimed in. "You were a captain last time."

Teddy added his two cents. "It's my turn. I ain't been one, yet."

"Yeah, you have, too," Buddy said, poking Teddy in the arm. "You're lying, and your feet stink."

Teddy glanced down at his feet. "I ain't lying."

Milt, an athletic kid, wore a New York Yankees ball cap over his blonde flattop haircut. He pointed at Marshall. "All right, Marsh, you kin be one-a-tha captains."

Teddy stomped his foot. "If he gits to be a captain, then I git to be a captain."

"Jeez, Teddy, be a captain. We don't give a shit." Milt happened to be the only one of the group with nerve enough to cuss out loud. Milt pointed at Marshall, then winked. "You get to pick first, Marsh."

Marshall pointed at Milt and winked back. "I pick Milt."

Teddy's turn to pick. "'Cause you chose Milt, we get four guys and you only get three."

"Hey, that's not fair, Teddy," Marshall said.

Teddy opened a wrapper of Double Bubble gum and popped it into his mouth. "Is fair. Wayne ain't here, so Milt's the best player."

The two captains traded picks until one team had four and the other had three. They were about ready to start when another kid showed up.

"Kin I play?"

The new guy carried a glove his father must have used when *he* was a kid. It was all puff and no padding, with five, big, fat, flower pedal fingers. The kid, mostly elbows, toothy grin, and freckles, wore baggy corduroys with ripped and tattered cuffs.

Teddy whispered in Marshall's ear. "Jeez, it's Billy Ray."

Milt spoke loud enough for him to hear. "I ain't playing if he's playing."

Marshall couldn't look Billy Ray in the eyes. "Uh, we already picked."

"Ain't you missing a player, Marshall?"

The two boys locked eyes. Marshall looked away. "Sorry, maybe next time."

Billy Ray's elbows drooped, his toothy grin faded, and he shuffled away. Milt hocked a loogie in the dirt and took a practice swing. "Man, that guy's a loser."

Everybody laughed.

The tall, gangly, right-handed *loser* ended up leaping off the mound after pitching a no-hitter and winning the state high school championship.

.   .   .   .   .

Marshall re-positioned his UNC ballcap on his head. Reaching down, he rubbed both knees and stretched the left one. The height of the attic barrel seat provided a less than comfortable bend angle, and this memory had brought back a few uncomfortable choices he wished he could take back. Seemed the memories, triggered by the letters, were exposing a plethora of questionable things he'd said and done in the heat of lots of moments. An inner voice didn't lose an opportunity to speak up. *Something you thought was okay at the time you said it, or thought it, makes you feel like a jerk, now, doesn't it, Marshall?* Being tagged as a jerk by one of your friends or even a stranger was one thing. Marshall stared down at the notebook and shook his head. Tagging *yourself* with the moniker was a far more uncomfortable thought entirely.

Marshall's Office

"Mama!"

Millie came running from the den.

"What!" she exclaimed. "What did you find, Beth?"

"His phone," she said. "Found it under a bunch a stuff in his office." She paused and shook her head. "And guess what?" She scrunched up her mouth and shook her head. "It's turned off."

Millie reached out and took the phone. "What's going on here?" she said, throwing up her hands in disgust. *Why would you hide your phone and deliberately turn it off?* She immediately regretted asking questions she wasn't sure she wanted answered.

Attic

Sunday
March 3, 1996

Dear Gammy Gat,

Randy came back to school on Friday. His arm is in a cast. He said he broke it after he tripped down the stairs. His neck had bruises, too. He said he got those when he fell. Then he told me to mind my own business. I heard some of the other kids say they had heard Randy's dad had come to town. I asked Randy. He said, "Yeah, what about it?" I'm wondering if having his dad back is a good thing.

A train wreck waiting to happen, Randy's father was a piece of work. Marshall remembers being suspicious about this guy right from the beginning. And after all that happened, his suspicions had been right on.

Jake was obsessed with trying to help this Randy kid. And no matter how Randy treated Jake, his son took it as if he absorbed this little boy's sad life into his own and allowed it to drive everything he did or thought about. *Is it possible for an eleven-year-old to be the poster child for empathy, Marshall?*

He rubbed his forehead, closed his eyes, and imagined himself standing in Times Square. All he could see were images of his son and the words "Empathy starts with Jake," plastered on the side of every bus and taxi, every billboard and lighted screen. He couldn't decide whether to smile or shake his head. He returned to the letter.

I heard later Randy's fall wasn't an accident. I think I kind of thought it might not have been. Somebody said his dad hit him. Daddy's never hit me. I mean, he gets pretty mad sometimes. He'd never, ever hurt me.

Marshall winced when he read those words. He'd pushed Jake once during his sophomore year in high school. *You crossed a line with your son when you pushed him, Marshall. Seems you crossed a lot of lines with this boy.* To backtrack over a crossed line seemed an implausible tap dance with reality, especially if the person you crossed a line with wasn't around any longer. *How many lines are you crossing with your girls or with Millie right now?*

Marshall shook his head and let his eyes move back to the letter.

Randy's not talking. He's stayed away from me. It's okay, though. He's hard to be around, sometimes. It's like he's sad even when he acts sort of happy. And I guess I've got enough stuff of my own to worry about.

Remember when I told you I had a pretty good idea about which group I'd be in? Well, the way Ms. Murray yelled at me last week kind of gave me a clue that it's not the good one.

I do feel like I ought to be nice to Randy, even if he's not being nice to me. He's my friend. It'd be nice if he wanted me around. Maybe he doesn't know how to ask me.

I've wondered about how you know when to stay away and when to mess in somebody's business. The kind of messing where you don't think you're being mean or a busybody. Which is not like Lisa at all. When she sticks her nose into my business, she means to get me in trouble. Eddie and I knew when to stop.

I wrote a poem this week. Here it is.
Randy ate some candy.
And then he kissed Mandy.
Mandy said to Randy,
Your kiss was sort of sandy.
Randy said to Mandy,
Well, I'm sort of a handy, sandy Randy.

It's kinda stupid, I guess. Ms. Murray said I should be more serious when I write and not so silly. I wish she thought words were fun. Most of the words she thinks up sound like,

"Get those carrots out of your ears, young man."

"Any questions? If you listened to the directions, you shouldn't have any."

"It's your turn to read the next paragraph. Everyone keep up."

"Go to the board and work problem number 10. Everybody watch to see if he gets it right."

"I need everybody's attention, right now."

"No, you're wrong. Does anyone else know the answer?"

"No talking."

"Stay in your seats."

"Look at your own paper and do your own work."

From a silly, willy, nilly,

Jake

P.S. I love you, Gammy Gat

P.P.S. If God hadn't made words, I couldn't write to you.

Marshall took a breath, albeit a shallow one, as it was his habit to do. Jake's poem and his teacher's reaction to it pushed another memory window open. He needed a prop for this one, if he could find it. He eased himself up off the barrel and shuffled over to a shelf he thought might be harboring what he searched for. The old, waxed box still existed.

Inside was a stack of old folders he had saved. They were filled with loose pictures of his elementary school drawings and paintings. Stubby, half-used pencils with no erasers, dried up ink pens, in addition to sundry knick knacks were scattered throughout the box. And from the North Carolina State Fair, what was left of one of those straw-filled stuffed animals. Nasty, cheap sawdust covered the bottom of the box. Sifting through the folders and mess, he found what he looked for. After picking it up, he remembered thinking it being thicker.

Ten notebook pages, written in his third-grade elementary year's chicken-scratch cursive, nestled alone in the folder. The title he had written at the top? *Marsh Man and The Flying Horse by Marshall Gatlin.* All on his own, he'd come up with the idea of writing a story about a monster who shot fire out of its four eyes. He re-read the story and then placed it back in its folder. A hero he called, Marsh Man, and his flying horse, Fire, saved the day by stabbing the monster with a magic sword. He'd ended his story by having them fly off on their way to another adventure, which he had intended to be a sequel. He never wrote it. The reason settled into his head like a dark cloud blotting out the sun. Jake had been right. Words were fun until someone told you yours weren't worth reading. His thoughts drifted back to a night under the covers, after everyone else had gone to bed.

.   .   .   .   .

"Marshall."

"Yes, Momma."

"Your flashlight still on?" She poked her head through the door. He knew she knew. Clicking it off, he stuck his head out from beneath his blanket and smiled at her. She blew him a kiss, like she did every night. "All right, then. Sweet dreams and sleep tight. I love you."

"Love you more."

As soon as she shut the door, he clicked it on again.

Marshall wrote with a vengeance. When he reached the end of each page, he added it to the stack beside him. Each time, before beginning a new one, he counted how many he'd written, smiled, then started on the next one until he had reached ten whole pages. The following morning, ten pages dog-eared together in hand, he jumped out of the car, ran up the broad concrete stairway, and down the third-grade hallway of J.R. Williams Elementary School. Out of breath, he made his way immediately to his teacher's desk.

"Mrs. Roland?"

She spoke to him, but her eyes looked somewhere else. "What is it, Marshall? We have to get class started." He handed her the ten pages. "What's this?" Before Marshall could answer her, someone shrieked in the back of the classroom, and his teacher launched her evil eye, aimed at no one in particular. She glanced back at Marshall. "Y'all know you're supposed to wait to turn your homework in when I call for it." Then, she looked at the pages. "Oh, this isn't homework, is it?"

"No ma'am, but..."

Mrs. Roland shook the papers at him. "I hope you didn't spend too much time on this and not get your homework done."

The smile on his face vanished, like the last piece of fried okra at a Sunday afternoon picnic. "No, ma'am, I didn't."

The papers crinkled in her careless fingers. "Well, good, because I can't look at this right now. We've got to get started on our work." Her eyes shifting around the room once more, she had handed his masterpiece back. He didn't show it to her again. She never asked to see it.

Six months later, his mother had helped to clean up his room. In actuality, the project involved Marshall being "*present*" in the room while his mother darted from one task to another, faster than he wanted to move. Holding the broom and dustpan in her hand like a sword and shield, she gazed with her eagle eyes around the room. A dust cloth tucked into her apron tie, she blew her hair up and out of her eyes, sighed, and frowned at him. "Marshall Gatlin, I don't know how you can live in this pig sty."

"Yes, ma'am. I, uh...mean no, ma'am."

"And these drawers are a disaster. Your underwear is falling out all over...what's this?" She picked up the mussed-up stack of loose-leaf notebook papers sealed by the dog-eared corner. He had forgotten to throw them away.

"Nothin'."

Marshall watched her read for a few minutes. When Mary Claire reached the last page, she stared at her son. "You wrote this?"

"Yes, ma'am," he mumbled.

She wiped her forehead with the unused backside of her dust cloth. "My gracious, Marshall. When?"

He did his "I know, but I don't wanna tell ya," shoulder shrug. "Don't remember."

She still held on to the papers. "Was it a homework assignment?"

"No, ma'am."

She flipped through the pages once again. "So, you wrote it because you just felt like it?"

"It's stupid."

Her scowl had long since eased into a soft smile. "Did you show this to your teacher?"

"Yes, ma'am. She didn't have time to read it."

His mother had spread the story papers flat on his dresser and carefully set a heavy dictionary on top. She moved to his bed and sat next to him, curled her arm across his shoulders, and caressed his face. She lifted his chin and raised his eyes to meet hers. "Your story is wonderful, Marshall. I loved reading your words."

.   .   .   .   .

Marshall's eyes and thoughts returned to the words in the notebook on his lap. Chicken-scratch, yet readable. One of those inner voices, sounding suspiciously like his mother's voice, whispered, *When someone tells you your words are worth reading, it's a whole new ballgame, isn't it, Marshall?* At the moment, he couldn't decide whether he loved reading Jake's words or if reading them scared him to death. *Both things are possible, Marshall. Both.* He didn't know, yet, how he felt about those two possibilities. As if enticed by some unknown force, he glanced down at his feet. His eyes stopped on Jake's little kid Stride Rites. One thing he knew for sure, he loved those little shoes.

Upstairs and Downstairs

Millie and the three girls wandered around the house. Lisa made Mary accompany her during the search. For what seemed like the umpteenth time, they traipsed upstairs and down, checking all the rooms.

"All right," Millie said. "Anybody check *under* the beds?"

"He'd never fit," Beth retorted, rolling her eyes.

"Do it anyway," Millie said, closing her eyes and shaking her head. She told herself to keep her daughters busy looking. Especially Mary. She was determined not to give in and reveal her intuition kept telling her Marshall was nowhere inside the house. If only for the reason to deny Marshall the satisfaction of suddenly showing up and acting like nothing was wrong.

Not yet.

But she was getting close.

Attic

Wednesday
March 6, 1996

Dear Gammy Gat,

Randy said his mom and dad may be getting back together. At least, it's what he said his dad told him. He said his mom didn't say anything. Sometimes, I think Randy likes to believe in what he wants something to be, more than he likes to accept what it is.

Later in the day, Randy got sick. He barfed all over his desk and on the floor. Mr. McQueen had to clean it up. He sprinkled this green, powdery-looking stuff on top of the chunks. I wish I hadn't looked. Mr. McQueen wished I hadn't, too.

Mama and Daddy aren't happy about me still being friends with Randy. They said they didn't want to be picking my friends, even though I still couldn't go over to his trailer. They don't like his parents.

I'll bet you said "but" to my Daddy, too, a lot, when he was my age.

Marshall nodded his head. The exception word, "but," had always seemed like one of the great qualifiers. "Yes, but...," came to mind. A modifier of opinions, suggestions, casual truths, and intentions, it seemed to define the level of power and control kids figured had to be tied to parental whims at the moment. Marshall was sure if he could ask his mother, she would confess to professing such a doctrine. He knew *he* did. But she would've told him anything concerning relationship building with your child boiled down to being able to create a balance. Somehow, his mother had been a master at creating the balance. *A balance appeared to be non-existent in the relationship you built with your son, Marshall.* He glanced away from the notebook and up at the ceiling. Sighing, he moved his eyes back to the letter.

I have this other friend. He's in another class. I met him on the playground. His teacher yells sometimes. Ms. Murray yells, too. She can even yell with her eyes. Mama and Daddy yell at us sometimes. I yell at Lisa and Beth all the time. They yell at me, too. Daddy yells at our dog, P.J., sometimes. Randy says his mom and dad yell at each other and him a whole bunch.

I think it's hard to listen when somebody's yelling.

Randy made me mad today, even though he got sick. I felt like staying mad forever. Eddie used to make me mad, too, sometimes. Where you are is forever, isn't it?

Forever yours,
Jake
P.S. I love you, Gammy Gat

The word "forever." A few synonyms came to mind—For keeps, always, permanently, for good...all such "extreme" words. Like the amplitude of a pendulum. The absolute highest point of the pendulum's swing? "I love you forever" would be stuck on one side. "I hate you forever" stuck on the other. *Is it possible to either hate or love forever just for a little while, Marshall?*

This damned conundrum, impossible to fathom, pushed the next image into his head.

.　　.　　.　　.　　.

An early summer morning arrived already hot enough to bring on a sweat. By mid-morning, those muddy, brown waters at High Rock Lake would teem with skiers, inner-tubers, sailors, sightseers, and swimmers. A car pulled out of the driveway across the street. For a whole month, Marshall had been living for this once-in-a-lifetime adventure with his friend.

Tears streamed down Marshall's cheeks as Teddy's family car sped away, towing their 16-foot Larson ski boat. The car turned left at the corner, the boat trailer fishtailing before it disappeared behind Mrs. Woolridge's giant boxwoods. His sisters giggled behind the door, and he started to come after them. His father grabbed him before he did something else stupid.

"Whoa, soldier."

"Let...me...go!"

His father's grip had been too strong.

His mother had stood in the kitchen doorway, her hands busy drying a cast-iron pot. "We're sorry, Marshall."

Angry tears waterfalled from his eyes. "Y'all said I could go."

His father made him look at him. "This was before you broke Mr. Barlow's window. Now, you're gonna have to do some work for him this weekend to pay for the glass."

Marshall stopped struggling. The tears didn't stop falling. His father loosened his grip, and Marshall took the chance to twist away. "I hate Mr. Barlow. I hate rocks, and I hate windows. And I hate you!" He bolted to his bedroom, stopped, and hesitated in the doorway. "I hate you, forever!" And then he slammed the door. His father's "pillow" head took a beating that day. He didn't have a "mother" pillow to punch, so he grasped his blanket and twisted it as hard as he could.

. . . . .

The memory of all the pillow beating and blanket twisting made Marshall's neck ache. He pressed it back against his hand, which helped some. Remembering Millie closed her eyes to help ease her migraines, he decided to try it too. Seeing and reading the "hate" word again didn't help matters. It was the "forever" word, however, that took his breath away and brought back something he tried hard to keep from showing up. Too late. And like a developing photograph, the flag-draped casket at Jake's funeral appeared. A funeral too long to endure, too short to be an acceptable goodbye. Like hinges soaked in WD-40, this memory image opened and closed like a saloon door and would probably never completely close. *Your son's gone, Marshall. He isn't coming back. And not just for a little while, but forever.*

Kitchen

"Make sure you check the bathrooms again. Pull back the shower curtains. Wouldn't put it past him to sneak down into a tub and fall asleep."

"Mama, we've already checked these places a zillion times," Beth said. "He's not in this house." She lowered her eyes and said quietly, "You just don't want to accept it."

Millie's eyes flashed anger and impatience, then quickly dissipated, as she closed them and hung her head. She rubbed her forehead and waved her other hand in the air. All three girls turned and stared at one another.

"C'mon," Lisa said, as she motioned for her sisters to search anyway. "We can have a contest. Whoever finds him first doesn't have to wash dishes for a week."

"It'll be Mary and me against you."

"You're on," Beth said.

Attic

Sunday
March 10, 1996

Dear Gammy Gat,

The secretary, Ms. Lovell, asked me why I came to the office on Thursday. I said I had a stomachache. She said I could lie down on the bed in the health room. I told her I thought I might feel better by lunchtime. The math lesson was going to be over by then, anyway. Ms. Murray said if I tried harder, I could do better. I'll think about it. When we do good work at school, we get smiley faces. I've gotten 27 so far. Daddy says, "Keep it up." I got two sad faces this week. One was for a spelling test I didn't study for, and one because I forgot my math homework. I lost TV privileges, had to go to bed early, and got a thirty-minute lecture on working hard and not goofing off. You know, I heard somewhere, a frown is a smile turned upside down.

I jammed my finger trying to catch a ball yesterday. Daddy says gut it out. All the time. Gut it out, if I get a splinter. Gut it out if I bump my head. Doing the right thing takes guts. Thinking twice takes guts. It takes guts to gut something out.

Guts, guts, guts.

Sometimes I just don't have the guts to want to gut it out.

Trying to get some anyway,
Jake
P.S. I love you, Gammy Gat

Marshall could hear his father's voice as if he sat right next to him. "Takes guts to stand up and be a man, soldier." The whole guts thing had been one of his father's favorite mantras. Marshall had adopted it for his kids. He used it to this day. This letter took him back to another summer day with four of his friends on an adventure in Miller Park.

.   .   .   .   .

"C'mon, dork! You're such a slowpoke!" Milt shouted as he pedaled up to the Gatlin front stoop on his bicycle. Teddy, Grover, and Wayne followed.

Marshall had rushed out the door. "I'm coming, I'm coming." He glanced back through the doorway. "Bye, Momma."

"Bye, Momma!" All four mocked him in unison.

"Y'all be careful," she said, ignoring the banter. "Don't do anything foolish, stay out of the mud, watch for snakes, and look after one another." She paused. "And have a good time."

Marshall's feet churned on his pedals down the driveway. "Last one's a rotten egg!"

Milt shouted. "First one has to eat it!"

The ride to the park was only a five-minute trip, quicker if you raced. The guys made it under four. They parked their bikes in the rack by the main concession stand and sprinted on foot around the big shelter. Scampering along the paved path, down the large stone steps, across the roller-skating rink, and through the playground, they finally reached one of their favorite sections of the creek. Milt took off his sneakers and socks and immediately jumped into the mud. "Yahoo! Everybody has to jump in the mud."

They all followed suit.

Like a cat, Wayne, the best athlete of the group, slipped on his shoes and jumped up onto an old tree trunk. "What's next?"

Milt washed his feet and put his shoes back on. "I know just the place." He paused. "If you guys got the guts."

Teddy looked at Grover, then over at Marshall. "Where's he wanna go?"

"We probably don't wanna know. Come on. Let's see anyway," he said. Teddy and Grover hadn't moved.

Wayne vaulted off his tree trunk perch. "I know."

"I'm going home, "Grover said. "Wherever he's going, I ain't."

"I'm with *you*, Groveman," Teddy said. "See ya, Marsh."

The two boys put on their shoes and ran off. Milt winked at Wayne. "Ah, only one of the dorkmeisters has guts."

After putting on his shoes, Marshall moved between the two. "Where *are* y'all going?"

Milt put his arm across his shoulders. "You'll see."

When they rounded a part of the creek Marshall had never explored before, the three boys came up on a large, exposed pipe stretching at least twenty-five feet across the creek and about six feet above it. The rusty, old, black iron pipe, perhaps three feet in diameter, had probably been around for years.

"Y'all aren't going to…?"

"Question is…are *you* gonna do it?" Milt said, interrupting.

"It looks dangerous and…and a stupid thing to do."

"He called you stupid, Wayne."

"Quit mouthing off and git up here." Wayne stood at the edge of the pipe.

Milt stood behind Wayne. "What's it gonna be, Marsh? Guts or no guts?"

Marshall studied the rusty pipe and spied a patch of slick, green moss growing in the middle. "No Guts!" He shouted, then walked away.

Two days later, Milt and his mother shopped for groceries at the same time Marshall had accompanied his mother. The boy wore a cast on his leg and walked with crutches.

.   .   .   .   .

This memory brought a smile to Marshall's face, as it eased away like the slowing drip from an old spigot. One of those snarkier inner voices muttered, *Can you gut out what you're reading in this notebook, Marshall?*

The voice quieted, and he stared at the next letter. Maybe some things weren't meant for gutting out. The death of a child, for instance. Reading and absorbing his dead child's story, in his own words, was not a gutting-out task. It was a gut-wrenching one.

Main Floor Hallway

"Mama!" It was Beth.
"What now?"

Attic

Wednesday
March 13, 1996

Dear Gammy Gat,

Ms. Murray fussed at Marie for not asking questions today. Johnny asked her one, and she told him his question was silly. Natalie gave a report this week, and Ms. Murray said, "I can't hear you." The class stopped at the hallway bathrooms after recess before heading back into the classroom, and Ms. Murray told Will to tone it down. We had to have silent lunch today in the cafeteria. Ms. Murray told Robert, "Listen to me when I'm talking to you." I told Daddy I thought Randy was unhappy, and he said he didn't want to hear any more about this Randy kid.

Talk? Don't talk. Talk louder? Be quiet. Listen to me? Don't want to hear about it.

Which is it?
Not much else has been going on. Hope you are having fun.
Thanks for listening,
Jake
P.S. I love you, Gammy Gat

Millie had told Marshall *he* didn't listen. She said he only "heard" bits and pieces unconnected to the actual act of listening. He had responded with a wisecracking, "Huh?" She'd smacked him on the arm. "Funny, hot stuff. I rest my case." Marshall scratched his ear and re-read, *Is anybody listening?* A memory from a field trip to Raleigh took him back to spring in the fifth grade.

.　　.　　.　　.　　.

Their activity bus pulled into the downtown parking lot. "We're here, Marsh," Grover said. The bus parked in one of those oversized spaces. The entire class filed out and lined up for their trek up Wilmington Street, past the Legislature Building, across Jones and Edenton Streets, until finally reaching the Capitol Square. Students were allowed to wander around at the site until time to head for the Museum of Natural Sciences. A cacophony of brake squeals, horn blasts, revving diesel engines, and goofy cooing pigeons filled the air in downtown Raleigh. Grover pointed across the sidewalk. "Psst, Marsh. Look at that guy."

"Where?"

"Over yonder."

An old man sprawled on the grass.

Springtime in Raleigh was warm. This guy wore an overcoat. Sporting a ripped front pocket and torn lining, the tattered, stained coat hung at least two sizes too large off the man's gaunt frame. Dirty-white beard stubble littered his face, and old man, sun-damaged skin rippled across his face and neck. A pair of scuffed-up black shoes covered his sockless feet. A short length of rope, tied in a crude knot in the front, laced through the belt loops of his baggy pants. Creepy, empty eyes darted everywhere and nowhere at the same time. A cardboard sign rested in his lap.

"Can you tell what the sign says?" Grover whispered.

Marshall squinted his eyes and stared. "It says '*I am a deaf mute. Need money. God bless you.*'"

Grover scratched his nose. "It's a dumb sign. What does 'mute' mean?"

"I don't know."

Grover rolled his eyes. "Man, must mean he's stupid."

Later, at home, Marshall bit into a piece of apple his mother had set out on the counter for an after-school snack. "What does 'mute' mean, Momma?"

His mother stood at the sink. With a vegetable peeler, she deftly peeled some yellow squash. "It means a person who can't speak. Why do you ask?" She brushed her hair off her forehead with the back of her hand, then scooped up a handful of squash skins from the sink and tossed them into the garbage can.

"We saw this sort of nasty, old guy in Raleigh today. He had a sign. It said he was a deaf mute. He wanted money."

Mary Claire smiled, wiped her hands, and sat down beside her son. "I guess you've seen your first homeless person, Marshall."

"You mean he sleeps on the streets?"

She nodded. "I'm afraid so."

"Well, if he can't talk or hear, does it mean he's stupid?"

"My goodness, why would you think such a thing?"

"Grover said it."

"Grover doesn't know what he's talking about. Anyway, people can be deaf mutes for many reasons. He might've been born deaf or gotten sick or had an accident. Because he can't hear and can't talk has nothing to do with whether he's smart or not. Sometimes, people with perfectly good ears and voices act like they're deaf and refuse to listen or understand what's going on in the world right before their eyes."

"What do you mean?"

She placed both hands on Marshall's shoulders. "I know it's hard to understand, honey. Someday, you'll know what I'm talking about."

.　　.　　.　　.　　.

The memory faded away, like Marshall figured the life of the old man did. He thought about his mother's response. He, like Millie, Jake, and the girls, had been enamored with his mother's wisdom, her gentleness, her patience, and her humanity. Marshall looked up from the letter and sat...in silence.

One of those inner voices broke the quiet inside his head. *Jake's talking to you, Marshall. Can you hear him? Are you listening?*

Marshall remembered reading in an earlier letter that Jake felt it was difficult to listen when someone was yelling. The essence of this truth was certainly not lost on him. Jake wasn't yelling some incoherent bluster. His letters were like a storied country song Jake was *singing*. A soulful tune whose melody and lyrics were cementing themselves in his mind.

Foyer

Beth stood beside the front door, next to the coat pegs. "His parka, Mama. And his Carolina cap. They're gone."

"They're what?"

Millie brushed past her daughter and opened the front door. A chill blast slapped her as she stepped through and out onto the front porch. Cold drops of rain plinked on the portico roof above her. Lisa stepped out beside her. "He went out in this rain, didn't he, Mama?"

Millie turned and looked at her daughter, who stood, eyes wide, staring out into the nasty, cold, wet night. Millie tried to hide the look of fear and anger on her face. The other two girls crowded around their older sister and mother. Millie's pride and internal denial still kept her from being ready to admit it. "I just can't believe he did, sweetheart. You know your father. He probably dropped his coat and hat on the floor or in a chair somewhere."

"That would be so goofy, even for him," Beth said. Millie frowned and rolled her eyes. Beth rolled her own eyes, threw up her hands, and said, "But we'll look."

Attic

Sunday
March 17, 1996

Dear Gammy Gat,

I had a heart-to-heart with Mama and Daddy after supper tonight. Some of it was about Randy and a lot about behaving and stuff. They think he's the one getting me in trouble at school. They said he can't help it because he doesn't have a good home life. I tried to explain about Randy needing me to be his friend. They said even though they felt sorry for him, because of his parents, I wasn't helping him by getting into trouble, too. I told them Ms. Murray just didn't like us. Daddy said hogwash, and I had better do some changing. He said I was the one who had to convince them I wasn't a troublemaker. He gave me this same lecture about five different ways. When he started on number six, I said I'd try to do better. I knew he was more than likely going for ten, and I was getting sleepy.

The reason we had this "little talk" was because Ms. Ledbetter called them about having to fuss at me on Friday. I swiped a bite of Jamie Stinson's hot dog off his tray at lunch. I remembered the whole conversation with Ms. Ledbetter.

She said, "How would you like it if he did that to you?"

I said, "I don't know."

She said, "What do you mean, 'I don't know?'"

I said, "I don't know."

She said, "Is this all you can say?"
I said, "I don't know."
She said, "What should we do about this?"
I said, "I don't know."
She said, "What do you know?"
I said, "I don't know."
You know I knew,
Jake
P.S. I love you, Gammy Gat

The hot dog trick had generated a chuckle from Marshall and elicited a groan from Millie. He *was* angry with his son, though, for not thinking and getting himself into trouble again for a goofy, stupid decision. Seemed "I don't know" had established itself as a prominent mantra for both he and his son. A painful, "I don't know" memory window opened, he'd rather not relive. This one blew open the window, rushed in, and chilled his heart—his eighth-grade year at Dalton Junior High School.

▪   ▪   ▪   ▪   ▪

Abby Williamson had entered his Language Arts classroom several days after the Christmas and New Year holidays. Jack Canton spied the new girl first. He whispered to Marshall across an empty desk. "Marsh, look. Who...I mean...*what* is it?"

The girl's dress hung almost down to her ankles, like something Marshall figured his grandmother might have worn growing up. Tall and gangly, with floppy brown hair and wearing clunky, black sandals over the top of poochy red socks, she clumped into the room. Snickers and giggles rippled through the class.

His homeroom teacher, Mrs. Honeycutt, glared around the room. "Class, this is Abby Williamson," she said. "Abby and her family moved here from Sylva, a small town in the North Carolina mountains." Mrs. Honeycutt paused and crossed her arms over her chest. "I *know* y'all will make her feel *welcome*."

Jack turned his head and covered his mouth with his hand. "I don't think it's a girl, Marsh. I think it's a giraffe."

Mrs. Honeycutt glared and tapped her foot. "Jack, do you have something to share with the whole class?"

"No, ma'am."

She moved down Jack's aisle and stood beside his desk. "I'm sorry, I thought I heard you speaking a moment ago. You sure you don't have something you want to tell us?"

"Yes, ma'am. I'm sure you don't wanna hear it." Jack flashed a self-approving grin.

Mrs. Honeycutt frowned and shook her head. "Marshall, will you help Abby get settled in the desk beside you?"

He wrinkled up his nose and mumbled, "Yes, ma'am."

A month and a half later, on Friday evening, February 15th, the annual Valentine's Day Dance in the gym started at 8:00. A local DJ spun tunes behind a long table. The Beatles. The Mamas and the Papas. The Four Tops. The Supremes.

Boys lined up on one side and girls on the other. Very seldom did they mix, except for a few couples going together. From time to time, girls would run out onto the floor and do a group dance thing. The boys stood around, pretending they didn't care, not daring to risk peer ridicule by asking a girl to dance. Assistant Principal Johnson walked up to Jack and Marshall. She approached Marshall first. "Marshall, I need you to do me a big favor."

From the sound of sweetness in her voice, he knew she had something in mind for him he, more than likely, did not want to do. "Yes, ma'am?"

"Do you see the young lady in the blue dress, standing all alone?"

He squinted. His eyes got big. "Do you mean Abby, Ms. Johnson?"

"Why, yes. The new girl."

"Uh, what's your favor, Ms. Johnson?"

"I think it would be a wonderful gesture if you'd ask her to dance."

Jack whispered in his ear, "She wants you to ask the giraffe to dance."

"Shut up," he whispered back. Her big favor was even worse than he had expected. Turning back to the Assistant Principal, he shrugged his shoulders, smiled, and said what he thought would be his ticket to freedom. "Ms. Johnson, I'm not a very good dancer."

"Nonsense, everybody can do the twist." She reached out to pull him across the floor. "One dance, Marshall, is all I'm asking you to do."

He shook his arm free. "Okay, Ms. Johnson. I'll do it if you just don't go with me. Please?"

He heard Jack's voice behind him. "I gotta see this."

Like popcorn kernels exploding in a hot stove pot, news of his impending dance with this new girl circulated throughout the gym. By the time Marshall reached the other side of the room, a large crowd had gathered. He found himself caught between saying he'd honor her request and hoping for some miracle to get him out of this unreal situation. Before a miracle could save him, he stood face to face with those stringy, brunette bangs. Abby kept trying to brush them out of her eyes. When she started biting her fingernails, barfing in his mouth crossed his mind.

"Ms. Johnson wanted me to ask you to dance," he mumbled.

Abby still sucked on those fingers. "I don't dance so good."

Marshall tried not to look. "Well, if you don't want..."

"Okay, I'll dance."

Marshall tried desperately to ignore the growing crowd. Soon, a huge, half-circle had formed, and the DJ announced, "Baby, I Need Your Loving" as the next song up. They couldn't twist to it. They'd have to *touch* each other in a slow dance. A voice shouted out. "Hey, Marsh! Are y'all gonna make up a new dance and call it the Giraffe?"

He recognized the voice and scowled.

Gritting his teeth, he reached out toward Abby. "Uh, give me your hand."

"Oh, yeah, sorry," Abby mumbled. She handed him the wrist free of nibble-drool. The whole crowd started singing, "Abby, I need your loving." It was the proverbial last straw. Marshall dropped her hand like a hot frying pan and took off. He didn't stop until he reached the boys' bathroom. A few minutes later, Jack found him hiding behind the bleachers. Jack laughed so hard he had to hold his stomach. "You won't believe it, man. You should've seen her. When you bailed on her, the skag bawled and ran out the door. It was great. Thanks, Marsh. You made my night."

Several weeks later, outside his parents' bedroom, the door cracked open, Marshall, unnoticed, could see and overhear them. His mother sat on the edge of the bed and smoked a cigarette. "Did you hear about the family who moved here from Sylva?"

His father, re-reading the sports section from the paper, didn't look up from his chair. "Nope."

"Well, they moved here because the mother had some disease," she said. Cancer, I think."

Cole folded his paper and leaned his head back against his chair. "Not good. I guess they were hoping for better care at Bowman Gray Hospital."

His mother shook her head. "Well, she up and *died* last night. The poor man is left with six kids."

"Six?"

"Yes. And one of them is in Marshall's class. She's the only daughter and the oldest." Mary Claire stood up and walked over to the window to adjust some twisted blinds. "I heard some folks say the father's gonna pull them all out of school and go back to the mountains." She paused, and her voice got quiet. "And this young girl. I don't know what her name is. She'll have to drop out of school to help look after the little ones."

Marshall gulped and figured he'd heard his cue. His guilt-ridden stomach had been extremely uncooperative most every day since the "dance." He eased around the door. "Abby. Her name's Abby."

His mother turned. "Oh, Marshall. We didn't know you were standing there."

"Yes, ma'am."

"So, she *was* in your class?"

"Yes, ma'am."

"I heard she was the target of a lot of jokes."

"Yes, ma'am."

"You weren't a part of any such thing, were you, soldier?"

Marshall hung his head and stared at his feet. His mother walked over and placed her hand on his shoulder. "Oh, Marshall. She needed a friend, didn't she?"

"I...I don't know."

.   .   .   .   .

The flapping overhead vent closed out the memory window. Over the years, Abby's image, that night at the dance, would appear out of nowhere in his mind. And he would wonder what had happened to her and her family. He was never sure whether he actually wanted to find out, but there remained a special ache in his heart he knew was related to her brief presence in his life.

Accountability and "I don't know" were like two sides of a single coin. The empathetic side acknowledged responsibility for one's actions and decisions. The other side pretended the mere illusion of ignorance warranted suspension of any acceptance of accountability. Marshall felt like he was constantly flipping this coin after each letter.

Kitchen

"Mama," Beth said, peering into the kitchen. Millie had retreated there while the girls searched the house for Marshall's coat and baseball cap.

"Find 'em?" Millie asked, turning at the sound of Beth's voice. She turned off the spigot at the sink and wiped her hands with her kitchen towel.

"We've been all over," Beth said. "No hat...no coat...anywhere." She put her hands on her hips. "That man is not inside this house, Mama."

Attic

Wednesday
March 20, 1996

Dear Gammy Gat,

I found a bunch of my school papers stuffed in the trash can. I thought parents were supposed to save all your school stuff.

Our cat, Callie, likes Lisa better than me. And I told her it wasn't fair. She said I smelled like a meat-headed hippopotamus.

I said, "Well, you smell like a slimy skunk."

She said, "It's better than having rotten, banana breath."

I said, "Your feet stink."

She said, "Yeah? Well, you look like a wart-headed, goon-eyed, spaghetti gook."

I said, "Squid head."

She said, "Rat breath."

I said, "Bitch."

She yelled, "Mama!"

I'm sure you can guess who got in trouble.

Why break a pattern?

Jake

P.S. I love you, Gammy Gat

Marshall chuckled at the name-calling inventiveness of his kids. Something to behold. When he glanced back at the salutation, one of those inner voices chimed in. *Remember the pattern you needed to break in your sixth-grade class, Marshall?* The appearance of this memory was as satisfying as losing something, remembering the last place you thought you put it, and finding it exactly where you left it.

.　　.　　.　　.　　.

Twelve-year-old Marshall entered his sixth-grade classroom first thing in the morning on a warm, spring day.

He whispered to Grover. "Oh, man, Mrs. Lowdermilk, again."

"Yeah, it's the pits, ain't it, Marsh?"

"She's gonna be mean," Marshall whispered back.

Soon, all the students had arrived. When the substitute teacher turned to walk across the front of the room, her hips collided with Elizabeth Schreiner's desk in the front row. The girl's pencil box landed on the floor and broke wide open. When the desk tilted forward, Elizabeth screamed, and her glasses flew off. Mrs. Lowdermilk shouted, "Young lady!" She glared at the young girl. "You nearly killed me. What is your name?"

"Elizabeth Turner Schreiner, ma'am," she mumbled.

Grover leaned over and whispered, "Schriney is so goofy."

"Yeah, but Mrs. Lowdermilk bumped into *her*," Marshall whispered back.

By late mid-morning, the substitute told the class they were going out for recess. Once outside, Marshall and Grover joined the softball group. The boys, begrudgingly, decided to let some of the girls play too. Grover nodded toward Elizabeth. "Jeez, Schriney wants to play, Marsh."

Elizabeth Shreiner made for the sweetest kind of target for teasing. With her strong prescription, which made her eyes look unnaturally large and goofy, and a high-pitched, whiny voice, Elizabeth received an unbearable level of scorn and derision from her classmates. "Let her play," he said, reluctantly, shaking his head.

Par for the course, when it was her turn at bat, Elizabeth swung and accidentally let go of the bat. It flew over Charlie's head. "Hey, you almost clobbered me! Jeez, girl, are you just stupid, or what?"

All this time, Mrs. Lowdermilk, emery-boarding her nails, sprawled in a chair. When it seemed like recess had barely started, she blew her whistle. Everybody dashed to line up. Of course, Elizabeth won the award for straggler. Mrs. Lowdermilk made her carry the ball and bat bag. Too heavy for her, she had managed to reach only halfway across the playground when Mrs. Lowdermilk shouted and stamped her foot. "Let's go, young lady. Hurry, hurry, hurry. Every minute you're not here in this line, I'm going to penalize the rest of the class one whole minute of its afternoon recess."

Everybody's encouragement sounded more like anger than support. "Hurry, Schriney!"

Still struggling, her glasses, catawampus on her face, one of her pigtails undone, and her blue dress covered in red dust, she stopped carrying and began dragging.

Foot still stomping, Mrs. Lowdermilk stared at her watch. "Well, five minutes of y'all's afternoon recess is gone." She sighed out loud, then lumbered toward Elizabeth. When she reached her, she paused briefly and glanced around. Without warning, she pulled out her ruler and hit Elizabeth on the butt. "Get–*Whack*–yourself–*Whack*–up–*Whack*–to–*Whack*–that–*Whack*–line. We've waited on you long enough, young lady."

Martha Gibson stood behind Marshall and whispered in his ear. "Mrs. Lowdermilk is so hateful."

"Yeah," he whispered back as he stared at Elizabeth, still holding on to the bag and trying to get out of the way of the ruler at the same time, tears running down her face. Marshall looked around and spied angry faces on all his classmates.

Elizabeth finally made it to the back of the line.

Marshall whispered to Martha, "We got to do something about this."

"What do you mean?"

"I have an idea. When we get back to our classroom, instead of sitting in our desks, we oughta sit down on the floor beside them and refuse to get up."

Martha thought for a second. "You mean a sit-in? Like those hippies do?" She smiled. "I love it."

Once inside, they stopped at the bathrooms. Martha gathered the girls together and told them the plan. Marshall told the guys. After returning to the classroom, Mrs. Lowdermilk directed the students to their seats. Martha and Marshall gave the thumbs-up sign, and they all dropped to the floor, crossed their legs and arms, and stared straight ahead.

"What in the world!? You children get up this instant!"

No one moved.

"Mrs. Lowdermilk," Marshall said, "we're on a sit-down strike. We don't like the way you've been treating our classmate, Elizabeth Turner Schreiner."

"You can't have a sit-down strike in my classroom," she said, glaring around the room.

"This is not *your* classroom, Mrs. Lowdermilk," Martha said. "Our teacher is Ms. Short. She's not mean like you. I don't think she'll be very happy when she comes back, and we tell her how you treated all of us, especially Elizabeth."

Mrs. Lowdermilk marched to the doorway, glared back at the class, shook her ruler at them, then stormed out. Everybody sat in silence. It didn't take Mrs. Lowdermilk long to come back. The principal followed, not far behind.

Principal Dean, tall with night-black hair tumbling down to the middle of her back, stepped through the doorway. All the students loved her but were extremely anxious about her reaction to their sit-in. Very calm and quiet, she informed the class that Mrs. Lowdermilk said they were rude, disorderly, and disrespectful. Marshall and Martha shared the students' side of the story. Mrs. Lowdermilk stood in the doorway, arms folded, eyes crazy-like, her lips all pooched out.

With a soft voice, Mrs. Dean turned and smiled at her. "Mrs. Lowdermilk, I'd like you to step out in the hall and leave me alone with the children for a few moments. Thank you very much." She walked over, ushered her out, and closed the door behind her. Mrs. Dean moved to where

Elizabeth hunched over and stooped down. "Elizabeth, are you okay, sweetheart?"

Elizabeth still snuffled, and she kept wiping her tear-stained, muddy cheeks. "Mrs. Lowdermilk hit me," she whispered, still snuffling.

"I know, Elizabeth. And I want you to trust I'm going to take care of it."

Mrs. Dean walked back to the front of the class. "Return to your seats, please, boys and girls," she said, in her calm, in-charge voice, one all the students had come to expect and respect. All the children stood up and, silently, went back to their desks.

"I know y'all believe what you did was right. I know your intentions were honest." She paused. "Mrs. Lowdermilk did some pretty mean things to you and one of your classmates. But she was placed in charge of your classroom for the day. When Ms. Short returns, I'm sure she'll be most distressed to hear about this incident."

"But...," Martha attempted to respond. Mrs. Dean interrupted her.

"Don't anyone talk right now. It's my turn." She moved slowly back and forth across the front of the classroom. "Mrs. Lowdermilk won't return to this class. Ever. But if y'all think she was tough, wait until you see what I have in store for you this afternoon." She backed up against the teacher's desk, the ends of her black hair tickling the surface. She lifted herself until she sat on the edge. "Silent lunch for starters. And you'll go home with sore hands, tired brains, and tired bodies. Y'all are going to work like you've never worked before, and when you think you're tired, we're gonna head outside and pick up litter around the school grounds."

All the students turned, wide-eyed, and stared at one another.

"I have one more thing I want to say." She looked down at the floor and had a half grin on her face when she looked up. "I was proud of y'all today. You stood up for a fellow human being. A fellow human being to whom *you*, over and over, have been more abusive than Mrs. Lowdermilk ever was." She paced across the room and stared, one by one, into everyone's eyes. "And in your hearts y'all know this." She paused and then broke into a big smile. "You broke this pattern today, didn't you?"

Everybody cheered and laughed. Mrs. Dean clapped her hands once.

"All right. Calm down. Don't let yourselves get too cocky. 'Cause if y'all ever do this again, I'll call your parents, bring them in for conferences, and suspend every one of you." She paused and then, in a quiet voice, said, "Do I make myself clear?"

"Yes, Mrs. Dean."

.　　　.　　　.　　　.　　　.

Marshall closed his eyes and allowed himself to savor the memory as he casually returned to the present. He smiled as he stared down at Jake's letter. They didn't tease Elizabeth again. At least not until her classmates elected Elizabeth Turner Schreiner president of the senior class in high school.

His eyes, inadvertently, flicked down to the Stride Rites again. He stared at them. The ends of the shoestrings weren't even frayed, and the soles seemed almost brand new, with barely a scuff mark. Their condition appeared to be the opposite of how he felt. The term "frayed" emotions came to mind. And the scuffed-up status of his soul was starting to concern him. He finally glanced at his watch and wondered how long he had been in the attic. Chagrined he hadn't checked the time when he got here, he worried he might hear Millie pounding on the ladder door any minute. Then he remembered he had deliberately failed to inform her as to his whereabouts. His half-baked, half-ass plan had included her discovering his missing jacket. She'd assume he had gone out for a walk. Being safe, at this particular moment, didn't leave him feeling comfortable with his decision, just stupidly oblivious to the consequences of such an action. *If you don't die up here from exposure, she's going to kill you, for sure, Marshall.*

Before going back to the notebook, he stuck his hands in his pockets for a brief warm-up and felt his son's letter from Afghanistan. He pulled it out and carefully unfolded it.

Read it again.

When he finished, he carefully refolded the letter and returned it to his pocket. An inner voice whispered, *You and your classmates broke your pattern of behavior back then, didn't you, Marshall? Jake's Christmas letter from Afghanistan reveals he wanted to sit down and talk about his pattern of behavior. A pattern he was ready to break. You're listening to Jake, right? You desperately wanted him to change his pattern of behavior. How about you? You capable of doing it again?* He'd never hear Jake's voice again. Through the notebook of letters...he could listen to Jake. He closed his eyes. Reminded himself he still had three daughters who needed to know that he heard them, too. And listened. And he *could* ensure that he changed the pattern of behavior of the only person he had control over.

He placed his thumb along the side of the notebook and gently thumbed through them. *Take a breath and just dwell on the letters, not on your lie to Millie. Jake's got a bunch left to say.*

Main Floor Hallway

"It's getting darker and it's 6:30, Mama," Beth said. "Time to call 911."

"And tell them what?" Millie said. "My husband...your father...has sneaked off somewhere to hide from all these wonderful people who came to support us tonight?"

"Something just doesn't feel right," Lisa said.

"I'm not calling 911." Millie shook her head and scowled.

"Serve him right if he got in trouble with the police," Beth said, scowling.

"You could call the sheriff's office," Lisa said. "One of the deputies is Johnny Bates. His folks went out of town for Christmas, and he, uh, has the duty tonight. We went to high school together."

"I'll think about it," Millie said.

"What if he doesn't come home?" Mary said, her lips quivering.

Lisa was the first to pull Mary to her. "He's coming home," she said. "You just wait. He'll be back before you know it."

Millie reached out and smoothed Mary's hair, then turned to head off down the hall, once more, to the kitchen. To pretend to clean something, anything, everything...again.

I can't believe you've done this to us, Marshall. Not tonight. When I...we...needed you.

Attic

Sunday
March 24, 1996

Dear Gammy Gat,

Sometimes, I don't want to do anything. I want to find someplace where I don't have to do or be or see or think about anything or talk to anybody. I especially don't want to talk to anybody who says, "Look at me when I'm talking to you." I want people to leave me alone. At least for a little while. It's no big deal.

Oh, yeah, by the way, your oldest granddaughter (I refuse to mention her name) is a big, fat tattletale. I'm never going to trust anybody, ever again.

Sometimes doing nothing is more like something than anything,
Jake
P.S. I love you, Gammy Gat

Forcing Jake to open up about anything was typically a dead end. He would clam up and go into some dark world of his own. To demand he look Marshall in the eyes and own up to whatever the perceived transgression happened to be, proved the essence of the proverbial definition of insanity. Marshall did it anyway. His father had tried the same thing on him. Marshall had his share of the "look me in the eyes" childhood memory windows available to him. The one to enter, now, had the added distinction of also reminding him of a pretty significant breach of trust incident. A nighttime snowfall had dropped eight inches of the best snow ever. The great snowball-making kind. It had been a magic time for Marshall and three of his sixth-grade buddies.

.   .   .   .   .

"I'll go around old man Crawford's oak tree, Marsh."

"Okay, Groveman. I'll sneak over to Ms. Mitchell's garbage cans. Watch for me, and I'll give the signal."

The game? Two, two-kid teams worked together to build a snowman in the center of Marshall's front yard. After completion of the task, both teams struck out for the end of the block, where they hid behind a house on opposite sides of the street. The key strategy was to circle around and be the first team to smash the snowman. Anyone hit by a snowball had to sit for a count of 50 before he could come back to the field of battle. Grover and Marshall comprised one of the teams. The Walker twins made up the other. Marshall toted ten pre-constructed snow grenades in a canvas bag. Grover knew the plan.

By the time the two had begun their separate approaches, snow had ceased to fall. The eight inches, plus, provided an unusual depth for the North Carolina Piedmont. Marshall kept moving toward Ms. Mitchell's garbage cans. Just as he was about to reach them, Marshall spied several Ninja shapes out of the corner of his eye. The appearance of three figures surprised him. He lost his balance and fell down. Sitting sprawled in the snow, with no time to grab a snowball, left him a sitting duck. They pounded him. His chest. His legs. His back. One struck him smack in the face. The ice chip shrapnel exploded all over his cheeks, in his mouth, through his open coat collar, and down his neck and back. The twin enemies dashed away before he could even stand up. Grover, the betrayer, held back for one last insult to injury. A final bomb smashed Marshall a second time in the face. Laughing, Grover took off and left his former comrade alone with his misery.

Marshall, fighting back tears, struggled to his feet and ran after the perpetrators. Their retreat—hasty. Their getaway—clean. The icy wetness beneath his coat soaked through to the skin and straight to his heart. Only one front yard away from his own, he trudged through the connecting hedge. Upon reaching the snowman, he let him have it.

Marshall stomped into the house and slammed the door behind him. The Gatlin winter rule demanded boot removal, gloves set out to dry on a shelf, and hats and coats hung on pegs in the mudroom. Marshall tossed everything on the floor, except for the boots. His father, sipping a mug of steaming coffee by the fire, sat up straight and shouted, "Whoa, soldier, get those boots off and stow your gear."

Marshall ignored him. Cole set his coffee down and rose from his seat, all in one swift motion. "Soldier. Front and center, now!" Marshall stopped, refusing to turn around. His father closed on him, fast, grabbed his shoulder, and attempted to twist his son toward him. Marshall shrugged off the twist and held his backward stance. He glared down at the floor. "Don't turn away from me, soldier. You look at me when I'm talking to you."

.   .   .   .   .

The sound of the rain he wished was snow brought Marshall back to the present. The betrayer incident had been one of those "gut-kicker" memories that lingered beyond the treachery. Forgiveness had been one thing. Forgetting another. Marshall chuckled. He didn't speak to Grover for about a week. And even afterwards, he'd brought it up often. He knew what betrayal felt like. The betrayal sentiments reflected in Jake's letters seemed incalculable. One of those pesky inner voices paraphrased the words from Toby Keith's country song. *Don't you wish you knew then what your finding out your son felt, now, Marshall?* He whispered his answer aloud. "Heaven help me."

Foyer

"I'm scared, Mommy," Mary said, leaning into her mother.

"Nothing to be scared of. You're Daddy's probably stepped outside to check on something."

"Check on something?" Beth said. "What could possibly need checking on outside?"

"I don't know," Millie said, her voice with a bit of edge. "Something." She opened the door again. "Marshall!" The sound of her voice was lost amidst the plink and splatter of the rain falling on the porch roof. She started to shout again.

"Mama, the neighbors...," Lisa said, glancing at Beth and rolling her eyes. She reached for her mother's arm and gently pulled her back inside. "I know what we need," Lisa said, turning to Mary and caressing her little sister's cheeks between her hands. "Would you like to hear some Christmas music?"

Attic

Wednesday
March 27, 1996

Dear Gammy Gat,

I lost my jacket this week. Ms. Murray asked me to think back to where I might have lost it. If I knew, I think I would have known right where to look.

I got a paper cut, too. Daddy wanted to put this red medicine on it. I asked him if it would burn. He could've told me the truth. I could've handled it. Gutting it out works better if it's not a surprise.

I told Mama if she made me take a bite of her asparagus casserole, I'd throw up. She said I'd like it once I tasted it. She wished she'd listened to me.

I've been meaning to tell you about PJ. He doesn't hear so good, anymore. Daddy says he's about fifteen years old in people years. This means he's like over a hundred in dog years. He likes to tell us he's had PJ longer than he's had us. PJ still loves to run. He gets tired real quick, though. When he was younger, he'd leap and hop around like a rabbit. His ears would flop too. He's still frisky for an old guy, but he can't dash around like he used to anymore. I like to take him on walks. We don't go as far as we used to. When we go off on a day trip, we leave him in Mama and Daddy's room, and he gets on their bed. Daddy made him these little steps so he could walk right up. When we get back, he'll be sound asleep. We can move all around and make lots of noise. He doesn't hear us. I like to wake him up right away. To make sure, you know.

Mama is getting fat. I won't tell her, though. Beth said it, not me. I told Beth, Mama is supposed to get fat. I reminded her a baby's growing in her stomach. What do little sisters know? You'd think God would know better than to give a guy so many sisters.

Remember when I said, "You know who" tattled on me? Well, she said I spit on her. I didn't. Well, what I mean is, I didn't do it like she said I did. She'd punched me in the stomach when I had milk in my mouth. She didn't tell Mama that part. And my sister, your oldest granddaughter, said she never touched me. Well, you know who Mama believed. She told me I had two punishments. One for spitting and one for telling a lie. Unless I told the truth and then I'd get one punishment. So, I told her I did it. It worked.

A lie works in mysterious ways,

Jake

P.S. I love you, Gammy Gat

When Marshall finished the letter, he heard Christmas music downstairs. Celebrating his own pity party up in the attic proved to be a welcome alternative to the efforts to make everyone else feel better downstairs. The sound of the music and Jake's false confession helped push open another memory window. On Christmas Eve, more than several decades ago, an early snow had covered the ground.

▪ ▪ ▪ ▪ ▪

The Gatlin family's car tires crinch-crunched as they pulled into the Methodist Church parking lot. A full moon hung as if pasted in the sky. A spotlight shone right in front of a Nativity scene, targeting the manger. Life-size mannequins stood in for Mary, Joseph, the shepherds, and the wise men beneath a wooden shelter constructed by several parishioners. His younger sister, Alice, pointed toward the display. "Look, Marshall, my Tiny Tears doll gots to be Jesus."

The midnight Candlelight Service would commence in about an hour, and the Gatlins had arrived early to help set up refreshments, along with several other families. It included two of Marshall's friends from church, Jim and Alex. Jim waved, ran, slid through the slush, and skidded to a stop before reaching Marshall. "Hey, Marshall." Jim said, "Let's you, me, and Peewee go exploring." Alex's friends called him Peewee for obvious reasons.

"Can I, Momma?" Marshall said.

Alex looked at his mom. "Yeah, can we?"

The three boys pleaded, in unison, *"Puhlease?"*

Mary Claire adjusted her hat. "I guess so, Marshall, just don't go far. The service begins in a little bit, and I don't want you to be a mess."

Cole Gatlin plopped his beefsteak hand on Marshall's shoulder. "And don't y'all go running around all over the church. They don't want three hooligans going in and out of all the Sunday school classrooms. And don't even think of going near the sanctuary. It's an order, soldier."

"Yessir."

The three hopeful hooligans took off, as if they had escaped from some high-security prison. For a few moments, they played chase in the church playground. Before long, the cold air nipped at them more than they could tolerate. They ended up sneaking inside the classroom building, while Mary Claire Gatlin and the other parents were setting up refreshments in the Fellowship Hall around the far side of the sanctuary. Emergency lights at the ends of hallways provided the only light in the classroom building. Jim had peeked around a hallway corner.

He laughed, ran down the hall, and started turning knobs on classroom doors.

Marshall unzipped his coat and let it hang open. "Our folks told us not to go into the classrooms."

Jim made a face and unzipped his coat, too. "You're such a drag, Marshall. Anyway, they didn't tell us we couldn't play in the *hall*. C'mon, last one to the other end has to be *it*." Both Jim and Alex took off and reached the end of the hall first. Laughing, Jim said, "You gotta wait with your eyes closed and count to a hundred while we hide. Then you have to come find us."

Marshall frowned and dropped to the floor. He started to count by ones, changed his mind, and finished counting by fives. It didn't matter, though, the other two boys were long gone. Marshall stood up and started to tiptoe down the hallway.

His mother had made him wear his Sunday shoes. On the freshly waxed tile floor, they squeaked like a herd of mice. The moon shone through the windows and illuminated the large, round clock, suspended high on the wall. It read 11:30 p.m., and it wouldn't be too long before families entered through the outside doors into the Narthex for the celebration. Marshall hoped he could sneak up on the guys and come at them from a direction they didn't expect. His squeaky shoes were going to present a problem.

His choices were to go back the way he came or enter the sanctuary here, exit through the Nave, and out the Narthex without anybody seeing him. Taking a deep breath, he reached for the door handles. As he entered, he heard the organ playing "Joy to the World." Tiptoeing, he crossed along the rail separating the chancel and choir loft from the Nave. A slight chill ran down his back when he thought about being this close to where the preacher preached his sermons. The Choir Director, Mr. Collier, his back to Marshall, rehearsed for the evening service. The carol filled the carpeted, empty room, which wouldn't be empty soon. Marshall stopped, closed his eyes, and listened to the music. After playing "Joy to the World," Mr. Collier moved right into "O Little Town of Bethlehem." As the notes to the carol ended, Marshall opened his eyes and realized Mr. Collier stared right at him. "Young man, what are you doing in here?"

"I, uh, I was just listening to the music."

"This is a place of worship, not a play place."

"Nossir, I...I mean yessir."

"Are you being smart with me, young man?"

"Nossir."

"What is your name?"

"Marshall Gatlin, sir."

"Ah, Mary Claire and Cole's son." He stood up and made his way down the steps. "I think your parents need to know what you were up to."

He grabbed hold of Marshall's arm and walked him back to the Fellowship Hall.

Marshall's father immediately walked over to meet the two. "Mr. Collier, what's going on?"

"Well, Cole, I caught your son here, playing around in the sanctuary. He interrupted my rehearsal for tonight's program."

"I'm sorry to hear this, Mr. Collier." Cole took hold of Marshall's other arm. "What do you have to say for yourself, soldier?" Marshall's father wasn't going to buy that he went into the sanctuary by accident and got caught up in the beauty of the music. The truth would be perceived as a stretch. He decided to jump right into the apology.

"I shouldn't have been in the sanctuary without your permission, sir." Then, he turned toward Mr. Collier. "I'm sorry, sir, for disturbing your rehearsal."

The man, a surprised look on his face, half-smiled. "Well, no harm done, I guess." Marshall's father released his hold on his son's arm. He even had a grin on his face.

The memory trailed away, like the vibrato on the last note Mr. Collier had played on "O Little Town of Bethlehem."

.   .   .   .   .

The truth of his own presence in the attic brought Marshall back to the present. He listened intently, for a moment, attempting to discern the music he'd heard playing downstairs. He thought it might have been *Frosty the Snowman*, but it suddenly stopped. Disappointed, he sighed and sat in the relative quiet, just trying to think of nothing in particular for a moment. The plinking of the rain on the roof ended up filling the sound void, until an inner voice spoke up. *How could you not have known how alike you were, Marshall?* He sighed and gently rubbed his eyes.

He didn't know when it happened, he just knew somewhere along life's growing-up and getting older journey, his childhood memories had evolved into a series of random "things." Not all-encompassing sensorial events. A past his mind had filed and then stuffed into hidden places. He had trouble identifying them, much less calling up an empathetic response to his son's behavior. But a self-evident truth was unfolding, like the photographs from one of those old Polaroid instant cameras. His memories revealed parallels between his experiences and Jake's. Parallels he had refused to acknowledge, much less understand they even existed. The letters. They were triggering these memories. Memories hidden somewhere deep in the recesses of his mind, like lemon juice reveals words on a page written with disappearing ink.

Living Room

As the last notes of *Frosty the Snowman* had trailed away, Millie suddenly stood and paced back and forth in front of the living room sofa.

"That was fun. One of my favorites," she said. Before the next song began, she reached over and switched off the CD player. "You girls go back and finish straightening up in the den and the dining room. I'm gonna, uh, go out and see if I can find your Daddy."

"Mama...we've cleaned everywhere at least fifty times already tonight." Beth puffed out a frustrated breath and rolled her eyes at her sisters. "Guess we're done listening to Christmas music, huh?"

"Clean again," Millie snapped. Thinking better of the quick response, she said, "I'm sorry, girls. Didn't mean to fuss."

"I don't like you going outside in this awful rain," Lisa said, shaking her head and starting for the kitchen.

"If we're not gonna call 911, then it's time to call the sheriff's office, Mama," Beth pleaded. She pointed to the clock on the side table. 6:50.

"Not yet," Millie said. "He's probably outside, close by somewhere."

Lisa looked over at her sister, Beth, and shook her head. "Why don't we all clean up together, again? This way, we can look around the house once more if you want." She paused. "I just hate to think of you going out..."

"I won't stay long. Remember, y'all are the ones who said he's not inside," Millie responded, a bit blunter than she had intended. "We've looked everywhere and unless he's hiding in a drawer somewhere..."

A whimper sounded behind her. It was Mary, snuffling. Tears formed in her eyes.

"Oh, little girl, I'm sorry. I didn't mean to be so...oh, C'mere, you." She reached out and threw her arms around her youngest. They walked to the den and just sat together on the sofa in front of the fire.

Attic

Sunday
March 31, 1996

Dear Gammy Gat,
　I'm not supposed to talk with my mouth full.
　I'm supposed to do my homework first thing when I get home from school.
　I'm not supposed to burp at the dinner table.
　I'm supposed to wash my hands after using the bathroom.
　I'm not supposed to pick my nose.
　I'm supposed to brush my teeth after every meal.
　I'm not supposed to bite my fingernails.
　I'm supposed to do my best all the time.
　I remember hearing somewhere there's not supposed to be any supposed to's.
　I'm not supposed to stay up this late, so I suppose I should stop,
　Jake
　P.S. I love you, Gammy Gat

Marshall closed his eyes and took a deep breath. A "not supposed to" window opened, and a memory slipped in. Something not supposed to happen had gotten him in hot water.

.   .   .   .   .

With his seventh-grade frame still as goofy as ever, Marshall walked down a hallway. He pinball collided with every eighth and ninth grader who happened to block his path. Grover accompanied him. On their first day of Junior High School, they had tried to take the most direct route toward their lockers. After finally wending their way down the correct hallway, they reached their side-by-side lockers.

"Groveman, hold some of these while I get my combination, will ya?"

"Sure, Marsh."

Grover tried to take the books. Two slipped and fell to the floor. While making a desperate attempt to catch them, both he and Marshall watched as the remainder of the books tumbled to the floor. Three ninth graders happened to be walking down the hall. The tallest boy reached out his arm to stop the other two as they approached. "Well, men, what do we have here?"

"C'mon, Marsh, let's get our books." A nervous Grover squatted and started to gather up the fallen books.

One of the boys turned to his buddies. "These guys are new." He smiled at Grover and Marshall. "Being as how we're upperclassmen, we're supposed to help you guys."

A second boy turned toward Marshall. "Do you know your combination? We'll even open your locker for ya."

"You put the combination slip in your right front pocket, Marsh." Marshall frowned a "Why'd you tell him?" look.

The third boy said, "That your combination slip? Hand it over here."

"I, uh, don't think I'm supposed to tell anybody."

The boy snatched it. "It's okay. We're ninth graders. We're supposed to be helping you guys."

"Marsh, I got first-period lunch, so I gotta go."

"Uh, okay, Groveman."

Grover located his books in the pile, picked them up, said a hurried goodbye, and scooted down the hallway.

"Hey guys, this slip's kinda hard to read," said the boy holding the slip. "Some of them numbers are kind of blurry. Maybe if I wet my finger, I can rub off some of them smudges."

Marshall shouted, "No! Don't!"

Too late. He turned toward Marshall. "Uh-oh. Smudged 'em. Sorry about that. Here's your combination slip."

It was unreadable. The only thing for him to do was to retrieve his books and leave as quickly as he could. "I'm gonna be late for my first gym class."

The first boy sidled up to Marshall and put his arm across his shoulder like they were best buddies. "Look, we just come from gym class, ourselves, and it's a good thing we stopped ya, 'cause I'll bet you don't even know about the change."

"Change?"

"Yeah, the change. Coach told us to tell all y'all the locker room is being cleaned. Y'all are supposed to meet for the first time in the girls' locker room."

"The girls' locker room?"

"Right, ain't no girls' class this period. Y'all are supposed to come straight on in. He'd be waiting on y'all. First locker room you see on the right when you walk into the gym. Since you're late, all the other guys'll probably already be waiting on ya." Marshall stood by his unopened locker. The three older boys passed on by and continued their walk down the hall.

Access to the gym meant going through the double doors at the end of the hall. When the late bell rang, Marshall panicked. Like a doofus, he tucked all his books under his arms as best as he could and hurried toward the doorway. The girls' locker room was on the right, like the ninth graders had said. Marshall heard faint voices inside, nothing coming from the boy's side. He walked right into the girls' locker room.

"Young man, you are *NOT* supposed to be in here!"

.   .   .   .   .

Marshall winced as the memory slipped away a great deal slower than he had fled the embarrassing scene in the girls' locker room. He'd found out later he hadn't heard anything in the boys' locker room because the gym teacher had already taken them outside. Jake had claimed a few "not supposed to's." Marshall had certainly experienced a whale of one of his own.

Foyer

"Look, I'm gonna put on a warm coat, get an umbrella, go outside and find your Daddy. He's just gone out for a walk...not very smart in this weather. You know him. He gets wild hairs sometimes. He can't be too far away. I'll be back in a jiffy."

"Mama, I don't think..."

"It's okay, Lisa."

"We're gonna wait right here and watch out the window." Beth scrunched up her mouth and stared hard at her mother. "If you're not back in ten minutes, I'm coming after you."

Attic

Wednesday
April 3, 1996

Dear Gammy Gat,

They should've asked me. I would've told them. The people in the school office sure made a fuss, though. They stretched me out and made a pillow for my head, then covered me with a blanket. I could tell they thought the bulge by my knee must've been something pretty awful.

The ambulance guys didn't even ask me. They picked me up real careful. Then they put me on a rolling bed. The ride to the emergency room was cool. Mama went crazy about the bulge. They told her I'd fallen off a merry-go-round thing on the playground. She didn't ask me, either.

The doctor poked around. HE asked me. I told him, then showed him. The bulge was my plastic container of green slime. It must've slipped down through a hole in my pocket and stuck in my pants by my right knee when I fell off. The doctor laughed. Mama wasn't amused.

I would have told them if they had asked.

When we got back home from the hospital, Mama fussed at me for not being honest with everybody. She didn't buy the part about nobody asking, and said I did it on purpose as an April Fool's joke to get to ride in an ambulance.

Maybe.

When it was time for bed, I had a chance to be honest, again, with Mama. I know I should be. Sometimes, for no reason, it takes a while to make yourself own up. I remember what I said and what she said.

"Will you help me get my bed ready?"

"You're a big boy, now."

"Will you get me up early?"

"I always do."

"Do I have to go to bed now?"

"You're stalling."

"Will you leave the hall light on?"

"I always do."

"Mama, I'm sorry about the ambulance thing."

"Yeah, well, okay, just don't let it happen again, kiddo."

"Will you stay with me for a little while?"

I hate it when Mama's mad at me.

I should have been honest from the start,

Jake

P.S. I love you, Gammy Gat

P.P.S. Mama stayed.

P.P.P.S. I miss you…honest.

Marshall figured he should've been angry as the dickens at Jake. The EMTs, the ambulance ride, and the doctors had hit his pocketbook hard. But the incident had cracked him up. He'd loved seeing his son getting the best of his mother. Despite her anger, Millie had been there for Jake. He had apologized to her. Marshall closed his eyes and thought about Millie and his own mother. They were like two peas in a pod. They could anticipate what everybody needed in the moment. Jake knew this about his mother and knew it about his Gammy Gat. Marshall reached up and rubbed his eyes. *Are you starting to understand what getting the "best of them" actually means, Marshall? Did he get the "best of you?"*

Marshall hated this question now. Before he found the notebook of letters, his answer would have been very different.

Neighborhood

Millie reached the end of the sidewalk and paused. She'd pulled the collar of her raincoat up close beneath her neck and held the umbrella down close over her head. Glancing first to the left, then to the right, she chose right. The sidewalk led toward the downtown area of Oakton, within walking distance of their home. Turning back toward the house, she waved to the girls watching from the window. All the stores would be dark by now, although the downtown Christmas lights and decorations remained lit and festive.

Taking a deep breath, she walked quickly, sidestepping along the already deeply puddled sidewalk.

Attic

Sunday
April 7, 1996

Dear Gammy Gat,

I think worrying about Randy helps me not to think about feeling sorry for myself. Is it okay? I guess it's like putting off one worry for another one. My brain gets clogged up sometimes. If I'm not busy worrying about Randy, I start thinking too much about how we moved away from our real home and left my best friend, or I have to put up with two sisters, or I have to go to yucky school every day.

I've been thinking about Eddie a lot. Mama and Daddy told me he can visit sometime. I used to see him every day. It kind of makes me think about you and cigarettes. Remember when you tried to quit smoking? You tried to do what you called going "cold turkey." You put your cigarettes down and said you'd never pick them up again. Remember how terrible you felt? You told us you didn't know whether you could stand going cold turkey or not. And you couldn't.

I feel the same way about what I had to do with Eddie.

The dishwasher in the school kitchen broke this week. We had to eat on those flimsy, foam trays. They're smaller than the thick plastic ones. Sections aren't as big, so everything doesn't fit. I got peach juice on my beans. The spoon and fork don't fit, so you have to hold them underneath your tray with the same hand you're holding your napkin with. We had soup today too. I needed Mr.

McQueen after the spill. He told me next time I should hold my tray with both hands after I put my milk carton in the upper left corner.

I've been meaning to tell you about something else. We have Show and Tell every day. Sometimes kids show. Sometimes kids tell. You can't do both on the same day. It's not like the kind of Show and Tell when I was a little kid in kindergarten. It's like, we're expected to be creative or bring something unusual we might have found or made. Well, one kid in my class has never shown or told anything before. On Thursday, he brought a baseball glove to school. He said he found it in the gutter. Ms. Murray told him if he kept the glove, it would be like stealing, and he should try to find out who lost it. It looked like a cool glove, so I whispered to him later he ought to play catch with it before he turned it in. He said he hadn't found a ball yet. I kind of thought he'd never be able to buy one, so I sneaked my new baseball to school in my backpack and gave it to him on Friday. Can't tell Daddy the truth, though. He'd be really mad at me for giving it away.

"I'll be damned," Marshall whispered out loud. He shook his head. The next memory window cracked open like a baseball smashed it.

．　　　．　　　．　　　．　　　．

"How do you like your new baseball, son?"

An uncomfortable silence followed.

"I, uh, it's gone, Daddy."

"What do you mean, 'It's gone?'

Jake wouldn't look at his father. "It rolled into the gutter."

"What was it doing rolling in the gutter?"

Jake kept his eyes on the floor. His voice barely above a whisper. "I was throwing it up into the air, and I missed it when it came down. Bounced into the drain before I could reach it."

"What were you doing throwing it up in the air so close to the street, Jake? Haven't I told you not to play close to the street?"

He lifted his eyes and stared up at Marshall. "Yes, Daddy, I forgot."

"Your forgetting costs money, son. Baseballs aren't cheap."

"I'm sorry, Daddy."

.   .   .   .   .

Marshall made himself replay this memory in his head. Connecting it to Jake's account in the letter, again, elicited another quiet, "Damn." He had made Jake work off the money the ball had cost. *Why couldn't he tell you what he did with it, Marshall?* He knew why. Marshall would've told him how foolish it was and not his job to give a baseball to this kid. Then he'd probably said, "What were you going to do, buy a baseball for every kid in your class who didn't have one?" After reading these letters, something told Marshall, maybe the Jake he didn't know at the time, would have considered it. *Keep breathing, Marshall.*

Back to the letter.

Our school has a classroom for special kids. I think Mama said they are artistic or something like that. They can't talk, or if they do, it's not like they're talking to anybody special. I heard this boy sort of talking one time. It was like he knew everything he was saying. It didn't make any sense to me.

I wonder what he was thinking. I wonder if he even knew what he was talking about. Their teacher is a real nice person. She's always smiling whenever I see her.

Guess what? Lordy, Lordy, Daddy's forty. It's what's on the big sign out in the front yard. He says his body is wearing down, and his back hurts all the time, and his knees don't work so good anymore. Is forty old? When is a person old? I guess you were old. You could still tell me neat stuff, though, and go swimming at the lake. I remember your stories about teaching water safety to all those big football players when you were in college. About how you could break all their holds, even though they were stronger than you and thought they were real tough. And I remember how you still used to sit on the floor and play card games with us. Sometimes Daddy wants to tell us he's getting to be an old man. He uses this silly, pretend scratchy voice. He deserves a punch in the stomach when he does this. I'm not stupid. I know what growing up and getting old mean.

Lordy, Lordy, I hate forty,
Jake
P.S. I love you, Gammy Gat

Marshall shook his head. Once again, what Jake wrote about triggered something from his own past. This time, the memory slithered up from the depths of his mind.

.　　　.　　　.　　　.　　　.

For Cole Gatlin, springtime mowing made the ritual list. Goose grass, dandelions, crabgrass, and chickweed were all fighting words. Every Saturday, Marshall's father waged war against those adversaries. He drafted his son into his weed killing, grass cutting, and mulching army.

Already up from the breakfast table and out the screen door, his father headed for the tool shed. "C'mon, soldier, I need you to help me work in the yard."

Marshall, as on every Saturday yardwork day, did the scrunch up his nose thing. "Do I hafta, sir?"

His father stopped long enough to shout and point his finger. "Yes, you *hafta*. This kind of work'll make a man out of you."

Marshall frowned and half-shouted a half-hearted, "I'm coming. I'm coming."

His father's wide body and head disappeared inside the shed, then, like a jack-in-the-box, he re-appeared. "Here, try these gloves on. Your mother uses 'em when she messes around in her flower garden. They oughta be about your size."

He disappeared into the shed again. Marshall stared at the pair of dirty, green and white gloves and frowned. He slipped one on. "It feels yucky, inside."

"Good grief, soldier, show some gumption," his father grumbled amidst the clanging of metal against metal as he rummaged around looking for tools. "Your mama puts 'em on and dudn't complain. And she's a woman."

Marshall shook the second glove. Some dirt fell out, followed by an empty beetle carcass. He shivered, then slid it on. His father met him at the door with an old, wobbly red wheelbarrow. "Here, take this and go over yonder to the compost pile and fill it up. Use the old shovel. And—not like the last time—remember to turn the compost over a couple of times with the pitchfork first. After you fill up the wheelbarrow, tote it around to the front yard." He paused. "Oh, and by the way, you got any notion where the clippers are?"

"Nossir. Maybe Momma used 'em, and they're in the house or something."

"I'll check it out," Cole said. "You go on ahead and get the compost. Meet you around to the front." He headed off through the grass like a giant stomping his way through an unlucky village.

Marshall had grabbed the wooden handles on the wheelbarrow and wobbled his way toward the site in the back, right corner of the yard. The rusted, broken-handled shovel and a pitchfork leaned against one side of the cinderblock enclosure. Bricks holding down the thick, green tarp on top of the cinderblocks had to be moved first. Reaching for the last brick, he spied something move close to his feet. A slithery tail with three narrow, yellow, horizontal stripes running to its tip disappeared through one of the open holes in the cinderblock.

"Daddy! Help!"

Cole Gatlin showed up in a flash at full sprint, breathing like a bull. "Soldier! What's wrong?" He gulped air. "You...hurt?"

"It was a snake, sir. And he was sorta green. And he had long yellow stripes on him."

His father threw his hands up into the air and dropped to his knees. His voice wheezed like a bagpipe with a hole in it. "For Pete's sake, you about gave me a heart attack."

Marshall had stood, staring. His father, still on his knees, continued to breathe hard. Marshall knew old people had heart attacks. Was his father old enough to have one of those? He couldn't get his mind to decide what to make his feet do. Should he run for help or stay with his father? Sure as anything, if he stayed, he was going to watch him die.

He didn't die. At least not on that day. While Marshall had stood there, paralyzed from indecision, his father yelled, "It was only a little bitty garden snake. Wouldn't hurt a fly." He gulped, took a deep breath, and finally stood up. "Don't be such a baby. You gotta *grow up*, soldier."

·   ·   ·   ·   ·

The memory slithered away as Marshall shook his head and involuntarily shivered at the thought of having come face to face with a snake that wasn't safely behind a glass barrier. His father had risked his life to save him. The image of him collapsing would be imprinted forever in Marshall's mind's eye. What growing old and growing up meant had smacked him in the face. For Jake, growing up and getting older had just become another cog in the wheel, distancing him from his father. Marshall went back and re-read, *He deserves a punch in the stomach when he does this. I'm not stupid. I know what growing up and getting old mean.* Marshall whispered aloud, "Was I so clueless...? He interrupted his self-chastisement and thought again about his parents.

A heart attack took his father, eventually. Coming face to face with the mortality of both his mother and father had shaken him to his core. After all these years, an IED and Jake's letters were shaking him all over again.

He still hated snakes. *Read another letter, Marshall. And breathe.*

Foyer

"Mommy's back!" Mary shouted.

"No Daddy," Beth said under her breath as she watched her mother cross in front of their next-door neighbor's yard.

"I want my Daddy," Mary said, beginning to snuffle again.

Lisa reached out and pulled her younger sister to her. "We'll find him," she whispered, glancing at Beth and rolling her eyes.

"You are soaked," Beth said, as she helped her mother remove her coat. They'd left the folded-up umbrella outside by the front door. She whispered in her mother's ear, "I gave you more than five extra minutes before I was about to start out the door."

Millie brushed her hair back from her forehead. "I don't think it would've mattered how many extra minutes you gave me," she said quietly. "I either went the wrong way or...or..." She couldn't decide whether to cry or shout out in anger, then chose neither when she looked down at Mary's tear-stained face.

"Girls," she started, "I..."

"Call the sheriff's office, Mama," Beth said, catching her big sister's eye.

"It's time, Mama," Lisa said.

Millie looked around at each of her daughters, then glanced at her watch. 7:15. She sighed. "Okay, okay, let me go put on something dry, right quick, and I'll meet you in the dining room."

Attic

*Wednesday
April 10, 1996*

Dear Gammy Gat,

Randy's cast came off this week. And all he's been talking about is trying out for after-school soccer at the park. He's trying to talk me into it. No way. I think he thinks getting on the soccer team will make him popular. Some of the guys are giving him the business. They're calling him a goofball and saying when he tries out, they're going to make it tough for him.

It's almost like Randy wants life to be hard. Like he wants to have to put up with the guys being mean, so he can blame them instead of blaming himself if he doesn't make the team. I don't think you can TRY to fit in anywhere. Seems like it'd be kind of like hitting yourself while somebody else is holding you down. I think you just fit.

Ms. Murray has been acting weird. I know why. She's worried about how we're going to do on the big test coming up. Every kid in North Carolina has to take it. It's the one where we have to sit all morning and color in little circles with a number two pencil. She tells us not to worry, but she sure does act strange.

We've been doing a lot of new stuff too. We don't spend much time on it. She says we have to cover everything for the test. The school sent a letter home to our parents about it. The test is mostly about reading and math. Ms. Murray was mean to Jeremy because he didn't get a problem right on the blackboard.

He's one of the black kids in my class. She yelled at him and said he needed to try harder because it was important for little boys LIKE HIM to do well on the test. Jennifer (she's a white girl) didn't know how to do the problem either. Ms. Murray didn't fuss at her. I looked over at Jeremy, and he had this sort of mean-looking frown on his face. I kind of don't blame him. The night before the test, we're supposed to get plenty of sleep. Oh, yeah, she tells us not to worry and to think about the fun stuff we do at school.

Having a ball,

Jake

P.S. I love you, Gammy Gat

P.P.S. I wonder if other teachers treat black kids different.

Marshall shook his head and knew which memory window would open next. His first day in third grade.

．　　　．　　　．　　　．　　　．

The family's blue Bel Air station wagon pulled up close to the drop-off zone at J.R. Williams Elementary School. "We're here." His mother delivered the phrase in her best "Aren't we all happy about it" voice.

Marshall had already reached for the door handle. "Momma, please just drop me off."

"Don't you want me to go in with you, Marshall?"

"Momma!"

"I want to meet your teacher."

He sank into his seat and let out a sigh. "Okay," he grumbled.

His mother pointed toward a crowd gathered around further up the curb. "I wonder what's going on?"

"I dunno," Marshall said, shrugging.

She had frowned and clutched her hand to her chest. "Oh, my goodness. I know what it is."

Marshall recognized several of his friends and their parents. They stood in two lines on either side of the sidewalk, and he could see their angry faces. Two young kids and their parents walked between those two lines.

"Children from a colored family are coming to your school, Marshall."

"How come they ain't going to their own school?"

His mother had leaned down and gently lifted his chin with her hand. "This *is* their school. In fact, all schools should be open to all children, Marshall."

"I never been in a class with a colored kid before."

"Well, how will you act if you do have a colored child in your class, Marshall?"

He had shrugged his shoulders and stared down at the grass. "I dunno."

She placed her hand on his back and eased him up the sidewalk. "I hope you'd be a gentleman and try to make friends."

He had dragged the toes of his shoes over the sidewalk concrete. "Aw, Momma, can't somebody else be their friend?"

"If not you, son, then who?"

He and his mother located his classroom. He chose a seat beside Jack Canton, who wore a tightly tucked, blue Cub Scout shirt, rolled-up jeans, and Chuck Taylor All-Stars tied in a double knot. Cub Scouts were authorized to wear their blue caps with the yellow stripe indoors on pack meeting days. Marshall stared at the yellow neckerchief pulled snug around Jack's neck. He envied the metal slide and wished he'd joined.

After talking with the teacher, Marshall's mother smiled at him. She pointed her index finger at her temple, indicating the "think" sign, mouthed, "I love you," waved goodbye, and left.

Jack leaned over and whispered, "Did you see them colored kids, Marsh?"

Marshall recalled seeing Jack and his mother in the angry line. He whispered back. "Yeah."

"I hope none of them's gonna be in our class, don't you? My daddy says they oughta go back to where they come from."

"Where's that?"

Jack looked at Marshall like he was stupid or something. "Why, Africa. Everybody knows that."

"I thought they's born in America."

Jack leaned back and crossed his arms over the tail end of his Cub Scout neckerchief. "Don't matter if they was or not. Don't want one sitting next to me."

"My Momma says we should be nice to 'em."

Jack adjusted the slide on his neckerchief. "You be nice if you want to. Anyhow, they don't fit in, you know?" He paused. "Hey, Marsh, you oughta join our scout pack. My daddy's the den leader." Voices at the doorway caught the two boys' attention. A young man and woman entered the class with their daughter. Jack whispered, "You're kiddin' me. We're gonna get one of them colored kids." Jack squeezed his nose with his fingers, like he suddenly smelled a fart.

The man and woman spoke to the teacher and smiled at their daughter. After a long hug, they turned and walked away. Marshall watched as the parents glanced back once and then at each other. The forced smiles revealed extremely worried faces. Marshall looked at the young girl. Her blank stare and the way she bit her lips revealed her anxiety. He looked back at Jack, who glared at the girl and stuck out his tongue. Several of the other kids did the same thing. He noticed his teacher scoping out the seating situation. She seemed worried. Marshall spied the empty seat beside him, one of several in the classroom. He raised his hand. The teacher smiled and said,

"Yes, young man?"

"She can sit here."

.   .   .   .   .

The memory faded, and Marshall re-read, *P.P.S. I wonder if other teachers treat black kids different.* His mother's unerring wisdom brought a smile to his face. Mary Claire Gatlin had passed on her sense of fair play and her sense of right and wrong about how we treated people to him, hadn't she? Although he felt no urge to pat himself on the back, the memory helped him to feel maybe some of her modeling behavior hadn't completely muddled away from inside of him. These letters reflected Jake knew, understood, demonstrated, and manifested a compassion for the human condition Marshall hadn't thought him capable of...meaning his son had inherited so many more positive genes than Marshall had given him credit for. *This begs two questions, then, doesn't it, Marshall? Why would your son, growing up, have been any different than you? And how did you, so totally, misread him?* Marshall sighed and gazed around the attic. He had a feeling the inner voice wasn't done. *What kind of parent were…are you, Marshall?* He grimaced. His answer to the *were* question had been unfolding uncomfortably. A clinched fist pressed against his lips reflected he needed a new approach to the *are* one.

Den

"Gatesville Sheriff's Office, how can I help you?"

"This is Millie Gatlin, on Capital Street. My, uh, husband has gone out in the rain. He's been gone for well over several hours and has not returned."

"Hey, Mrs. Gatlin, this is Meredith Lilly."

"Hi, Meredith, you get stuck with the Christmas duty?"

"Yes, ma'am. It's all right, though. I can go home in the morning." She paused. "Did you say Mr. Gatlin has gone out and not returned?"

"Well. We've searched the house and..."

"Did he take the car?"

"No, the car is still in the garage."

"Did anyone see him leave?"

"Well...we did have right many people over tonight, you know, in honor of Jake. But no one said they saw him leave."

"I heard about your son, Mrs. Gatlin. I am so, so sorry."

"Thanks, Meredith. We're hanging in over here. Marshall being gone certainly isn't helping."

"I assume you've looked everywhere in the house?"

"We've looked everywhere, even under the beds. His heavy coat and hat are missing from the front hall." She paused. "It...it's a Carolina blue cap and his coat is a dark green parka with a furred hood. No umbrella is missing. I did go out briefly and walk down the street toward town. Looked around for about ten or..." She glanced over at Beth. "...fifteen minutes. Oh, and, uh, he doesn't have his phone with him." She paused. "Lisa mentioned Deputy John Bates may be on duty this evening?"

"Both John Bates and Deputy Natalie Dawson are on duty tonight. I'll let the two of them know what's happened. If you'll just give them a few minutes, one of them will get to your house shortly."

"Thanks, Meredith."

"You're welcome. I'm sure we'll locate him. Don't you worry, now."

Millie looked around at her girls. "Bye and thanks again," she said, turning toward her daughters. "How 'bout you girls go watch for the deputies."

Attic

Sunday
April 14, 1996

Dear Gammy Gat,

Randy didn't make the soccer team. He said Coach Mack made this big speech to all the guys. He told them about trying their best and about being winners and about how you're supposed to play the game. Then, he told them if they didn't make the team, it was only because they weren't good enough.

Randy didn't act mad. It was more like he knew it was going to happen. He said he wanted to be somebody. Now, he feels for sure he's a loser. I told him I didn't think he was a loser. I told him I was his friend. He told me thanks for nothing, and then he walked away. I didn't know what else to say. Maybe he didn't want somebody to tell him he shouldn't feel like he was feeling. Maybe he wanted to feel sorry for himself for a little while.

Even kids get the blues sometimes,
Jake
P.S. I love you, Gammy Gat

All those times Jake got in trouble, the school tagged him as one of the losers. But he had been willing to look like a loser, if it meant standing up for this troubled kid. This convoluted thinking triggered another one of those winner or loser adventures. It happened on an unusually warm evening in October at the North Carolina State Fair.

.   .   .   .   .

"Marshall, you boys meet us outside by the Red Cross building in two hours." His mother turned to the other ten-year-old boy standing beside him. "Grover Woodside, your momma'll skin me alive if I don't bring you back home safe and sound." She paused. "And promise me you'll look after one another."

Grover pulled his ball cap down tight around his ears. "Yes, ma'am, Mrs. Gatlin."

Marshall snapped to attention and saluted. "We will, Momma."

Marshall's father pointed to the knuckles on his balled-up fist. "Y'all stay out of trouble. And don't even think about going near those girlie shows. That's an order."

"Yessir," Marshall said. "C'mon Groveman!" They took off toward the midway.

One last shot from Momma. "Don't spend all y'all's money in one place!"

"We won't!" They shouted over their shoulders.

"Where to first, Marsh?"

Marshall grabbed Grover's arm. "I got a idea," he said. "When we buy food, if we get one order and share, we can save our money and get more stuff."

For an hour, they filled their bellies with French fries, cotton candy, elephant ears covered in powdered sugar, popcorn, a corn dog, and a barbecue sandwich. They rode the Wild Mouse five times and banged around in the Bumper Cars. Shuffled sneakers ended up covered in dust, and conversations had to be shouted over the blaring music. Nothing existed quite like the Fair fragrance of popping corn, charcoal grills sizzling from dripping fat, oil frying, red dirt, sweat, and animal poop. After they tumbled out of the "Largest Horse in the Known World" exhibit, Grover grabbed Marshall's arm. "Look, Marsh. Over yonder."

"Oh, man," Marshall muttered. "She ain't wearing hardly nothing."

Grover wore a big grin. A big feather hat on her head, the woman pranced back and forth across a stage. Grover pulled Marshall. "Let's go see."

Marshall pulled back. "Daddy'll kill us."

Grover leaned close, his eyes wide and crazy-like. "He'll never know. C'mon. Just for a minute."

Marshall glanced around, checking to see if his father might be spying on them. He swallowed hard. "Okay, for a minute."

The two sneaked their way through the crowd and hid behind a light pole. A barker, wearing a straw hat, stood up on stage with the scantily clad woman. He smoked a big, fat cigar and spit his spiel into a large microphone. "Come on in and see for yourself." The most beautiful girls in the world in all their natural born glory. The rowdies, crowding around the stage, howled. She ended her prance around the platform with a quivering smile, blank stare, and a lackadaisical hip wiggle.

"How old you reckon she is?"

Grover looked at Marshall and shrugged his shoulders. "About twenty-five, I guess."

Marshall grabbed Grover's arm. "I think she looks like she don't wanna be there. And anyway, she's gotta be older'n my Momma. Let's get outta here." Marshall pulled him back up the midway. Stopping and out of breath, they stared at each other and broke into guffaws.

"I wanna win something," Grover said, after finally catching his breath. How much money you got left?"

Marshall checked his pockets. "A little bit." He paused and scrinched his nose. "I hate playing those games. You never win nothing good."

"My big brother won a giant teddy bear one time."

"Does he still have it?"

"Naw, he give it to his girlfriend. I think she told him it busted open, and all them pieces of sawdust stuff fell out."

"We could do Pick Up Ducks," Marshall said. "At least you know you're gonna win something."

"Aw, picking up goofy ducks is for babies." Grover headed for the "toss your dime and land on a plate" game. "Let's try something cool."

"You ain't gonna git your dime to stay on the plate."

Grover had already pulled out a coin. He set nine more dimes in a circle drawn on a ledge in front of him. The barker stood right beside him.

"One thin dime is all it takes!" He announced. "If it stays on the plate, you win your choice of what you see hanging right here! Just one thin dime!"

"Gotta be about a zillion dimes in the bottom, already," Marshall said, as he watched Grover flip a dime into the air. "You're just givin' away your dimes. You ain't doing it right."

"Am too." He flipped another dime the same way and kept doing it until all his dimes were gone.

"I told you flipping 'em wasn't gonna work."

Grover stomped his foot. "If you're so smart, why don't you try it?"

Marshall held a dime in his hands. "Naw, won't work my way, neither."

Grover flapped his arms. "Aw, you're chicken. Ain't but one dime. Won't kill ya."

Marshall stared at the plates. He stared at his dime.

"You gone kiss it or toss it?"

Marshall frowned, then closed his eyes. He tossed the dime like he threw a Frisbee. The coin sailed flat-sided toward the glass plates and landed on the plate nearest to Marshall. It skidded across and to the next one, then the next one, like a skipping rock across a pond. The dime went all the way to the other side and slid across the last plate. Marshall held his breath. The dime finally stopped and dangled, holding up on the outside edge.

"We got a winner here! And all it took was one thin dime! Whataya want, kid? You can have a dog or a chicken.

■　　　■　　　■　　　■　　　■

Marshall returned to the present, and he glanced over at the box containing his flying horse story. The bottom of that box held what was left from the stuffed chicken. For both boys, winning proved to be getting an eyeful of a sad, demeaned young woman and a bunch of sawdust. *If winning isn't important or all it's cut out to be, does it make somebody a loser, Marshall?*

Jake's version of winning, all along, meant being willing to lose if the outcome was more important than the perceived glory. For Marshall, coming to this understanding about his son proved to be one of those "I feel more like I do now than I did before" kind of "ah-ha's." It didn't make sense. Then again, maybe it did. His son was knocking the hell out of the contention that being tagged a loser meant you were one.

Living Room

"I see a car with Sheriff written on it, Mommy," Mary shouted.

Attic

Wednesday
April 17, 1996

Dear Gammy Gat,

Randy ran away. His parents came to our house tonight because they think I might know where he went. I told them I didn't know. His mom said he was real upset when they told him they might be splitting up again. I know he thought they were going to stay together. I think they were either fooling him or he was fooling himself. She said Randy got angry after their news. He yelled at them and banged on walls and stuff. Then he took off.

While they were at our house, his mom started crying. His dad acted weird. And he smelled and talked goofy, too. It would serve them right if he didn't come back.

His parents said they were going to the police. When they left, Randy's dad kept staring back at me. Daddy stared at me, too. I could tell neither one of them believed me. Even if I knew, I'm not sure I would've wanted to tell. I know it would've been the right thing to do. He could be in trouble.

I wish Daddy believed in me more,
Jake
P.S. I love you, Gammy Gat

Marshall re-read, *I wish Daddy believed in me more.* He *had* thought Jake knew where Randy had gone. Reading the word *"in"* was particularly disturbing. Not believing what you thought was a one-off lie was one thing. Hearing someone thinks you don't believe *in* them was an entirely different ballgame. His memory of this night didn't float in on a breeze—it blew in on a hurricane wind.

·　　　·　　　·　　　·　　　·

Randy's father, short and stocky, stood on their front porch, his greasy hair hanging down across his shoulders. Some of this guy's teeth were green. Marshall had been convinced he'd been drinking or was on drugs. Randy's mother, with dark circles beneath her eyes and bruises on her arms, looked like a walking advertisement for an eating disorder and spousal abuse. Marshall had no intention of allowing these people to enter their home. They wanted to know if Jake knew where Randy was. Jake had said no.

"Your kid's lying, man."

Millie saved Marshall before he lost his temper.

"He said he didn't know," she said quietly.

Randy's parents had lingered a moment. His father had aimed an evil eye at Jake, then Marshall, who returned the favor. Suddenly, the man turned, grabbed his wife by the arm, and hustled away in a huff. After they left, Marshall knew he had to grill his son. His words were measured and slow. "Was his father right, Jake? You know where Randy is, don't you?"

Jake stood straight and tall, arms across his chest. He had stared Marshall straight in the eyes. "No...sir."

Marshall had leaned in close. "Look, Jake, if you know where he is, you have to tell us right away."

Millie reached out and touched his arm. "He *said* he didn't know, honey."

He gently removed Millie's hand. "Those two kids have been pulling all kinds of shenanigans all year." He had turned back to Jake. "You've made it pretty tough for me to trust you, son." Jake had stared at the floor. Marshall took his son's chin in his hand. "I want you to tell me the truth. If this boy is your friend, then you'll understand it's not safe for him to be out all alone. Now, one more time, do you know where he is?"

Jake's eyes never left his father's. "Nossir."

Marshall let Jake's chin go. He had stared at Millie, then back at Jake. "What's it gonna take to get you to be honest with me, son?"

Millie, her voice controlled and quiet, walked over and put her arm around Jake. "You'd tell us if you knew, wouldn't you, honey?"

He looked up at his mother, then tossed a glance at his father. "Yes, Mama."

Marshall threw up his hands. "Go to your room, Jake," he had muttered. "I hope for your sake, young man, something terrible doesn't happen to him."

Jake had walked in silence down the hall. Halfway down, he stopped and looked back at his parents. He wiped away a tear. After Jake closed his door, Millie socked Marshall on the arm.

"You're unbelievable."

"He knows where this kid ran off to, Millie."

"You're wrong about your son, Marshall Gatlin." She turned and walked away. "Dead wrong."

.   .   .   .   .

Marshall adjusted his butt on the barrel seat. He sighed and moved his eyes back to the letter. He read it again. *I wish Daddy believed in me more.* Painful truths hurt worse when your heart and mind ultimately confirmed their veracity. Marshall imagined Millie tying his arm to a post and then pushing a button on a mechanical Millie-fist designed to, deservedly so, punch him over and over.

Foyer

Lisa opened the door before Deputy John Bates could knock.

"Hi, Johnny," she said, a smile on her face.

"Hi, Lisa," he said, returning the smile.

Beth poked her sister in the side, looked at Mary, and winked. Mary stifled a giggle. "You gonna let him in, Lisa?" Beth whispered.

"Oh, yeah, sorry, Johnny."

"Hello, Mrs. Gatlin," he said as Millie walked up. "First, I want to say how sorry I was when I heard about Jake."

"Thanks, Deputy Bates," Millie said, trying to smile. "Now, with Marshall nowhere to be found, it's been quite a Christmas Eve."

"Yes, ma'am, I'm sure it has. Deputy Dawson stayed at the station in case any more calls come in. Mrs. Lilly filled us in a bit on what you told her. Can you go over it again, for me, one more time, please?" He paused. "And, please, call me Johnny." He smiled.

Attic

Sunday
April 21, 1996

Dear Gammy Gat,

They found Randy on Thursday morning. He was hiding under the bleachers at the high school football stadium. He'd stayed all night. Mr. Carruthers, the custodian at the high school, discovered him sleeping and called the police. He got to ride in the squad car. I don't know what his dad did after he got home.

After school, I told Mama and Daddy I was going out to ride my bike for a while. I sneaked over to Randy's trailer park and went around by his window. They had locked him in his room. He didn't say much at first. He was real calm. And then he started talking a lot.

He said he wished his parents weren't his real parents. And bunches of other crazy stuff I can't remember. I mostly listened. I did tell him he was a jerk for running away and hiding under the bleachers. I told him he should have picked a better hiding place. This made him laugh a little.

I wonder how bad it has to be to make your brain tell your feet to run away?

When he came back to school on Friday, we talked again. Guess he needed to keep talking. And I think he knew I would listen.

He said his mom and dad kept fighting, and it's over him and money stuff. He overheard them arguing. They thought he was asleep. He said his dad kept talking about how much trouble he was in. And how they didn't have enough money. He said he wished Randy had never been born. His dad said everything would be all right if Randy went to live at the Oakton Orphanage. He said it would make everything better for all of them. His mom yelled and then got scared she might wake up Randy. She came in to check on him. He pretended to be asleep. Randy said when his mom left his room, he couldn't sleep, and he stayed awake all night.

I've never heard Mama and Daddy yell at each other before. I know they probably do because I'm sure they get mad at each other sometimes. I've seen Mama give Daddy the evil eye a lot. I guess they yell when we're not around.

Listening to Randy got me to wondering if they'd ever had one of those "I wish the kids weren't around" kinds of conversations. I have a feeling Daddy might feel this way lots of times. I have to admit I wish HE wasn't around sometimes. I did some staying awake this week, too.

Wide-eyed and wondering,

Jake

P.S. I love you, Gammy Gat

Marshall closed his eyes. Seemed like a natural thing for a kid, after a heated exchange with a parent, to just wish the parent would "go away." He wondered what thing or things, specifically, had pushed Jake over the edge. An inner voice—with a bit of snark to it—filled him in. *Take your pick, Marshall. With your track record, it shouldn't be too hard to figure out.*

He sighed and read the ending of this letter again. *Listening to Randy got me to wondering if they'd ever had one of those "I wish the kids weren't around" kinds of conversations. I have a feeling Daddy might feel this way sometimes. I have to admit I wish HE wasn't around sometimes.*

The thought of having no kids *had* crossed his mind, even after having them. He figured he couldn't be the only guy ever to think it. And the "no kids" thought haunted him. Now, *he'd* lost one. Marshall had been the one who had forced his son to join the military. "Learn to be a man," he had said. He'd convinced himself the rationale for his decision consisted of believing it would help Jake straighten up and get right with his life. It seemed, now, it might have been more of a copout and rationale for his reluctance to confront the difficulties involved in truly understanding his son and his needs. An inner voice sneaked in a comment. *Sounds like you thought the solution to your frustrations was to send him away, Marshall. Did you think, back then, if he wasn't around, it would remove your responsibility to have to deal with his everyday presence in your life?* His son's death seemed like the ultimate, tragic "be careful what you wish for" scenario. So many pages revealing so much about his son. A son he thought was someone else. A son he may have wronged in ways he may never atone for.

Something was happening to Jake then. Something was happening to Marshall, now.

Living Room

After listening to Millie, Deputy Bates said, "Sounds like, for sure, he's out in this rain either still walking around or maybe he's slipped and accidentally fallen and injured himself. And since he doesn't have his phone, he can't call for help." He paused, glanced over at Lisa, smiled, and then looked back at Millie. "Mrs. Lilly informed the guys on duty at the Fire Department. I'll touch base to see if we can get them to help in the search. Oh, just to ask one more time, you looked everywhere in the house and saw no indication of where he might have gone. Right?"

"Daddy's gone," Mary blurted out. And one more time, the tears started to flow.

The young deputy placed his hand, gently, on top of Mary's head, then leaned down and spoke softly, "I'll do my best," he said. He turned to Millie and the older girls. "I'll keep you posted." And he turned to leave.

"Thanks, Johnny," Millie said. "Lisa, will you show him to the door?"

They watched, silently, as the young man left, Lisa walking by his side.

Attic

Sunday
April 28, 1996

Dear Gammy Gat,
    I'm tired of writing and thinking. We finished the test on Thursday. I hope I never have to hear the words, "You may begin," again.
    Feeling dumb,
    Jake
    P.S. I love you, Gammy Gat

A past conversation entered Marshall's mind. It was one he thought he'd been rather proud of at the time. The night before Jake took the first part of the California Achievement Test, Millie had asked Marshall to tuck him in. She made him promise to try to ease his son's fears about the test.

• • • • •

Jake pulled up his covers. "I'm getting too old for you to tuck me in, Daddy."

"Well, it's your mama's thing, son, so why don't we try to make her happy, what do you say? Anyway, I want to talk to you about the testing tomorrow."

Jake screwed up his nose.

"This is important stuff, son. You ready for it?"

Jake turned away from him. "Uh, I guess so, Daddy."

With a bit more energy than he had intended, Marshall grasped his shoulder and pulled him back toward him. "You guess so? Don't be guessing, Jake. Ms. Murray's spent a lot of time trying to prepare you for these tests. And your mama and I expect you to be on your "P's" and "Q's" and do your best. You may get what you deserve with all the goofing off you been doing this year."

·　　　·　　　·　　　·　　　·

Marshall sighed. A fluttering ache crept into the pit of his stomach after reliving this memory. He shifted a bit on the barrel, reached his hands into his pockets, and grasped the handwarmers. Gripping them tightly, he let the remaining, gentle warmth ease the chill in his fingers. Not unlike the handwarmers, Marshall had a task to perform. His was to ease his son's anxiety the night before the test. Instead, he had turned the pressure vise a few more turns. He likened it, now, to reaching into his pockets and grabbing two ice cubes instead of handwarmers. *You were some kind of inspirational speaker, Marshall. You told him he was gonna screw up.*

Like death row inmates taking the long walk, Jake and most every kid who ever took the test probably fretted for hours, believing, in their hearts, they had to take a test to prove they were either smart or stupid. And sure enough, Jake's best took a hit. When they got his scores later, he had underperformed. Marshall was smart enough to know self-fulfilling prophecies pretty much did their own dirty work. He felt like removing the top from his barrel seat and stuffing himself inside. He'd ask to have the top resealed and have someone *please* push him over Niagara Falls.

Living Room

Lisa stood and watched as Deputy John Bates ran through the cold rain to his car. Upon opening the door, before he got behind the wheel, he gave Lisa a quick wave and a thumbs-up. Then he slid in, closed the door, and drove away.

Attic

Wednesday
May 1, 1996

Dear Gammy Gat,
Randy said he had a plan. I said I would help him. It's wrong, but it seems
right, somehow.
I promise I'll do some more thinking, anyway,
Jake
P.S. I love you, Gammy Gat

Do some more thinking was an understatement. Jake had gone into deep secret mode. He had been even quieter and more distant. Marshall had thought it to be a part of his rebellion. What he didn't know was those boys were hatching a plan that changed their lives forever. Finding out how it had transpired was not unexpected. Of course, the unexpected happened when one least expected it. And Marshall didn't know *what* to expect.

A junior year in high school memory window opened. About expectations and plans, it marked an important time in Marshall's life. For the first time, he had an out-loud conversation about his future with someone other than himself.

．　　　．　　　．　　　．　　　．

At dinner time, Marshall's younger sister, Alice, had turned on her sweet, innocent face. His older sister, Helen, was off at college. "It's your turn to help with the supper dishes, Marshall," she said. "I get to go watch TV while you help Momma."

"It can't be my turn again. Can it?"

"Honey, I'll finish up in here with Marshall. You go sit down and relax," Cole said.

Marshall's mother stopped on her way to the sink, a pleasantly stunned look on her face. "Seriously, Cole?"

He stood up. "Won't offer twice. Anyway, I want to have a little talk with our son."

"I won't pick up another dish." She handed what she held to Marshall, then walked over to her husband and gave him a peck on the top of the head. "Thanks, honey. I'll be in the bedroom reading if y'all need me."

His father wiped the kiss off his head and whispered, "Not in front of the youngins, Mary Claire."

She laughed.

"Oh, pooh on you, Cole Gatlin."

Marshall headed for the sink. "We won't need you, Momma." He had no clue why or what his father wanted to talk about. Usually, it meant he was angry or upset or needed to lecture Marshall about something. "Am I in trouble?"

"No, son, not at all. I, uh, wanna talk with you about your future."

"What do you mean, 'My future,' Daddy?"

"I want to know what your plan is."

"My plan?"

"Yeah, you know. What you wanna do with your life?" He paused. "Have you given any more thought to joining up after you graduate? You never know what your draft number'll be. And if you sign up, you'll at least have some choice in your duty. If not, you could find yourself in a rice paddy in Nam."

"I don't *dislike* the military. But I wanna do something different with my life. Go to college. Study business. Maybe even get an MBA." Marshall paused. "Not worried about my number yet. I think I have a little more time to do some thinking." He hesitated. "It, uh...the military's not right for me, Daddy."

Cole took a plate and set it down in the dishwater. He picked up a glass, stuck it beneath the sudsy water, washed them both and handed them to Marshall. "Don't wait too long, son. Before you know it, opportunities'll pass you by and you'll have to settle instead of choose."

.　　　.　　　.　　　.　　　.

Marshall re-read, *I promise I'll do some more thinking, anyway.* Then thought back to his draft plan gamble. It had ended up being a lucky bet. His gamble had delivered his hopeful outcome, based on an APN draft number that had been higher than the highest one called at the time he was eligible. Jake's gamble with Randy seemed like one of those *right vs right* moral dilemmas. After the two boys did what they did, Marshall had feared his son's life plan might involve *doing* time. *He surprised you with all the extra time he put in, didn't he, Marshall? All along, you wanted Jake to learn from what you felt were his mistakes. What are you learning from yours?* Marshall closed his eyes. He figured he might need an entire notebook to list it all. And another one to write down everything he needed to change. Sighing, he went on to the next letter.

Living Room

Mary cuddled up beside her mother. "What do we do now, Mommy?"
"Wait," Millie whispered, as she caressed her daughter's hair.

Attic

Friday
May 3, 1996

Dear Gammy Gat,
We did it. Don't ask me to tell you anything right now. I'm trying not to think about it.
I think you're going to be upset,
Jake
P.S. I love you, Gammy Gat
P.P.S. I hope you will still love me.
P.P.P.S. Is it ever all right to break the law?

Marshall paused. He did the neck stretch again, then immediately went to the next letter.

Living Room

"What's Daddy thinking?" Beth said. All three girls sat on the floor in the living room.

"He's hurting," Millie said, standing in the doorway.

"We're all hurting," Beth said.

"I think having this crowd of people over here tonight was too much for him. He, uh, had to get away, and his solution was to sneak out of the house."

"Sorry to say this...it was a stupid solution, Mama," Beth said. "It's cold. It's dark. It's raining. It's Christmas Eve. And Daddy left without taking a phone?" She paused. "He'd ground me for a month if I did something even close to what he's doing."

Lisa, holding Mary's hand, said, "I'm gonna go fix me some hot tea. Anybody else want some?"

"I'm in," Beth said.

"Sounds great," Millie said, smiling.

"Can I have some hot chocolate, please?" Mary asked, between sniffles. She continued to hold tight to her older sister's hand.

Attic

Wednesday
May 8, 1996

Dear Gammy Gat,

Okay, I guess I'm ready to tell you.

I had to talk to the police. Randy's at home too. He's with his mom. Randy found out where the landlord at Randy's trailer park left the bag of rent money every month. And he knew Mr. Williamson liked to keep it around for a few days before he took it to the bank. So, we sneaked in and took it. When Randy showed his folks the money we took, he said his dad acted real mad and everything and said he was going to take it and turn it in to the police. Instead, he never turned it in. He kept it and took off. The police are after him.

It was all over the local TV station, about how these two kids stole money so the family of one of the kids wouldn't have to break up. It didn't work because Randy's family was broken already. I think I put a crack in mine.

Do you think I'm terrible? Lisa and Beth have been hard to live with this week, and it's even worse with Mama and Daddy. I know I let them down. It seemed like doing something wrong was the right thing to do. I can't explain it, though. You know something is wrong to do, but you do it anyway? I know Lisa and Beth will never let me forget it. And I don't like looking in Mama's eyes. She keeps staring at me like she doesn't recognize me or something. Daddy won't look at me at all. He probably wishes I wasn't his kid. Can't blame him, I guess.

I'm gonna hate going to school and having to see all the other kids. How come when you think about all the bad stuff happening to you after you do something wrong or stupid, it feels worse than when you were thinking about it before you did it in the first place? Going before the judge today was scary. It hurt the back of my neck looking up at him. I think he meant what he said about me making sure I never had to come back into court for anything. He'd said our punishment would be for Randy and me to work for Mr. Williamson, to make up for what we'd done. We have to cut grass and pick up trash and stuff every day for two months. We can't do it together, though. All Daddy said when we left was, I had gotten off lucky. He probably wished they'd put me in jail, or something like that. Guess he only cared about me if I was one of the "good" kids. I think I'll be grounded until I'm an old man, anyway.

School's almost over. Daddy and Mama talked with Ms. Ledbetter, and they thought we should stay out of school all this week. It was like being suspended. Besides working for Mr. Williamson, Mama and Daddy said I have to do volunteer work at the Goodwill Store downtown this summer.

They haven't found Randy's dad yet, so the money's still gone. It's crazy, isn't it? We took Mr. Williamson's money because we thought it would help Randy's mom and dad stay together. Too many wrongs and not enough rights, I guess.

Trying to get it right, now,

Jake

P.S. I love you, Gammy Gat

P.P.S. Do you still love me?

P.P.P.S. Mama's upset, but I think she still loves me. Not so sure about Daddy.

No clear memory window opened for Marshall. A mish-mash of images and conversations—more like heated discussions—weeks of sleepless nights, tears, sympathetic looks from co-workers, unsympathetic looks...filled his head and his heart.

Marshall's anger level with Jake had reached its highest point. Although all of the money taken had been intended to go to Randy, Marshall had refused to listen to anything his son had to say. Compliant had been Jake's demeanor, as if he had anticipated the outcome and had prepared himself for the consequences. He never argued or made excuses. He never complained about having to work for Mr. Williamson. He never asked to change anything about the plan to work at the Goodwill Store.

Marshall had not been able to look Jake in the eyes. Of course, the boy's sisters had razzed him day and night. They were merciless. Marshall didn't encourage it. He didn't stop it, either. Millie had been the calm one, holding her emotions in check. Until, of course, after they went to bed.

Before the court date, Marshall had relished anticipating his son's confrontation in court. He rationalized a great lesson would be learned. His whole mindset changed when his young son stood before the judge. Jake never flinched. He stared right into the Judge's eyes. Marshall had been the one to flinch. He had wanted to grab Jake up and hustle him out. Instead, he piled on to Jake's misery. He'd lectured to him one more time. Thinking about it, now, he smiled one of those, "I'm such a jerk," smiles, remembering it had ticked him off, he'd been conflicted between wanting his son to suffer and wanting to save him.

Marshall glanced back down at this May 8th letter. *Your son might not have, exactly, had a life plan, Marshall, but what he was doing and thinking sure showed he was thinking a hell of a lot about his life, wasn't he? And part of his thinking involved wondering whether you even loved him or not.* He massaged his head again. It didn't help. "Damn it, I did care about...love you, son," he whispered to himself, out loud. *You just didn't let him know it was unconditional, did you, Marshall?*

Kitchen

Lisa, Beth, Mary, and Millie stood by the stove waiting for the kettle to whistle. "This has to do with Daddy and Jake not getting along, doesn't it?" Lisa said. "The two of them have been at each other for a long time, haven't they?"

"You noticed that, did you?" Beth said.

Lisa rolled her eyes slightly. "It was difficult to miss. Having to leave Eddie hit him hard." She paused. "The family of one of the kids in my classroom moved right before Christmas, and her last day was the day before vacation started. We had a little celebration for her. But she was so sad to be leaving all her new friends."

"I know ya'll knew your Daddy and Jake had their ups and downs that year we moved," Millie said.

"All of us hated the move," Beth said. "All of us, 'cept for little miss —merely 'twinkle in your eye— Mary." She reached out and tousled Mary's hair.

"The...the move was important. For your father's career," Millie said.

"Didn't make it any easier," Beth said. "We adjusted. I love my new friends here."

"Jake took it extra hard, though, didn't he?" Lisa said.

"Daddy got really po'd at him for it," Beth said.

"Well, the angrier Jake got, the angrier your father got," Millie said. "And the more messes Jake seemed to get himself in."

"We saw it, too, Mama," Lisa said. "Jake wouldn't talk to us."

"Wouldn't talk to anybody," Millie said. "When he hooked up with that poor little red-headed boy, it was the straw that broke the camel's back for your Daddy."

"The letter from Jake right before Christmas...right before...you know...." Lisa hesitated. She reached out and touched her mother's arm. "You didn't let us read it, Mama."

"I don't know why we kept it from you," Millie said. "Stupid and thoughtless of us. I'm sorry." The kettle whistled, and she removed it from the burner. "When we got the news about Jake, what he wrote in the letter crushed your father." Millie paused. "He's kept it with him ever since. Never removes it from his pocket. I made a copy, though. Would you like me to read it to you now?"

Millie left to go upstairs to retrieve the copy of the letter.

Attic

Friday
May 10, 1996

Dear Gammy Gat,

They're gone. Randy and his mom left town. Mr. Williamson told us when Daddy dropped me off at the trailer park. He said Randy's mom had a friend who brought a truck and packed up everything they had. And as far as he knew, they weren't coming back. I didn't even get to tell him goodbye. He left me here, only after a couple of days, to do this work for Mr. Williamson all by myself. Oh well, you always said, "When it rains, it pours." I'm going to find out where he went and write him a letter. Our school counselor, Mr. Jones, will know how to find him. I hope he'll tell me.

I wish they hadn't run away. It seems like it's what his mom and dad have been doing all the time. And Randy got caught right in the middle. I guess his mom wanted to get away from her husband, again. I'll bet he finds them. I hope the police find him first. I wish Randy had told me they were leaving. Saying goodbye's better than not getting to say anything.

Daddy's thrilled,

Jake

P.S. I love you, Gammy Gat

When Mr. Williamson shared the news, Marshall could barely contain his excitement. When he rushed into the kitchen after returning home, he hugged Millie.

.   .   .   .   .

"Millie, honey, like Elvis, they've left the building."

"Whoa, cowboy," she said, as she wriggled away and laughed. "Who left?"

"The red-headed kid. You know, Randy and his mother." He pumped his fist. "Yes!"

Millie, holding a potato masher, stopped laughing and stared at him. "When?"

The energy in the room slipped away like being up two points and watching the opposing team hit a half-court three-pointer to win the game with no time left on the clock. Marshall lowered his voice. He stumbled over his words. "Today. Old man Williamson. He told us. When I...you know...dropped Jake off to do his work."

Millie stepped closer and locked a Death Star tractor beam stare at him. "You didn't act this way in front of Jake, did you?"

Marshall attempted to look away. The pull of Millie's glare proved more powerful than he could overcome. "What way?" He managed to mutter.

She threw up her hands, tossing mashed potatoes everywhere. "Like this. All giddy and thrilled."

He scowled, hoping to appear grievously offended. "Of course not. You have to admit, Millie...they're gone, so we've got a much better chance of getting back in control of our son. It's gotta be worth celebrating."

Millie tossed the masher. Miraculously, it made it to the sink. "I don't suppose Jake *leaped* with joy when he heard the news."

"Of course not."

"You said something to him, didn't you?" She stood up and put her hands on her hips. Those tractor beam eyes made contact again.

Marshall leaned back against the counter. "Well, I, uh, said something about things finally getting back to normal."

Millie wiped her hands on her kitchen towel. A scowl across her face, she let him have it with both barrels. "Let's see if I can get this straight," she snarled. "He lost another best friend. *He* left the first one, and *this* one left him. He poured out his heart and soul to this kid and supported him in something—oh, God—never in a thousand years would we have suspected of him, and then, to add salt to his wound, you offered up some comment about normalcy being important. *Your* definition of normalcy, of course." She wadded up the paper towel and tossed it into the trash can. "About cover it?"

"Damn it, Millie, all I did was..."

"All you did was belittle his feelings," she said, interrupting, her voice level commensurate with the energy behind it. "His decisions. His life."

"This kid was bad news, Millie. You've even agreed with me."

Millie shook her head and rubbed her eyes. "Yeah, you're right. I thought it. Said it. To Jake, he *wasn't* bad news. This kid's leaving was one more thing piled onto a tough year for our little boy. And sometimes, I'm not sure whose welfare we were looking out more for. His or ours." She paused and combed her fingers through her hair. "You...we...didn't just rain on our son's parade, Marshall." She turned on her heels and headed for the door. Stopping as she passed through, she looked back at Marshall. Tears welled up in her eyes. "We soaked it to the bone."

.   .   .   .   .

Marshall set the letters down and listened to the rain as it struck the metal vents above him in the attic. *You didn't care whether your son's parade got rained on as long as yours stayed dry, didn't you, Marshall? Were the decisions you made primarily intended to make your life easier and keep you safe from the everyday life-storms hitting you? Had you rationalized that you had to allow your son to face the full brunt of just living life...on his own?* The brunt of that realization struck him in the heart like a storm-blown, broken limb against a window. Surely, he had not created such a scenario for his daughters.

Frantically, he did a quick flip of the remaining letters and realized he was nearing the end of this notebook. Reading these letters had not been easy, to say the least. Now, he didn't want them to ever stop. It had been as if Jake sat beside him, helping him to turn the pages. He couldn't decide if he thought he could read the last one when he reached it. He knew he'd lose Jake all over again. For a brief moment, he considered putting the notebook somewhere safe and coming back to it later. *You can't stop, now, Marshall. Not now.*

Den

Millie returned with the letter. The three girls, with their tea and hot chocolate in hand, gathered together in the den and waited, seated on the floor, backs against the sofa. Millie unfolded it and began to read.

Dear Mama, Daddy, Lisa, Beth, and Mary,

I can't believe it's almost Christmas. I know you'll be getting the tree pretty soon. Wish I could be home to decorate it with you.

Lisa, make sure to make one of Gammy Gat's chocolate pies. Since I won't get to eat one this year, it'll give you something to write to me about. Beth and Mary, you can describe how all the chocolaty goodness looked and tasted.

I do hate to tell you this next thing. I thought you should know, not too long ago, one of the guys in our company—Private Green—shot himself. Our MA unit had to process him. He had a wife and kid back in South Carolina. And now he's headed home, just not the way his family expected. I didn't know him very well. It didn't make what he did any easier to accept. You know, I even read somewhere, counting those who come home, more soldiers kill themselves than get killed in combat.

Mama and Daddy, I know I've never sat down and talked with you about my fifth-grade year. I guess when Greeny did what he did, it brought it all back, big time. It made me realize I owed you a long talk.

I kind of shut myself down, then, I know. Like I wanted to keep everybody out. I haven't let anybody in on anything I've felt for a long time. And I know it wasn't and hasn't been fair. Being only eleven at the time, I guess I can convince myself I didn't know any better. I know I royally screwed the whole father-son thing, and I have awful regrets. Maybe if I'd known then what I know now…but things don't work that way, do they? Not sure what I'm getting at, except I think I'd like to try to talk about it, you know?

Now, I didn't tell you all this because I want you to worry about me. It's…well, when I get back, I hope we can sit down and get to know each other again. Means even you girls (Ha ha).

Oh, yeah, one more thing. They say December is nasty over here. We thought the dust storms had been bad. All the red dust builds up and turns into a muddy mess because of all the rain and snow. It's cold, too, and going to be worse than Oakton in December.

We've been involved in a few recoveries these past few weeks. Don't fret, though. (I know you, Mama.) Khost has been pretty dull lately, and the road to Gardez has been pretty quiet for the most part. Before long, the weather will clog up the road, anyway.

Well, I've got to go. Sorry this one had to be so short. Didn't mean for it to be so mental either. This stuff's on my mind, and Christmas is tough enough without family around to spend it with. The holiday won't be the same without being at home. I miss you all so very much and wish I could be there with you. We have a job to do. Will try to write more later.

Love ya and hugs,

Jake

P.S. Merry Christmas

P.P.S. Don't worry about me. I'll be home before you know it.

Millie folded the letter and glanced around at her daughters. Not a single dry eye met her gaze. A sad smile crossed her lips, and a tear dropped from one of her eyes. Lisa broke the silence. "I think it's time for a group hug, Mama."

Attic

Sunday
May 12, 1996

Dear Gammy Gat,
We only have about three weeks or so left of school. And tomorrow's also going to be my first day back. I know the kids at school are going to bug me wanting to know everything about what Randy and I did. I wish they didn't. I don't want them to ask me anything. I want to forget about what happened and for school to be over.
I still don't know anything about where Randy is.
That's all,
Jake
P.S. I love you, Gammy Gat
Strangely, Marshall remembered this particular Monday, and it felt like anything but a maple-sweet kind of memory.

.　　　.　　　.　　　.　　　.

Millie had made blueberry pancakes for breakfast, Jake's favorite. They were pretty much Marshall's, too. Jake hadn't taken a single bite and had pushed his plate away. "You're going to go to school, Jake."

"But Daddy."

"But Daddy, nothing. Make a man out of you."

With his proverbial blank stare and shoulder shrug, Jake had picked up his book bag and shuffled out the door without another word or any breakfast in his belly.

.   .   .   .   .

A short gust of wind blew across the vent, overhead. It rattled slightly. Marshall glanced up at the noise and listened for a moment to see if it would continue. After a few seconds, it ceased, and he eased his eyes back down to the letter he had just read. He tried to imagine how many times he had said, "Make a man out of you," to Jake. He tried, unsuccessfully, to chuckle when his mind twisted the mantra into, "Go on outside into the storm, by yourself, son. Make a man out of you."

Just trying to make sense out of it all, messed with his mind. Marshall had acted like he knew what "becoming a man" meant. Saying it and not knowing what to truly look for seemed counterintuitive. *Becoming a man* was such a limiting term, anyway. *Becoming a person...* capable of making a positive contribution in this world. Wasn't that what it was all about? A person ought to be able to define what it looked like when they told someone else to live up to it. And it sure as hell didn't involve an unprotected dash into life. It would take more than neck massaging, knee straightening, stretching, and eye rubbing to deal with the turmoil inside him right now. What he was learning from these letters and the sentiments generated by that turmoil were the driving forces behind doing something about it. *Keep reading them, Marshall.*

Den

"I think a game of UNO is in order," Lisa said, wiping her eyes.

"I don't wanna," said Mary, rubbing her sleeve across her wet cheeks.

"Let's do it," Beth said, grabbing a Kleenex and blowing her nose.

"C'mon, Mary," Lisa said. "It'll take our minds off waiting."

"I'll go get the cards," Beth said.

Millie smiled and nodded at Lisa, then gazed down at her youngest. "Beth and Lisa are right, honey. It will help to take all our minds off worrying." She glanced at the clock. 7:47. "We have to let John Bates do his job, don't we? He's only been looking for about thirty minutes."

"Mama's right," Beth said, returning with the box holding the UNO Attack cards and card launcher. "And it gives me a chance to whup up on you guys."

Attic

Sunday
May 19, 1996

Dear Gammy Gat,
Callie delivered her kittens this week. And one of them looks like his daddy, who just showed up one day. We called him Fuzz. Except this little kitten's only got one eye. We're going to keep him and call him Fuzzer. If he's half as good a cat as his daddy, he'll be great. We're going to keep him inside, though, and not let him become a warrior like his old man, who ended up accidentally eating some rat poison somebody left outside. Gosh, Fuzz was something.
I hope Daddy can say it about me someday,
Jake
P.S. I love you, Gammy Gat

Marshall stared at the salutation. Couldn't take his eyes off it. Sighing, he closed them and tried not to think about the implications of his son's hope. A memory crept in about a conversation he overheard just a few days after the kittens had been born. At the time, a conversation he had noted was cute but insignificant.

.   .   .   .   .

Millie had set up her kitten nursery in the laundry room. Marshall had hidden behind the door and spied on his son through the crack. Jake held the tiny, yellow, one-eyed runt in his lap. He had tilted the kitten's head up and looked him right in his one good eye.

"We're gonna keep you, little fellow," Jake said quietly. Jake had stroked the tiny ears, then tickled beneath the downy soft chin. "You'll never get to know your daddy, and he'll never get to know you. I'll try to tell you some things about him now and then. Fuzzer's gonna be your name. Your daddy's name was Fuzz. He was something, and I'll bet, someday, we'll say you were too."

.   .   .   .   .

"He was something," Marshall whispered the words out loud as he gently ran his fingers across them on the page. Even though whispered, the words filled the air in the attic like an announcement at a ballpark. He smiled. Saying them helped bring back another memory. It had been a late Friday evening, in October, at Winston-Salem's Union Train Station.

.   .   .   .   .

Five-year-old Marshall stood beside his father as massive iron wheels creaked and jostled when the passenger car clunked into place. The taste of the nasty odor of diesel fuel hung in the air. His mother had hugged him and kissed him on the cheek. "You boys have a great time."

"We will, Mommy."

The conductor shouted, "All Aboard!"

Cole scooted Marshall ahead. "We better go find our berths in the sleeper car."

Marshall spied his mother outside on the platform. He caught her eye and heard her shout, "Go Yankees!" Marshall placed his palm on the glass and pressed his face beside his hand. The train picked up speed. The two walked through the coach car to get to their sleeper. A narrow doorway, halfway down the hallway, opened into the sleeper car, where they had a double bedroom, courtesy of Cole's boss. They would travel all through the night and arrive in New York mid-morning. His father pushed the door open. "Here we are."

"This room is little, Daddy."

"Sure is." Cole pointed to a narrow door. "The potty room."

"Where's the beds, Daddy?"

Cole laughed. "Right here. Folded up against the wall." He unhooked them and they lay flat, like bunk beds.

After brushing his teeth, putting on his pajamas, and using the bathroom, Marshall, with a boost from his father, climbed up to the top berth. A bed rail stretched across the outside edge of the mattress. Marshall snuggled under the sheets. "Do you think Mickey'll hit a home run tomorrow, Daddy?"

"Never can tell. It wouldn't surprise me."

"He's the best ever, isn't he?"

"He's one of the great ones. Now, no more questions. Close those peepers or you'll be sleeping when 'The Mick' smacks one over the wall."

"Night, Daddy."

"G'night, little soldier."

After traveling all through the night, Marshall and his father left the train and Penn Station. The two ate a big breakfast at a corner café. As the game was not until 2:00, they fed the pigeons at a small park and watched some mounted police on patrol. A hook and ladder fire truck screamed down the street, and the two rode in a taxicab. Both got sore necks from looking up at buildings. Finally, the time arrived for the subway ride to Yankee Stadium. "Since we been snacking all morning, what say we wait until we get to the ballpark to eat lunch? They'll have some great hot dogs."

"I kin wait."

After a short ride, the subway pulled up at their stop, and the two traveled up a set of stairs to the street. Marshall pointed and jumped straight up in the air. "There it is, Daddy!"

"Yankee Stadium," his father said, smiling. "The most famous ballpark in the country. We made it, didn't we, little soldier?" Marshall and his father pushed their way in and found their seats on the second deck behind home plate. "These are pretty good seats," Cole said. "We're lucky my boss couldn't use 'em, eh?"

"Look, Daddy! I see him! Number seven!"

"Number seven it is, little soldier. Mickey Mantle himself."

"This is gonna be great, Daddy, even if he don't hit no home run."

"You're right. It's already been great, hasn't it?"

Marshall pointed toward a guy carrying a big box. "There's a hot dog man."

"I'm ready for one. How 'bout you, little soldier?"

For eight innings, Marshall and his father shouted and cheered and ate. They got mad when the Yankees messed up. They booed when the Cardinals got a hit. Mickey Mantle grounded out. He walked and hit a double. By the bottom of the ninth, the Yankees and the Cardinals were tied one run apiece. Mickey was up.

Marshall crossed his fingers.

Mickey Mantle walked up to the batter's box. The Yankee fans went crazy. Everybody chanted, "Mick! Mick! Mick!" The Cardinals pitcher wound up and threw the ball toward the plate. Everybody got quiet. Mickey swung on the first pitch. At the sound of the crack of his bat, the whole crowd stood up and went crazy. The ball sailed up and into the upper deck. The game ended, and the Yankees had won.

"He did it! He did it!" Marshall shouted. His father held him high in the air.

On the subway ride back to the train station, Marshall, exhausted, fell asleep. He woke up to his father taking him to the bathroom. When he tucked him in, he whispered in Marshall's ear. "Go back to sleep. When you wake up, we'll be home, and your momma'll be waiting at the station for us."

Marshall rolled over and smiled a sleepy smile. "Mickey Mantle was something, wasn't he, Daddy?" He yawned.

"Yes, little soldier, he was really something."

Marshall could barely keep his eyes open. "Do you think people will say that about me someday, Daddy?"

"You bet. Now, go to sleep."

.　　　.　　　.　　　.　　　.

Marshall sat quietly on the barrel for a few moments and let the memory linger. This was the only time Marshall and his father ever went anywhere, just the two of them, together. It was as sweet and savory in his head and his heart as the tang of the stadium spicy brown mustard had been on his tongue. They ate five hot dogs apiece. Marshall considered it his best day ever as a kid. *Your father told you people would say you were really something, someday, Marshall. Jake told his Gammy Gat, he hoped you might say the same thing about him. While you're pondering these thoughts, what do you think Jake would consider his best day ever as a kid? Would it have involved you?* Marshall quickly moved his eyes to the next letter. Dwelling on an answer to the question would prove to be too painful. But he paused before moving on and took a deep breath. He committed to ensuring there would be no doubt when it came to the days he had left to spend with his daughters. He sighed and returned to the letters. He still had so much more to learn about his son. He smiled...and about his daughters.

Dining Room

"UNO!"

"No way you can have just one card left, Mary," Beth said, frowning.

"Yep."

"You're a great player, Mary," Lisa said, chuckling. She glanced at her mother and Beth.

"One of us has to stop this little urchin," Beth said, sticking her tongue out at her younger sister.

"Do I hear a car out front?" Millie held up her hand for everyone to be quiet. All three girls started to get up and run to the door. Millie stopped them. "Hold your horses, it may be nothing." She nodded toward Lisa.

"I'll check," she said, setting her cards on the table and going to the window.

Attic

Sunday
June 2, 1996

Dear Gammy Gat,
   SCHOOL'S OUT.
   I'm sorry I didn't write to you during the week. I was worried about Randy. I still haven't heard anything about him. Mr. Jones, our school counselor, said he would let me know if he finds out something this summer.
   Lisa got all A's on her report card. Beth got all Very Good's. I could've gotten all A's if I'd wanted to. I might want to next year. And it will be okay with me if I get to see Eddie this summer.
   You're number one in my class,
   Jake
   P.S. I love you, Gammy Gat

Marshall shook his head after reading this letter. Reading about the school counselor's assurance he'd let Jake know about Randy reminded him how upset he'd been when he found out about it. A conversation Marshall had with Millie pushed out the Mickey Mantle and tangy mustard memory and replaced it with a bitter taste.

.   .   .   .   .

At the end of the last day of Jake's fifth-grade year before summer, Marshall and Millie were in the kitchen after putting the kids to bed. Marshall searched the refrigerator for a beer. He glanced at Millie. "You were kidding when you told me Jake talked with his counselor about somehow getting in touch with Randy, right?"

"Not kidding. He called me today to let me know. He's been concerned about Jake, you know—both boys—all year." Millie made herself a gin and tonic.

"Outta limes," Marshall said, popping the top on his can and taking a swig. He swallowed and looked over at Millie. "Why is Jake so determined to stay attached to this kid?" Ignoring his comment, she found the lime juice in the refrigerator and drizzled some into her glass. "The counselor crossed the line, Millie," he said, taking another long swallow. "I knew for sure, once he was gone..."

She interrupted. "His counselor *cares*." Then, under her breath, "Unlike somebody I know."

"I heard that," Marshall said. "And it's below the belt. I *do* care about our son."

"You care when it's convenient. Remember when you *didn't* want to go to school on his first day? 'You go,' you said. 'You're the one who's good at handling the school stuff,' you said. And then you had the gall to beg me not to ask you to go because—what was it you said? Oh, yeah, something about having enough paperwork to choke a goat. And you said—this one I still don't believe—he didn't need you because he was a big boy."

Marshall shrugged. "You remember all that?"

Millie rolled her eyes and took a sip. "It's not just what you *say* to our son," she said quietly. "It's what you *don't* say. And what he sees you *do*, Marshall. Like the faces you make when he doesn't meet your expectations. Or *not do*, like when he does want to tell you something, and you won't put down your paper long enough to listen."

"Okay, okay. I get the picture."

"Do you, sweetheart? Really?" She paused. "You underestimate your son—it's not the first time, I might add—and his passion for friendship and love." She paused again. "He not only needs you, Marshall. He needs to know *you* need him."

He set his beer on a coaster. "Look, if it'll make you happy, I'll go talk to him."

Millie reached out to grab him and nearly spilled her entire drink. "You'll do no such thing. He's in bed and you will not go in and wake him up, now."

.　　　.　　　.　　　.　　　.

Marshall shook his head and reached for the warmers again. Millie kept painting him a picture back then. She'd put it right in front of his face. *You didn't have a clue, Marshall.* Jake hadn't pushed *him* away. It had been the other way around.

A conversation with Jake streamed into Marshall's mind.

.　　　.　　　.　　　.　　　.

His son had returned from his "escape walk," the one he took after he learned Gammy Gat had died. Everyone had sat, teary-eyed and quiet, in the living room. Jake came up to his father and reached out. He had placed his hand on Marshall's shoulder. "I'm sorry your mother died, Daddy. You loved her very much, didn't you?"

"Thanks, son. We all loved her very, very much. And I'm gonna miss her something awful."

"Me too, Daddy." And then Jake hugged him.

.　　　.　　　.　　　.　　　.

A brief flash of light through the small attic dormer—car headlights—caught Marshall's attention. The vehicle kept going, and he thought no more about the brief disruption in his musing about the memory. Jake had comforted *him*. Millie was right. After his father died, Marshall remembered his children couldn't imagine any other place for his mother to live than with them. And because Mary Claire did stay, the entire family had been the better for it. His son had shown an incredible capacity for love...and for empathy. Marshall had both denied and been oblivious to its presence in his son's character. Jake, through his words and thoughts and actions, had poured out the essence of his character to his grandmother. *These letters have been painting this picture for you, haven't they, Marshall?*

Dining Room

"Just a passing car," Beth said, as she rejoined the group at the dining room table. She picked up her cards, looked around with a pretend frown on her face. "Nobody cheated while I was gone, did they?"

"Nope," Mary said, smiling, as she played her remaining card and won the game.

"I knew it," Beth said.

"Can we play one more game, Mommy?" Mary asked.

"You just wanna play again 'cause you won last time," Beth said, reaching over to tickle her little sister in the belly.

"If you go ahead and put your PJs on," Millie said. "It's 8:30 already." Mary jumped up and ran upstairs to her bedroom. "And go to the bathroom before you come back down."

Attic

Wednesday
June 5, 1996

Dear Gammy Gat,

I found out where Randy is, and I've got his address. Daddy was mad at me and said I couldn't write to him. Hope you don't mind if my letter to you is short. I'm going to write to Randy, anyway. Mama said I could.

Talk to you later,
Jake
P.S. I love you, Gammy Gat

Marshall remembered when Jake had burst into his parents' bedroom with the news.

.   .   .   .   .

"Mama! Oh...hi, Daddy." Jake had stopped short. "I...I didn't know you were here."

An indignant Marshall had put his hands on his hips. "Well, this *is* my bedroom, son."

Millie frowned. "Never mind him, Jake. What is it?"

He started to turn away. "Uh, nothing. Never mind."

Millie placed her hand across his shoulder. "Jake, honey, you ran in here all excited about something. Tell us."

Jake had stood silent and merely stared at the floor. When he finally spoke, he mumbled like the words left a bad taste on his tongue. "I found out where Randy is."

Marshall had thrown up his arms in disgust. "Well, this certainly explains your disappointment in finding me here, son. You know I don't think it's particularly exciting news."

Millie started to sock Marshall on the arm, stopped short, and shot him an evil eye instead. "This is terrific, honey," she said, turning back toward Jake. "Is this why your counselor, Mr. Jones, wrote to you?"

His voice grew excited again. "Yes, ma'am. And...and he gave me an address so I could write to him."

"You're not to contact this boy, Jake."

"Please, Daddy..."

"No. I've had all I can take of your relationship with this young troublemaker and his family." He'd glanced over at Millie, hoping for support. Got nothing. He pushed the issue, anyway. "His father's a drug addict and a crook, and I've got a feeling his son isn't far behind. The sooner you accept your so-called friendship is over, the better off you'll be."

"Now, honey, he just wants to write Randy a letter."

"I'm right on this, Millie. He's got no business staying in contact with this boy. He's bad news, that's all there is to it." He had put his hand on Jake's shoulder. "He didn't want to be your friend, Jake. Don't you understand he was only using you?"

Jake had stood up straight, his jaw firm. "You're wrong, Daddy." The resolution in his voice had been disarming. "He needed me...for real." Then, he had lowered his eyes to the floor and whispered, "And I needed *him*."

.   .   .   .   .

A toilet flushed downstairs, and it reminded Marshall he probably wasn't far from needing to go himself. Unfortunately, the flushing planted the thought. But he determined he'd be able to hold it. He took a deep breath and thought about the memory of that conversation he and Millie had had with Jake. At the time, Marshall had never anticipated this kind of reaction from Jake. After spending several remarkably revelatory hours in a cold attic, the truth of his son having traded him for Randy and his grandmother still crowded his mind like stale air in a cramped room. *A double whammy, Marshall.* He reminded himself he hadn't made it a difficult choice. The impact of his "Jake should weather the storms by himself" philosophy had created a perfect, guilt-ridden storm of his own. One he had boldly ventured out into, convinced he knew what he was doing, but whose aftermath, now, he wasn't sure he could survive.

Dining Room

While waiting for Mary to return, Beth stood up and stretched. "Got a bad feeling about this," she whispered.

"Don't think like that," Millie said. "He's outside. Somewhere."

Beth shuffled the UNO deck. "It's been over an hour, Mama."

"Is the water still hot on the stove?" Lisa frowned at her sister. "Johnny'll find him."

Attic

Sunday
June 16, 1996

Dear Gammy Gat,

It's been almost two weeks since I wrote a letter to Randy, and I haven't heard from him yet. I'm sorry I haven't written to you in a while. I'll try to catch you up. Lisa is off at music camp. Beth goes to this summer program at the YWCA every day. Eddie is at Disney World. Mama is miserable and seems to be getting bigger every day. Daddy goes to his office and stays late. I'm still helping out at the Goodwill Store. They needed the help, so I figured I would work a little longer each day. Even though I just have a few more days to work for Mr. Williamson, I've decided I still want to go back and help him out once in a while. Mama says she is proud of me for wanting to do it. Daddy hasn't said anything. I heard him tell Mama they shouldn't be patting me on the back for something I should be doing, anyway. Oh, well, I didn't expect any thanks from him, anyhow. Guess nothing much else is going on. I almost think Randy and his mom will show up one morning out of the blue.

It does seem like I'm hanging around waiting for something to happen.
Waiting,
Jake
P.S. I love you, Gammy Gat

Marshall remembered Jake had been restless and anxious at the beginning of summer. He had routinely checked the mailbox every day and insisted on helping Mr. Williamson and the folks at the Goodwill Store. This had impressed Marshall. But he thought it would have set a bad precedent to give his son too much praise. He hadn't been convinced, nor did he trust his son had learned anything from his experience, because he had continued to hang on to Randy. Marshall figured it was Jake's job to demonstrate to *him*. Show his father he had straightened up and learned to be a man. Waiting on *Jake* to change, Marshall had ignored something pretty basic. He had forgotten the only person he had the power to change...was himself. A memory slipped in. A cloudless, Carolina blue, noonday sky in July had settled over Holden Beach.

.   .   .   .   .

Marshall, no more than five, squatted on the damp, clean, white sand. He looked up at his mother. "Mommy, will you build a sandcastle for me?"

She smiled and reached for one of the sand buckets. "Good idea, Marshall. Let me show you something." She filled the bucket with wet sand, packed it, and then turned it over.

"Whee! Make another one, Mommy."

"You make the next one, Marshall."

"I don't know how."

"Sure, you do, honey. Here, I'll help you."

They filled the bucket, together, and patted the sand until level and smooth. "Now, pick it up." He slid his small hand under the full bucket. "Careful, now. Turn it over."

"Like this?"

"Yes. Now pat it." He patted. He lifted. A firm, sand mold of the bucket shape stood without a single blemish. His mother laughed and clapped her hands. "You did it. Now, let's build a castle."

A moat circled the sandcastle walls, and a long canal ran down until it reached the water. Broken scallop shells decorated everything. Ramparts and walls and towers stood tall.

"It's a wonderful castle, Marshall," his mother said.

"Can we play with it tomorrow?"

"Don't you remember what I told you about the tide, honey?"

He stomped his foot. "I don't want the tide to take it away."

She leaned down and hugged him. "We can't change what the tide does, son. What we *can* do is build *another* castle, tomorrow."

. . . . .

Marshall had been trying to change Jake. To fit *his* image of what he wanted his son to be. Jake had been doing it, though, the whole time, on his own. *All along it was you...waiting on yourself, Marshall.* He stretched his left knee. What felt like a mild electric shock startled him, and he realized he'd probably held his knee bent in the same position for too long. Reaching down, he massaged the pained area until the stiffness in the muscles and tendons eased. He took a deep breath and revisited the special sandcastling experience he'd had with his mother. Marshall convinced himself he *did* have a chance—like the ability to come back and build another sandcastle—to rebuild all those things important in his life.

Dining Room

"I'm ready, Mommy," Mary announced.

"Did you brush your teeth, too?" Millie asked.

"Aw, do I hafta?"

"Yeah, you hafta. Now scoot." Millie watched her youngest drumble down the hall toward the stairwell.

Mary stopped before going up. She turned her head and stared at her mother. "Daddy just got lost somewhere, didn't he?" Without another word, she stepped up onto the first step and continued upward.

Attic

Wednesday
June 19, 1996

Dear Gammy Gat,
It came. A letter from Randy. He sounds so strange and sad. I showed
Mama, and I wrote all the words down so you could read them too. He didn't
spell some right, so I fixed those.
"Dear Jake,
Why'd you write to me? I won't never see you again, so what does it
matter? I don't know why I'm writing you back. I guess I owed you. I think
you thought we was friends. I don't need no friends. I knew we'd be leaving.
You don't need no friends when you know you ain't staying. Don't write
again.
Randy"
Gammy Gat, do you think he means all those things he said?
I'm glad you're my friend,
Jake
P.S. I love you, Gammy Gat

This next memory window opened, not the least unexpected, as had so
many. Both Millie and Jake had kept the existence of this letter a secret from
Marshall after he returned from work later that day. Millie had later
confessed after they had gone to bed.

■   ■   ■   ■   ■

"Ah, a bit of treason going on here, I believe."

"We weren't treasonous. A *little* bit sneaky, maybe."

"I thought we agreed Jake would not communicate with this little guy."

Millie turned over. Leaned her head on her elbow. "Hold on, dear heart—your ultimatum not mine. If you recall, I supported Jake on this one."

Marshall got out of bed and walked over to the window. Fireflies still flitted around the yard. "I wish you hadn't gone behind my back, Millie."

She got up out of bed, came up behind him, and put her arms around his waist. "Guilty as charged, sweetheart. And I'm sorry. I couldn't bear to see the look of disappointment in our son's eyes."

Marshall kept looking out the window. "We should've talked about it."

"You're right."

He turned around and faced Millie. Gingerly, he placed his hands on her shoulders.

"Disappointment's a part of life, honey. We've got to prepare him to face it when it comes."

She, gently as well, removed his hands and sat on the edge of the bed. "It seemed this year has been so full for him already." She patted her belly. "You know this is probably going to be a little girl, don't you?"

"Meaning the odds of one more disappointment added to Jake's pot?"

"Will you be disappointed?"

"You kidding? Ten fingers. Ten toes." He chuckled and rolled his eyes.

"Works for me," Millie said. "Now, let's go back to bed. My back's killing me."

Marshall, still standing and staring out the window, said quietly, "I want what I say to mean something, sweetheart."

■   ■   ■   ■   ■

Marshall shifted his butt on the barrel and leaned back ever so slightly. He raised his arms and clasped his hands together, resting them on his head. Closing his eyes, he took a breath. His clasped hands generated a subtle warmth through his hat to his head. *Don't you think your son probably felt the same way, Marshall?"* Sighing, he released his hands, lowered his arms, and glanced back at Randy's words from the letter. A predictable lack of faith in humanity from a boy who couldn't believe someone like Jake could exist in his life. Marshall shook his head. He hadn't believed in Jake's humanity either.

Dining Room

"Show me your teeth and let me smell your breath."

"Mommy! Beth's being mean."

Millie rolled her eyes and smiled. "Cool it, hot stuff," she said. "She's only teasing you."

Lisa walked in with a steaming cup of tea. "We're playing one more game, right?"

"And I'm gonna win," Mary replied, a smirk on her face.

"Little girl, it is Christmas Eve and past your bedtime," Millie said.

"You can't put her to bed now, Mama," whispered Lisa. Another car engine sounded outside. They all jerked around at the noise. It quickly passed. Millie, Lisa, and Beth all looked at each other and shook their heads.

"Deal," Beth said.

Attic

Sunday
June 23, 1996

Dear Gammy Gat,
  Randy's dead.
  Jake
This letter had been bound to rear its head soon. Marshall also knew which memory was going to roll in. Jake had been outside practicing his pitching, aiming at a spot on the chimney. Marshall closed his eyes and recalled the sound of the baseballs as they thudded against the bricks.

．　　　．　　　．　　　．　　　．

"Son, come in here, a moment. Please. Your mama and I need to talk with you." He had promised Millie he would be nice, sensitive, and respectful of Jake's feelings.

"What'd I do?"

"You didn't do anything, son. We, uh, we have some news to share with you."

Jake walked in and cast a curious glance at his father. His mother's eyes were red, her cheeks flushed. Millie patted a chair beside her. "Sit right here, Jake."

Jake put his ball and glove down. He sat beside Millie, and Marshall sat across from them. "Y'all are scaring me. What's up?"

Millie spoke, her voice quiet, soothing. "The school called today. Randy...died."

Jake stared at her. A few agonizing, silent moments passed. He spoke, his voice calm and in control. "What happened?"

"The only thing we know is he took his own life, honey." Millie reached out to take his hand. He pulled back. "The school said as soon as they knew more, they'd call us." She paused and wiped a tear from her cheek. Jake stayed quiet. He cast his eyes down toward the floor. "I am so sorry, honey." Millie turned to Marshall. Her eyes implored him to say something...anything.

"This is a, uh, tough thing to have to hear, we know," Marshall said. "Seems, with the tough life this boy had, he was destined for some sort of tragedy."

Jake looked up at his father with what might have passed for a partial sneer across his lips. He stood up from his chair, picked up his ball and glove, and turned away from his parents. "Can I go to my room now?"

"Honey, if you want to talk about it, we're here if you need us." Millie stood up and started to go after Jake.

Marshall stopped her. "Let him be, Millie. Give him some space."

She grabbed Marshall's hand and gripped it with more force than he would have expected. "He's going to shut down. I know it. I know him. He's going to retreat to the place he goes in his mind, and he's gonna shut us out."

"C'mon, honey. Don't get crazy on me, here."

Millie socked him on the arm. "What if he needs professional help?" Her next words squeezed through her gritted teeth. "And you certainly softened the blow. 'The kid was *destined* to *die*?' You promised me you wouldn't be negative. You *promised* me."

He spit out his next words quicker than he'd intended. "It was not negative. Jeez, Millie. Can't you support me a little when it comes to expecting him to show the ability to face up to the truth about this boy?" He paused. "And anyway, Jake didn't act like he needed help."

"He's a *kid*, Marshall. He doesn't know what he needs. Isn't that *our* job? To help him know?" She paused. "*We* might even need to talk to someone, too. I feel so inadequate right now."

"Don't you mean send *me* to get fixed? After all, aren't I the one who's caused all of Jake's problems? It's what you mean. Isn't it?"

She socked him again on the arm. "Don't go there. And keep your voice down." She paused. "It's not what I meant, and you know it. He's struggling, and we're his parents. He can't "fix" himself by himself. Clearly, what we're doing isn't working. We've got to consider getting professional help for him...and for us."

■　　■　　■　　■　　■

Marshall took some deep breaths of the cool air in the attic. He hoped they might help to soften his memory of the sting in Millie's words and his own denial. This wishful thinking didn't help. Jake shut down like Millie had said he would. Strangely, in a few days, like a miracle, he acted as if nothing ever happened. Millie had tried for several months to bring it back up. He'd put her off, shrug his shoulders, and tell her to stop worrying about him. At the time, Marshall had rationalized, since his son had begun acting normal, he must be okay. They ended up not sending him to a counselor or going themselves. Millie had given in and decided not to fight Marshall's reluctance and resistance. His solution involved not confronting problems. If he didn't deal with them, they didn't exist. He had said something like, "The messes you made were *your* messes, nobody else's," to Millie. She had told him it sounded like something his father would have said.

Marshall shook his head, removed his ball cap, and ran his fingers through the few strands of hair remaining on the top of his head. Another memory rolled in. Like waves at the beach. This late-night conversation happened during Jake's junior year. The family had had a typical quiet suppertime. Out of the blue, Millie had brought it all up again.

. . . . .

"Jake, honey, wouldn't you like to talk about what happened with Randy?"

"No." And then he stood up. "Can I be excused?"

This little exchange had stuck in Millie's craw until around midnight. Marshall, almost asleep, felt her customary punch in his side.

"Well?"

Like a broken record, Marshall mumbled, "He doesn't wanna talk about it."

She shouted a whisper. "He's not *okay*! He's been holding it in for too many years. He's got to get it out."

"I agree, sweetheart. He's dealt with it by checking out of life."

"When you say stuff like this, Marshall, it scares me."

"I don't mean like, well, you know, *checking out* means he might commit, uh…"

She placed her hand over his lips. "I know what you meant, Marshall. Don't say it. Please don't say it."

He gently removed her hand and turned on his side so he could stare out the window. "He's got no passion for anything, Millie."

"He's struggling to find himself," she whispered.

"You're not gonna like this, but I think the military's the answer. After he graduates." He didn't mention anything about the confrontation they had the previous year or Jake's promise.

"Did you say what I think you just said?"

Marshall turned over and stared at her. "He needs discipline and direction, sweetheart. He needs something to get him focused on living his life again."

Millie sat up on her elbows and glared at him. "You know, you and the military have not been on the best of terms. Did you forget you turned your father down when he suggested *you* join up?" She paused. "If you suggest this to him, I'll never forgive you."

"Lighten up, honey. I know it's not for everybody. I have a feeling it's the right thing for him."

She turned away from her husband. "We should've sent him to counseling, Marshall. We should've made him at least talk to somebody."

.   .   .   .   .

Marshall returned to the present. For only a moment. Because these memories tumbled through the window, one by one, like cascading water down a multi-tiered fountain. This next one haunted Millie.

.   .   .   .   .

A clear November sky joined with a warmish Thanksgiving Day. Jake's senior year. Adirondack chairs on the backyard deck made for a perfect way to end a fun family day. A bit of bourbon and water on the rocks and uplifted faces exposed to the warm sun hadn't hurt. He had snookered the girls into cleaning the kitchen. Jake agreed to bag the trash and walked by, hauling it to the Rubber Maids by the side of the house.

"Thanks for doing the trash, honey," Millie said.

"Uh, sure thing, Mama. Done." Jake lingered. He ran his fingers through his shock of blond hair and shifted from one foot to the other. "I'm enlisting after I graduate."

Marshall couldn't miss Millie's hard glare. Jake got the softer version. "Did your father put you up to this? 'Cause if he did..."

"No, Mama. It...it was my idea."

For the remainder of the school year, Millie had tried to talk him out of it. Marshall had had to hand it to him. He had stuck with his decision. On the morning following graduation, Jake planned to go to the recruitment office. Millie woke Marshall early. "Ask him if he wants you to go with him."

"Jeez, I, uh, I don't know if..."

Millie sat up and took his head between her hands. She whispered. Her words were firm and clear. "He's your *son*, and he's about to make one of the most important decisions in his life."

A few minutes later, Marshall had stuck his head into Jake's bedroom doorway. He was lacing up the latest version of Air Jordans. "I'll go with you today, if you want, son."

"Mama told you to ask me, didn't she?"

Marshall hung his head. "Guilty."

Jake sat up, even though he still had one shoe to finish lacing. He faced his father square on. "No thanks, Daddy. I'm keeping my part of our bargain."

"Jake, I..."

"It's okay, Daddy, really." His words were confident, not confrontational. "It's the right thing to do. I, uh, feel good about it." He paused. "And don't worry about Mama. I don't need you to go with me."

．　　　．　　　．　　　．　　　．

Before this memory could even fade to an end, one of those inner voices immediately shoved its way into the conversation. *There it was, Marshall. Millie's prediction. Pretty ironic, wasn't it? Even though you might not like to admit it, when you needed him to need you, he didn't.* The cold air in the attic, combined with the stress, made his head pound. He thought this must be what one of Millie's migraines felt like. It provided him with a new appreciation for what she went through regularly. He pressed his fingers against his eyelids. The pressure helped a little. He tried pressing on his temples with marginal success. An agonized Marshall moved to the next letter.

Dining Room

"You are the champion of the universe," Beth said.

"Can't we play one more, Mommy?"

"I think we're all played out, sweetheart," Millie said, reaching out and smoothing Mary's hair.

"C'mon," Lisa said. "Let's go to the living room and wait on the couch."

"Will you read me a story?" Mary asked.

"Sure," Lisa said.

"*The Polar Express*?"

"You got it."

Millie watched as her three daughters curled up on the sofa in the living room with one of their favorite Christmas stories. She noted the clock on the table. 9:00. Walking over to the doorway, she gazed through one of the sidelight windows. Wiping away a bit of fog, she stared out at the street. The temperature had dropped just a bit, and the rain sounded more like ice than like water droplets. The street was silent. The glare of a lone streetlamp shone through the falling precipitation.

Oh, Marshall...what have you done?

When Lisa began to read, Millie motioned she was going to head upstairs.

Attic

Wednesday
June 26, 1996

Dear Gammy Gat,

Randy swallowed a bunch of some of his mama's painkiller drugs, and the doctors couldn't save him.

My school counselor, Mr. Jones, told us the police caught his daddy. They put him in prison. Mr. Jones met with me and gave me a note Randy wrote. His mama gave it to Mr. Jones. All it said was, "Tell Jake thanks for wanting to be my friend."

I didn't know what to say. Mr. Jones told me how wonderful I was for being nice to Randy, even though we got each other in trouble. He said Randy was angry at the world and couldn't deal with all his problems. Mr. Jones said Randy had a big chip on his shoulder. I think those kinds of feelings are hard for people to accept, sometimes. Because it's so hard to figure out how to help kids like Randy. At least, this is what Mr. Jones said. I didn't want to hear it, so I asked if I could leave.

I think I know what it's like to be so sad you think things will never change or get better. It seems like it takes so much energy not to be sad.

I hate what his parents did. They helped make it so easy for him to choose to give up. They gave up on each other and Randy. I think he wanted to feel alone to make it easier to feel sorry for himself. I wish I could've made it harder for him to feel alone. Randy wasn't a troublemaker at school. Ms. Murray thought he was. All she cared about was whether he could sit still, stop talking, and follow the rules. It wasn't because he wanted to cause trouble. Randy was talking. She just wasn't listening. Nobody listened. And now it's too late. I think what was going on in his head and in his heart was more important than schoolwork.

I do hope he's with you. Some of my friends said you can't go to Heaven if you kill yourself. I know killing yourself must be a terrible thing to do. He was a kid. Not to go to Heaven would be like getting two punishments for one mistake. God doesn't work this way, does he?

I hope Mr. Jones doesn't try to help me feel better anymore. I don't want to feel better, yet. I don't want to "pick up the pieces." I want to get rid of them and never see them again.

Feeling all to pieces,

Jake

P.S. I love you, Gammy Gat

Marshall thought again of all those times he'd said to himself, "He needs to grow up." "I'm tired of putting up with him." "Let the military handle him." Mini manifestos of an abdication of his responsibility. One of those inner voices didn't fail to bring it up. *Being a parent's hard, isn't it, Marshall? Did you give up on your son because being a parent was…is tough? Don't you think he felt it? Knew it?* Jake's voice throughout these letters was loud and clear. A voice that was now challenging Marshall in ways he had never anticipated. Challenges he was determined to face. But now this notebook was running out of letters.

Jake's Bedroom

Millie, her face drawn and eyes teary, made her way slowly up the steps.

After she reached the top, she turned and stepped toward Jake's room. Hesitating for an instant, she took a deep breath and walked in. Pausing just beyond the entrance, she stared into the darkness. Sighing, she reached over and flipped on the light switch. Jake's room was as he left it. *I need you here, Marshall. Now.*

Then she broke down. With both hands covering her face, she stifled the sound—so the girls wouldn't hear. Making her way to Jake's bed, she sat. Reaching out, she touched the folded flag and the Purple Heart. Then, like the slow-motion toppling of a tree, she fell onto the pillow and cradled them both close to her cheek.

Attic

Sunday
June 30, 1996

Dear Gammy Gat,

    I found out I won't get to see Eddie this summer. It isn't going to work out. Daddy said maybe in the fall. Yeah, sure, we'll see.

    I've been thinking. I wish you had one more heaven superpower. One morning, I'd wake up and I'd find an actual letter from you beside my bed.

    Mama's stomach is getting bigger and bigger. She still gets sick sometimes. It's weird to think about a baby growing inside somebody's tummy. How come people can't remember what it was like inside? The baby's moving a lot. We can feel HIM when HE kicks. What's the baby thinking? We think with words. This kid doesn't even know Mama is his mama. He doesn't know what people are. Or if he's even a kid. For all he knows, he could be a rabbit. Just kidding. It seems strange I was in Mama's stomach once. Hard to believe Daddy was inside you. You died, and I know our family's going to have another baby.

    I've been trying not to think too much about Randy. I know I don't want to talk about what happened. Maybe never. Mama wants me to. I can't. Right now, I just want thinking about it to go away. I can't imagine what his mother is going through. She lost Randy and his daddy. Of course, maybe having her husband out of her life may not be such a bad thing. It's like their family just stopped. It hurts too much to think families can stop. Families don't stop, do they? I do know things will never be the same, though. I still wish some things about our family hadn't changed. Somehow, life's got to keep going for everybody in the family who's still alive when someone dies.

Here's to keeping on keeping on,

Jake

P.S. I love you, Gammy Gat

Did you hear what your son said, Marshall? Life's got to keep going for everybody in the family who's still alive when someone dies. Marshall shook his head and re-read, *Families don't stop, do they?* Jake nailed it. At eleven years old. He had recognized even though things changed, he wanted to have some control over his life, like everyone did. Marshall had recounted a plethora of memories so far. It had taken Jake's death and letters written to his dead grandmother to trigger them. And the stuff his son had experienced? *You lived through many of those same kinds of things, didn't you, Marshall?*

Now that it was too late to share this with his son, just being sorry somehow didn't cut it. Doing something to honor that was the only alternative. Another window swung open. He hated this memory. On a Saturday in December, around 4:00 in the morning during his freshman year in high school, he was up and raring to go. Hunting season in North Carolina.

.　　.　　.　　.　　.

The clear December morning sky appeared as if hole-punched full of stars. The chill brushed across Marshall's cheeks like the rush of cold air on your face after opening a walk-in freezer. Mary Claire fussed with his heavy coat and tugged on his toboggan hat. "Are you sure you want to go, Marshall? You know, this is something you've never done before."

He grinned at her and pushed her hands away. "It's gonna be great, Momma."

A dirty-white Jeep Wagoneer pulled into their driveway. It jolted to a stop. Marshall shouted and waved toward the truck. "Pudge's here!"

"Hey, Marsh, get a move on! Them white-tailed deer ain't gonna wait on us."

"Coming!"

Pudge's dad, Bo, and Bo's hunting buddy, Pete, sat in the front seat of the 4X4 Jeep.

Marshall dashed across the front yard and leaped into the backseat. A crooked-tooth grin split Pudge's broad face as he and Marshall settled into their seats. "You ready?" He said, in his slow southern drawl. "Ain't nothin' like it, Marsh."

Marshall leaned over and whispered in Pudge's ear. "I never shot a real rifle before." He paused. "Never killed nothing neither."

"Aw, Pete'll learn you. He's the best hunter around."

After about forty-five minutes, the Jeep turned onto an old, dirt drive. A short time later, they pulled up to the old Melburn homestead. An elderly man waited under a light on his front porch. Bo stuck his head out the window. "Howdy, Homer, good to see ya. Pete's here, my son and a friend of his."

Mr. Melburn scratched his full, white beard and adjusted his horn-rimmed glasses off the tip of his nose. "I ain't let as many hunters come on the land this year. Seen one or two spikes. But feel free to take a doe. They's too many of 'em out thar as it is. Them stands y'all built are still up out yonder," the old man continued. "Y'all remember where y'all done built 'em, don't you?"

"Yessir, I do remember," Bo said.

Pete jumped out, made his way to the back of the Jeep, and started to unload. "All right, girls. Let's get our gear and head out. We're gonna stand here jawing and them white-tails are gonna go back to sleep 'fore we even sit down in a tree."

Pete showed Marshall how to handle and shoot the rifle. After they all put on bright orange vests, they headed out on foot down a makeshift path. At a fork, Bo whispered, "Good huntin', boys."

It wasn't long before Pete and Marshall reached their stand.

"If we see one, where will it probably come out?" Marshall asked, his nervous whisper a bit quieter than he'd intended.

"Good question." Pete pointed out toward a small open area. "Over yonder's a spot as good as any. We just gotta wait. Deer hunting's about waitin' and bein' ready." He smiled. "And lucky."

The sun continued its slow climb. Right when the early morning, soft, golden glow lit up the open area, Pete put his hand over Marshall's mouth and held his finger to his lips. He pointed toward the edge of the woods about thirty yards away. A head appeared, like a hand slipping through a curtain. The deer took three steps, then stopped. Marshall raised the rifle. His heart raced. He held the rifle as steady as his sweaty hands would let him and slowly squeezed the trigger. An explosion, like a bomb going off, broke the silence. Marshall winced from the force of the recoil against his shoulder. The doe dropped dead on the spot. Pete slapped him on the back. "Hell of a shot."

The doe didn't move. She'd dropped straight down, her head across her front legs like she was sleeping. Marshall couldn't take his eyes off the still body stretched out on the ground.

Pudge and Bo approached. Pete and Marshall climbed down from their stand.

"Who got her?" Bo asked.

"The boy here," Pete said. "Dropped her with a single shot." He'd already reached the deer. Pulling out a large hunting knife, he sharpened it on a whetstone.

Bo patted Marshall on the back. "Mighty fine shooting, son. You sure you never shot a rifle before?"

"I, uh, I was lucky," he mumbled, still unable to take his eyes off the deer.

"Y'all boys come on over here," Pete said. "So's you can learn something about field dressing a deer."

"C'mon," Pudge said. "This is neat. Pete's gonna slit her whole gut open. Hurry up." Pete sliced down the entire middle of the doe's stomach, all the way to the area beneath her tail. Something small fell out of the deer's stomach.

Bo leaned down and picked up a tiny fetus. "Well, I'll be dogged. This doe was pregnant."

"I...I didn't know."

"Not uncommon at this time of year," Bo said. "Unfortunate but unavoidable."

Pudge slapped Marshall on the back and smiled. "Marsh got two for one, Daddy," he said. Then he turned toward Pete. "Reckon it put the skids on this deer family, didn't it?"

Marshall threw up. This day had been the first and last time he ever shot a gun.

.   .   .   .   .

Marshall struggled to breathe. It had nothing to do with his asthma or being in the attic, however. *You did the same thing, Marshall. You put the skids on your relationship with your son.*

His brain felt like a computer with a hard drive infected by a virus. It was slowly deleting all his old files. He'd become his own desperate hacker trying to keep the virus from crashing his system. *Close your eyes, Marshall, and relax.*

The notebook fell from his lap before he could catch it. It landed on top of Jake's toddler Stride Rites. A folded piece of paper fell out. It was the actual note Randy had written before killing himself. The chicken scratch scribbling was worse than Jake's. He refolded it and placed it in the back of the notebook. When he flipped back to turn the page for the next letter, he discovered a blank page. Quickly, he flipped through the remaining pages.

Empty.

Could another notebook exist, Marshall?

Nothing.

Those letters had let him in on a son he never knew—a son he let slip away. Like discovering an unfinished painting, too much was still missing. In all his life, he'd never had the breath knocked out of him. Sitting, after hours of emotional ups and downs, agony, guilt, his own life passing before him, and now staring at his son's empty notebook had to be what it felt like. *You've thought about making some changes in your life, Marshall. What, exactly, are you going to do next?*

His eyes happened to fall on something he hadn't noticed before. The tip of a white, business-sized envelope peeked out from beneath another folder in the box. He reached for it and lifted it out. *Gammy Gat,* in Jake's handwriting, was scrawled on the front. Updated chicken-scratch, it appeared much improved. The envelope didn't look as old as the notebook. He stared at it for a moment. The flap had been sealed. He knew he had to open it. *Your son isn't through talking, Marshall.* He tried to smile. He was not through listening. With trembling fingers, he reached inside and carefully pulled out several pages of another letter. Marshall took a deep breath and began to read.

Jake's Bedroom

"Mama!" Lisa's voice from downstairs.

Millie heard the front door open. Voices sounded this time. She could not understand what they were saying. Lisa's voice again. Loud enough to hear. "They...they can't find him, Mama."

A pause.

Followed by a sob.

Attic

Wednesday
November 27, 2002

Dear Gammy Gat,

Tomorrow's Thanksgiving. I'm sorry I haven't written to you in a long time. It's been hard because to write, I had to think, and I just can't think. It hurts too much. I needed some time. Guess nothing's worse than an idiot who thinks he can figure out everything he needs to know about what to do with his life all by himself. Would you believe I'm a senior in high school now?

Mama's going to cook a turkey with all the trimmings. The weather is a bit "coolish" as you used to say, but it's not too bad. A sweatshirt and jeans work great for walks and playing football. You know, hanging around. Can't wait for the smells tomorrow. Especially the chocolate pie. Lisa learned how to make them like you did. Nothing better.

I have to admit something. Some of my memories of you are starting to get fuzzy. Like remembering when some things happened or exact details. It drives me stupid 'cause I don't want you to think I've forgotten the important stuff.

Sometimes, I try to remember what you looked like. Not when you were sick or when we visited you in the hospital, hooked up to all those machines. But when you were...you. Like the times you gave us birthday parties and made special cakes. Or when you worried if the birds were getting enough to eat in the wintertime. Or when you still treated Daddy like he was your little boy and teased him or fussed at him about something. Or when all we had to do was open a door at our house. A smile on your face is what I try to remember.

It's been about seven years since Randy died. Years, I know, of driving Mama and Daddy crazy. I do worry about not wanting to remember Randy. I get so confused about what's important to remember and the memories I want to go away. I think I haven't treated Mama and Daddy right about the whole Randy thing. I don't mean the dumb decision Randy and I made at the end of the school year. I know I embarrassed them and made their lives miserable. What I mean is, I still haven't been able to talk to them about everything. I don't know why. It's like I can't or won't. I don't know which. Mama told me they would be ready to listen whenever I was ready to talk. Maybe I'll be ready someday. Just not quite yet.

I think it's why I couldn't write to you for such a long time. I didn't know what to say or what to think anymore. I felt an emptiness that wouldn't go away. I think Mama thought I might go and do something stupid, and Daddy got on my case and stayed on it. I know they both meant well, and I guess I haven't done anything to help change their minds. Oh, I haven't gotten into trouble, again. I have done what both of them think—coasted along with no direction. You know, through school and life. This was and is what mostly drives Mama so crazy. So many times, I can see it in her eyes. Even her hugs. I can tell she wants to hold on to me for a little bit longer than usual. I also know I haven't done anything to help her not feel, somehow, I'm slipping away from her or something. Daddy's eyes are different. Instead of wanting to hold on to me, he just wants to push me away. I confess I felt the same way for a long time.

Oh, I know, Mama's had big plans for me all along. Lisa's made for college, and it's made for her. I think the more successful she is, the more I'm sure I'm determined not to go. Remember my best friend, Eddie? He wants to go to college, too. I remember, at one time, we talked about trying to get in at the same place so we could room together. I think life has something else in mind for me. At first, when Daddy talked about me enlisting, I was angry. You don't know this, but when I was a sophomore, I got so fed up, I decided I was going to run off. I told Daddy I wanted to quit school and leave home. Anyway, he told me I couldn't leave and if I tried, he'd send me to some military boarding school. He wouldn't if I stayed and finished out high school, then promised to join up.

I said sure, to get him off my back. At the time, I figured he had no right to "make" me do anything. Now, I feel kind of like Forrest Gump when he asked his mother to tell him what his destiny was. She told him he had to discover it for himself. You know, I never thought people were supposed to try to fit in somewhere. Destiny's got to be when you "fit in" without trying. How do you know where that is? Something has to let you know if you're on the right track, doesn't it?

Maybe it's why—would you believe it—I've decided I want to join the military. I know you know all about military life because of the first part of your life with Grandpapa. And I've been thinking real hard about it. Remember the last letter I wrote you after Randy died, and how I wished I'd been able to make it harder for him to believe he was all alone? Well, I've heard lots of soldiers come home from Iraq and Afghanistan and have problems "fitting" back into their lives. I learned this from my history teacher, Mr. Willis, this year. He's a Vietnam Vet. When he came back, he got his teaching degree. He's been here at my high school for several years. He does some coaching, too, and is a great guy. Remember, in one of my letters, I wrote I said I didn't think I could ever be a teacher? Well, I've been rethinking it a bit after being in his class. I think I might join up and then maybe come back and do what he's doing. He talked about what being a soldier was like and how some of them struggle when they come home. It got me to thinking that being a soldier must make them feel alone. I know they have all their buddies around, and they talk about watching each other's backs. Maybe a special kind of feeling alone reaches deep into their souls—when they know every day could be their last. So many of them come home confused and depressed. It's gotta be the kind of alone Randy felt. I couldn't help Randy. Maybe my destiny is to join the military and then come back home and teach, because I know about this kind of alone and what it can do. I know Mama won't understand about the joining the military part. She'll freak out. Daddy will say the discipline will be good for me. Maybe so. I don't want to coast anymore or go after some career I don't have my heart in, or hang around and work at McDonald's until I "find myself." Anyway, just thought I'd throw that out as something to think about.

We went to the beach last weekend. November is a great time to go. Still warm enough to build a sandcastle and walk on the beach. We went back out

Saturday evening to see if our sandcastle was still standing. Ship's lights dotted the dark horizon way offshore. The tide hadn't come in yet. We think the college kids we had seen walking on the beach, drinking beers, came by and knocked it down. It was like they didn't care someone had spent hours working and building something important. We sure wanted it to stay around a while longer. Those jerks tore it down too soon.

Your cancer was like that, wasn't it? It tore you down. And Randy's family was torn down by all their problems. I hope I haven't torn down my family. I have to be honest with you, I don't like going to the cemetery to visit your grave. Even though it's where your body is buried, I believe who you were, your essence, and your soul are not. Know what I mean? I often think about where you are, for real.

I remember when I first started writing to you, I thought maybe God would give you some kind of superpower so you could hear and see what I was writing to you. I know it was pretty much little kid thinking. Maybe, in some ways, you did read all my letters because I have this feeling in my heart, I know what you'd be writing back.

You'd tell me to work hard and do my best. You'd say hard things are a part of life. And I shouldn't make them more difficult by worrying about them all the time. You'd tell me you were proud of me, and I can be anything I want to be if I work hard enough.

You'd tell me to listen to Mama and Daddy. Even though I may not agree with them or like what they tell me, they love me. You'd tell me to make sure I get along with my sisters. And it's okay to fuss with each other now and then. It's part of growing up. And you'd tell me you know I love them and they love me.

I think you'd tell me I shouldn't feel guilty about Randy and what he did. And, as terrible a thing as it was, all of us will learn from it. You'd tell me never to forget who I am. And to remember, people aren't perfect. You'd tell me I'll make mistakes, and I'll have to put up with other people's too. And I should never forget, feeling happy is better than feeling sad, although I'll always feel some of both. And it's a good thing. You'd tell me to say, "I love you," even when it's hard.

I think you'd tell me, too, not to worry about you or Randy. Your pain and his, your worries and his, are things of the past. I know it's taken a long time for my heart to listen to you, and I never told you thanks for being my "super" listener. I don't know all that's in store for me, Gammy Gat. Do you think I'm ready to face it now?

I'll try not to worry about stuff. If it's all right with you, now and then, when things aren't quite like I'd like them to be and a little bit of worry starts to creep in, I'd like to "talk" to you. Daddy used to after you died. He'd go outside and sit by himself in the dark.

Well, I'm getting sleepy. The night is clear, and I think I can see a zillion stars. It's nice. Real nice. I'm looking forward to tomorrow. Might even spring the military thing on Mama and Daddy then. If I do, I'll probably hold off bringing up the coming back to teach part. Still just keeping that idea on the back burner. Or the part about knowing what alone feels like. I still don't think Daddy's ready to hear me talk about Randy yet.

Wish so much you were here. Goodnight.

I think I'm finally ready to pick up some pieces,

Jake

P.S. I love you, Gammy Gat

P.P.S. One more thing I never told you about, but you probably already knew. I didn't get a baby brother, but...SHE'S pretty cool. Oh, yeah. They named her Mary, after you.

After Marshall read these last words, the pages of this letter slipped from his hands and dropped to his lap. When his son was growing up, he thought he could read him like a book. *You just read the wrong book all along, Marshall.*

Marshall felt empty. *A teacher?* This last letter drained every ounce of whatever he had left of a soul. His fingers stumbled over the pages in his lap. He found the words he looked for and read them again. *"I think I'm finally ready to pick up some pieces."* He sniffled and wiped his nose on his sleeve. The tears welling in his eyes, he left alone. Carefully, almost as if he were handling some newly discovered Dead Sea scroll, he folded Jake's last letter, returned it to its envelope, and placed it at the back of the notebook.

Searching in the box, he located an empty brown clasp envelope and placed the notebook inside. Being careful not to break the still unbroken metal clasps, he guided them through the hole in the flap, gingerly parted and pressed them down, and sealed the envelope closed.

Before standing up, he stretched both knees out in front of him. This time, he felt and heard cracks from them both. The stretching, once again, proved therapeutic, and it helped to prepare him for the "get up off the barrel seat" effort. An image of the broken cherub ornament on the floor popped into his mind. Still clutching the brown clasp envelope, he stood and made his way to where he had left Millie's angels. "Why do they make these angels so damn fragile?" He said out loud. Something he had read suddenly came to mind. When the military flew fallen soldiers home, they called it the *Angel Flight*. An inner voice whispered over and over, *Two angels. Broken apart. Two angels. Broken apart. Two angels. Broken apart...* Taking a breath, he cradled the pieces in his hand and wrapped them back up in a piece of red tissue paper he found. *Breathe, Marshall. It's time for you to put your own "Angel" pieces back together.*

Jake's Bedroom

Millie pulled herself up off the bed, sighed, and attempted to steel herself to prepare to be strong for the girls. She started to head for the door. Before she was halfway across the floor, she heard a noise. It came from above, where a large section of the attic extended over the ceiling in Jake's room. The sound wasn't rain. It was more like someone walking or moving about.

GIFT

Attic

Cradling the wrapped-up pieces of Millie's angels, Marshall heard something creak. It wasn't his knees.

"Mr. Gatlin?"

He didn't recognize the voice.

"Are you up here, sir?"

A head appeared in the now-open attic stairway. The jig was up. A young deputy sheriff, who couldn't be much older than Jake, stared at him. He wiped off the wet tears on his cheeks. "I'm Marshall Gatlin. What can I, uh, do for you, deputy?"

The deputy turned and glanced down the ladder. "He's up here, ma'am."

Marshall watched as the deputy's head disappeared. He knew who he'd see next. He smiled. A feeble attempt. A smile, nonetheless. Millie showed no detectable smile of any kind on *her* face. She didn't speak as she continued up the ladder and sat down on the plywood floor. She broke down in tears. It wasn't a loud bawl. It was a quiet, head-in-hands sob. *Don't just stand there, Marshall.* He couldn't think of anything else to do. He was still riding an emotional roller coaster, with no protective bar down across his lap. He sure as hell knew he'd likely put Millie on one too. Part of him wanted to blurt out and tell her she wouldn't believe what he had been doing and share everything all at once. The letters. Everything he had felt reading them. All Jake's words. His thoughts. His perceptions about life. His story. And how his son had shared it all with him. To drop it all on her at once?

He didn't have a clue where to start. He decided she wasn't ready. In reality, he knew he wasn't either. He would wait until she got what *he* had done to her tonight off her chest. Hiding the brown clasp envelope was the first thing to do before she looked up. He stuffed it inside his jacket and zipped up. Millie dropped her hands and wiped her cheeks. *Breathe, Marshall. Here it comes.*

"Do you know it's freezing up here?"

"Yeah," he mumbled. "Uh, I put on my heavy jacket and a sweatshirt...and I, uh, have some handwarmers."

"Have you been crying?"

He silently chastised her eagle eyes and regretted his reddened cheeks. "I was, uh...looking at something."

"Looking at something made *you* cry?"

"Oh, yeah. Funny, huh?"

Millie glanced back down the ladder. "Johnny, thank you so much." She hesitated. "You can go on, now, if you think you *need* to."

Marshall recognized the "please don't go yet" in her voice.

"Thank you, ma'am. I'd like to stay a bit longer, if it's all right, to make sure everybody's okay."

Marshall figured him for a pretty perceptive guy. He knew if someone had checked, they would not find the name, *Marshall Gatlin,* on any perceptive guy list. Millie's relieved voice chimed in. "You are certainly welcome to stay," she said. "You've been so wonderful to help us on Christmas Eve." She turned back toward her husband. *Brace yourself, Marshall.*

"After you'd been gone for a while, I called you. You didn't answer. And...and when we found your phone, turned off, in your office, I figured you'd gone off without it like you always do. Then, I thought, no, on a miserable weather night like this, on Christmas Eve after our son's funeral—with a house full of people and daughters sad beyond belief—under no circumstances would you even *think* of leaving me to go off somewhere without any way to get in touch with you."

"Millie, I...."

"And then time kept going by. The girls and I searched all over this house looking for you. We even looked under the beds and in the bathtub, for God's sake. Then, we decided to go into the garage to check to see if maybe you'd decided to sit in the car awhile instead of going out, and typically, had fallen asleep. The car was still in the garage. Would you believe, no *you*? I went back into the house. What was I to do, you ask?"

"I, uh...."

"I called the Gatesville Sheriff's Office. I told them you were missing. I was afraid you might have decided, heaven forbid, to take a walk—perhaps you thought a cold, sobering rain would help to clear your head—and somehow got yourself in trouble, had a heart attack, lost your way or, in your state of mind, I don't know, called a taxi and gone to a bar, maybe." She paused. "I even thought...." She didn't finish her thought because she couldn't bear to say it, much less think it.

"No bars open tonight in Oakton," he said, then regretted it.

"Not the point, Marshall," Millie growled.

He figured it was time to deploy an old tactic. Deflect his guilt onto her. "The Sheriff's Office, Millie? Really?"

"I didn't know what else to do, Marshall."

Beth's voice saved him.

"Mama, Daddy, what's going on up there?" She, Lisa, and Mary stood at the bottom of the stairway.

Millie, as if afraid he'd disappear again, didn't take her eyes off Marshall. "We're coming down in a second, sweetheart. Please offer Johnny something hot to drink."

Marshall's shoulders drooped when those tears formed in her eyes again. He regretted his petty deflection tactic. "I'm sorry, sweetheart. I got no good excuse. At first, I thought I might take the car somewhere. Changed my mind. Decided to get away up here. Not letting you know was dumb and inexcusable."

Trying to hide the tears, Millie looked away. "We needed you," she said, snuffling. Tears flowed. "And you...you left us."

"I know, I know." He walked toward Millie and took her hand. "I'm here, now."

She took his hand, and for a moment, she didn't say anything. She merely rubbed her thumbs across his knuckles and the back of his hand. Staring at his hand, she whispered, "What in the world did you do up here for nearly five hours?"

"I sort of went through some of Jake's old things. You know. Looked through albums. Messed around."

"For nearly five hours?"

"Well, I lost track of time." He opened his hand and showed her the red tissue. "Did find this."

Millie took the tissue.

"Be careful."

She unwrapped it. "My goodness, it's the little cherub angels." Then, she frowned. "They're broken in two."

"Must've gotten overlooked when we were bringing down all the Christmas stuff. I accidentally bumped into a box and knocked it onto the floor. We have some Super Glue downstairs. It'll fix 'em right up." He smiled, hoping Millie reciprocated. "We can hang it on the tree."

She made a fist and threw a light punch, then she smiled. "You're something else, you know that?" She noticed the shoes. "Are those Jake's old Stride Rites?"

"Yeah. When I was fumbling through stuff, I found the darn things. Pulled them out to look at 'em."

Millie picked them up and rubbed the leather. "Oh, Marshall."

He placed a hand on top of the one holding the shoes. "I know. I know." He placed her chin gently in the palm of his hand. "I let you down, honey. Unforgivable, I know. I...I..." He released her chin and brought both hands up to his face. Sobbing, he allowed himself to let go. His eyes filled with tears. Millie reached out and took him into her arms. They stood together, both weeping, for several minutes. Finally, Marshall reached behind Millie's head and caressed her hair. Sighing, he forced himself to take a few deep breaths to quieten his sobs. Tears still streaming down his face, he whispered, "We'd better head on down. Surely this deputy has a home he needs to get to before it gets any later."

Upstairs

Millie made her way down the ladder first. Marshall followed. All three girls, along with Deputy Bates, stood at the base of the ladder, waiting anxiously.

"I hate to be rude, you guys," Marshall said, turning immediately to head for his bedroom. "I have to pee. Officially introduce me to this young man when I get back."

"Daddy!" Beth rolled her eyes and shook her head. She winked at Mary and said, under her breath. "At least we know the guy Johnny found in the attic isn't an impostor."

When he returned, he had removed his jacket and hidden the envelope under his pillow.

"This is Deputy John Bates, honey," Millie said. "His folks had gone on a Christmas trip this year, so he volunteered for the duty tonight. And I'm glad he did, because he's been wonderful."

Marshall glanced over at Lisa, a big grin on her face. "Nice to meet you, young man," he said. "I'm sorry your trip out here was a false alarm."

"Well, you gave us quite a scare, Mr. Gatlin. We believe it's better safe than sorry. I'm glad it *was* a false alarm, sir."

"You, uh, look familiar. Have we met before?"

Lisa spoke up. "Johnny was in my class in high school, Daddy."

Without cracking a smile, Beth elbowed Lisa in the side. The deputy smiled at Lisa. "I knew your son, Jake, too, sir. I'm sorry for your loss. Especially at this time of year and all."

"We've all taken it pretty hard."

"I didn't know Jake real well," he said. "What I knew came mostly from what other kids and Lisa told me about him." He paused. "Jake was one of the good guys, Mr. and Mrs. Gatlin. Of course, I'm sure this is something you already knew."

Marshall, after hearing those words from a stranger and thinking he had at least gotten off the roller coaster, felt like he'd slipped back on the track and been run over for a second time. Once again, tears flowed down his cheeks. He gazed at this young deputy, hat in hand, and standing proud. Jake had stood in his camos like this. Never to see this image again, except in a photograph, was too much. But then he thought about what was under his pillow, and what its existence meant to him. What it had done for him. A weight fell from his shoulders. It washed away years of a shadow hanging over him. *You've been waiting for something you didn't know you were waiting for, Marshall.* "Deputy Bates?" He whispered, tears still trickling, "Can I give you a hug?"

Upstairs Hallway

Without waiting for an answer, Marshall grabbed him and pulled the young deputy to him. His eyes closed, he imagined he had wrapped his arms around Jake in a hug that had been a long time coming. He sobbed, like a baby, on the young deputy's shoulder. John Bates hesitated a second, then hugged him back. Millie and the girls stood silent, eyes wide. A huge grin spread across Millie's face. Her cheeks glistened as wet as Marshall's. "Johnny," she said, "my husband is doing something we've *never* seen him do."

The two men both let go, and Marshall stepped back.

"Ma'am?"

Mary smiled, tears in her own eyes, and answered for her mother. "You're a stranger, but my daddy hugged you."

Beth stood, hands on her hips, with tears in her eyes, too. "He won't even hug *us* in public."

A tearful Mary grabbed her father and hugged him. "You scared me, Daddy," she said. "We didn't know where you were."

"I know, little girl, I'm so sorry," he said, still holding on to his youngest child. "Will you forgive me? I was so sad about Jake, I just wasn't thinking." He paused. "Anyway, you are way up past your bedtime, honey. You've got to go to sleep so you can wake up Christmas morning."

"I think we all need to hit the sack, Daddy," Beth added. "Oh, and by the way, we won't tell anybody you actually grabbed a sheriff's deputy and gave him a hug."

"Nobody'll believe it," whispered Lisa, smiling.

"You can tell anybody you want to," Marshall said. He paused and looked at the deputy. "I, uh, hope I didn't embarrass you, young man."

John Bates placed his hat back on his head. "Not at all, sir." He paused for an awkward moment. "I, uh, guess I don't need anything else from you folks tonight. I'm glad you're okay, Mr. Gatlin."

Lisa casually touched Deputy Bates's arm and looked at her father, her stare eerily reminiscent of her mother's eagle eye glare. "Lucky he didn't arrest you for assault."

Beth gave her sister a slight punch on the arm. "Good one, sis," she said, winking at her mother.

"Oh, Jeez. Deputy Bates, I..."

"No. No. It's okay, Mr. Gatlin. Really, it...it's okay."

Time for another cleansing breath, Marshall.

"We need to let this young man go home," he said. "Girls, will you escort him downstairs? Send him home with some of the food, I'm sure is left. Your mother and I'll be close behind."

Mary and Beth followed Lisa and Deputy John Bates down the hall. Millie threw her arms around her husband. Those arms were a welcome comfort. Both of them watched as their girls walked what had to be a bedazzled young deputy out. Marshall smiled as he thought Lisa looked a bit bedazzled herself. Millie, eyes still sparkling from the tears, turned her eyes on Marshall and then toward the attic. "What *really* happened up there?"

He kissed her wet eyes. "A miracle?" He whispered.

She looked up at him, her gaze soft yet questioning.

"You gonna tell me about it?"

He gazed back into her eyes. "Yeah," he said, a soft smile across his lips. "Just not tonight."

Den
9:45 p.m.

The house and the five were alone again.

The tree still stood tall and beautiful, as did all of the Gatlin crew standing around it. Thinking about the missing sixth allowed the quiet sobs to creep back. Page after page of letters, written in a child's handwriting, remained hidden under Marshall's pillow. Hidden from some folks, he knew needed to see them sooner or later. Getting to know his daughters better was a thought now imprinted on his brain. He wondered what each of *them* would have shared if they'd written letters to his mother. Marshall stepped back and opened his arms wide. "Lisa, Beth, Mary. Before you go to bed...come here. I think I have a few decades of lost hugs to catch up on."

"You got that right," Beth muttered, winking at her sisters. Millie joined the group hug.

"I love y'all more than you'll ever know," Marshall said. "Somehow, I want us to do all we can to honor Jake's life. By honoring each other better from now on." He paused. "And it starts especially with me."

Lisa reached up and touched his face. "We love you so much, Daddy."

Mary's tears tumbled down her cheeks. She buried her head into his chest. "And we miss Jakey lots."

"I know. I miss him too, little girl...more than I can say."

10:15 p.m.

Waiting until he knew everyone was asleep, Marshall slipped out of bed and reached under his pillow for the envelope. He placed Jake's last letter from Afghanistan inside and reclosed the clasp. Tiptoeing out of the bedroom, he headed downstairs to the kitchen. What to do with the notebook of letters remained a quandary. He knew it would have been crazy to hand them all to Millie and the girls and say, "Oh, by the way. I found these letters Jake wrote to Gammy Gat after she died. Read them. You'll find them *interesting*."

Although the incredible tragedy of their loss still overwhelmed him, a strange relief hovered over him like a canopy of warm sunshine. He just didn't know what to make of it. He thought about the Afghanistan letter. Jake had promised his mother and the girls he wanted them to be a part of his "sit down and talk" when he came home. Marshall realized the "sit down and talk" had happened. With him. It needed to happen again...with them.

He didn't want the sit-down to come simply because of Jake's letters. Marshall wanted it to come from him, too. He owed them. Jake had given them a gift. It had to be shared in the right way. Talking and apologizing could never be enough. Something had to change. Something else he believed he owed his family. Now he had to act on that responsibility. Still, he couldn't get his head around how to prepare them.

10:20 p.m.

A glass of bourbon, with some eggnog to cut it, sounded good. He would use the sipping time to help him think. He looked for those cherub pieces and found them on the kitchen counter where Millie had left them for the promised glue-back. He scrounged around the catch-all kitchen drawer and located a small bottle of still usable Super Glue. After repairing the small decoration, he set the cherubs aside to let the glue set. It should only take a couple of minutes, and the two little angels would be as good as new. He reached for his eggnog, added a touch more bourbon, and took the last sip. The mixture was one of those "get every drop" kinds of tastes. And as he tilted the glass back, how to share his "miracle gift" came to him.

10:30 p.m.

Millie stored her box of wrapping paper in the hall closet. He searched in the long, shallow plastic storage box and selected a small, night-blue roll with sparkly stars covering the entire surface. He took it and the envelope into the den and sat himself down by the Christmas Tree. With tape, scissors, a blank Christmas card and its envelope, and one of those stick-on bows, he wrapped the notebook.

On the card, he wrote,

To my family,
Merry Christmas!
Wanted you to know I'm okay and in a wonderful place.
Don't ever forget to keep talking and listening to one another.
I love and miss you all,
Jake
P.S. Gammy Gat and Grandpapa give hugs and kisses and said to tell you they love you.
P.P.S. I left you a gift under the tree.

He gazed at his handiwork and decided the red bow on top was an especially nice touch. He placed a piece of rolled-up tape on the back of the Christmas card envelope and balanced it on a limb. He hung the small cherubs beneath the note and placed Jake's "Gift" directly beneath it. Marshall attempted to get up, realized he'd been on the floor too long, and his knees didn't want to cooperate. He figured he'd given them enough aggravation, so he grunted, crawled over, and pulled himself up using the couch. He rested for a moment to allow his knees to recuperate. Sighing, he finally stood up and walked back to the tree, where he leaned over to get a better look. He smiled and then quietly said out loud, "Thanks, Momma...for being there for him. Somehow, you knew when we needed you most. You didn't get your 'superpower' in heaven. It's *always* been a part of you. Look after him. He's a good kid." Marshall paused. "He was like you, you know." He reached down once more and touched the wrapped gift. *You know what you have to do next, Marshall.*

Jake's Room

10:45 p.m.

Take another deep breath, Marshall. Switch on the light and walk through the door.

A pair of jeans, holes in the knees, still hung over the back of his son's desk chair. Millie had left them right where he had tossed them before leaving for Afghanistan. She had wanted his room to look exactly as he left it when he came back. A picture of Jake, holding his baby sister in his arms, alongside his other two sisters, sat on his bedside table. A poster of Michael Jordan, covering up the holes from a misguided dart game, hung on the wall. Something caught his eye on Jake's dresser. He reached over and picked up the pearl tie pin. Lifting it to his lips, he kissed it and then placed it back on the dresser.

Jake's smell lingered. In the soft gray paint covering the walls. In his comforter. His curtains. His jeans. Everything Jake. It had absorbed his essence over time. Maybe Marshall imagined it. It didn't matter. He breathed his son in as if he were inhaling the freshest air ever. *Exhale slowly, Marshall. Don't let it escape forever into the air too quickly.*

Jake's bed was a twin. It jutted out from the wall on the opposite side of the room. His comforter hung symmetrically off both sides. This was Millie's doing. He figured the slight ruffled indentation on the side of the bed had to be evidence of Millie's presence. Since Jake's death, she had visited alone several times. Marshall sat in the same spot. The folded flag and Purple Heart nestled beside his pillow. He hadn't wanted to handle them at all before. He started to touch the flag, then changed his mind. He didn't want to disturb the distinct folds of the unique triangle. Glancing around, he spied something peeking out from under Jake's bed. It was a pair of red and black high-top sneakers. Worn edges showed along the left and right insteps. Jake's stride was the culprit. The laces hung loose. The shoes were ready for his son's size ten feet. *You wear a ten, Marshall.*

Hesitantly, he reached down and slipped his feet inside.

Study
11:00 p.m.

Marshall sat behind his desk.

The streetlight through the window behind him lit up the precipitation spilling down from the dark sky. Like tiny, liquid darts, the freezing rain sliced through the glare. Staring out the window, he began to spy large, wet flakes interspersed between the drops of rain. More and more fell until the new snow replaced the cold, wet rain and filled the dark sky. He loved how his daughter Mary once described it. "The snowflakes look like dancing snow fairies and jillions of white-winged butterflies, Daddy." His mother had loved butterflies.

Marshall stretched out his feet and wiggled his toes inside Jake's sneakers. *Smile, Marshall.* He reached into his "Best Daddy Ever" coffee mug and pulled out his favorite mechanical pencil. *Now, talk.* He leaned forward and selected one of the new, yellow legal pads sitting on the corner of his desk.

Christmas Eve
December 24, 2004
Friday

Dear Jake,
I need to talk to somebody. You know, about things. By the way, this is your daddy, and it's Christmas Eve. But you know this, don't you? The first thing I want to tell you is you are really something. And, if it's okay, I thought we might

invite Eddie to come for a weekend visit now and then. Also, I'd like to get to know your teacher, Tom Willis. He seems like a nice guy. Something else is on my mind, too. Something I've neglected to let you know for a long time.

I love you, soldier...

Acknowledgements

My father always told me to hitch my wagon to a star. I am so thankful that I have the good fortune to "hitch" up with Black Rose Writing. To have someone tell you what you have written is worth reading is an honor and a humbling experience.

My mother's capacity for empathy, compassion, and wisdom…in essence, to "walk in someone else's shoes," has served as an inspiration for my story.

My most ardent critic is my wife, Judy. A tough editor, she continually keeps me honest and constantly challenges me to push and stretch myself.

Over the years, I have had the privilege of working with a number of folks who have read and critiqued various versions and excerpts. Their guidance, suggestions, and ideas are much treasured. I want to particularly thank Beverly Wilson, our Atlantic Beach neighbor, for her wonderful insights and editing suggestions, especially her tease that it appeared I hadn't "met a simile or metaphor I didn't like!" And to Developmental Editor, Katie McCoach, who, in the early stages of my book, provided me with invaluable editing suggestions and ideas.

My two daughters, Carrie McKeown and Stacey Webb, with their capacity to care for others and their commitment to their respective families, continue to be shining lights for both Judy and me. Each of our grandchildren, Marian, Sullivan, Madelynn, and Finley, has a zest for life that takes my breath away and warms my heart. They are a constant reminder that there is yet, still hope, that the future of this planet is in good hands.

About the Author

Andrew Phillips was an Ensign during the Vietnam War. Upon his return, he started teaching kindergarten in North Carolina. Years later, as a retired elementary school principal, he pursued performing children's music, writing picture books, middle-grade novels, and an adult novel. He and his wife developed a seminar: "Singing to Read."

At their renovated beach house in North Carolina, he delights in their traditional Fourth of July celebrations, showering in the best outdoor shower on the beach, and relaxing on the screened-in porch, where he writes and rewrites stories in his mind while breathing in the ocean breezes.

His podcast, *The Journey Inside*, utilizes original children's songs, stories, and excerpts from his adult novel to share thoughts and dreams about and for our children.

Note from Andrew C. Phillips

Word-of-mouth is crucial for any author to succeed. If you enjoyed *In Jake's Shoes*, please leave a review online—anywhere you are able. Even if it's just a sentence or two. It would make all the difference and would be very much appreciated.

Thanks!
Andrew C. Phillips

We hope you enjoyed reading this title from:

www.blackrosewriting.com

Subscribe to our mailing list – *The Rosevine* – and receive **FREE** books, daily deals, and stay current with news about upcoming releases and our hottest authors.
Scan the QR code below to sign up.

Already a subscriber? Please accept a sincere thank you for being a fan of Black Rose Writing authors.

View other Black Rose Writing titles at www.blackrosewriting.com/books and use promo code **PRINT** to receive a **20% discount** when purchasing.